Golden Heart Winner

A Place to Call Home

Front Porch Promises
Book 2

Merrillee Whren

Merrillee Whren
www.merrilleewhren.com

Publisher's Note: This is a work of fiction. Names, characters, places, and incidents are a product of the author's imagination. Locales and public names are sometimes used for atmospheric purposes. Any resemblance to actual people, living or dead, or to businesses, companies, events, institutions, or locales is completely coincidental.

Book Layout © 2014 BookDesignTemplates.com

A Place to Call Home/Merrillee Whren.
ISBN 978-1-944773-26-7

[Scripture quotations are from] THE HOLY BIBLE, NEW INTERNATIONAL VERSION®, NIV® Copyright © 1973, 1978, 1984, 2011 by Biblica, Inc.® Used by permission. All rights reserved worldwide.

For if you forgive other people when they sin against you, your heavenly Father will also forgive you. But if you do not forgive others their sins, your Father will not forgive your sins.

Matthew 6:14-15 NIV

CHAPTER ONE

Kurt Jansen sat in his rusty, red pickup and stared at the Victorian house surrounded by tall pines and bare-branched hardwoods. Faded black shutters hanging cockeyed by a single hinge and peeling white paint on the clapboards testified to many years of neglect. The place didn't look much better than the penitentiary where he'd spent the last six years, but it was better than staring at prison bars.

The structure resembled his life. A life in disrepair.

He stared at the photo in his hand. His heart twisted at the innocent faces of his two children. He vowed to put aside all the bitterness and anger from his unjust incarceration in order to get this restoration job. This was the first step to seeing his children again—the children he hadn't seen since they were six months old. He put the photo back into his wallet.

Approaching the house, he wondered whether the inside looked as bad as the outside. Outward appearances didn't always tell the whole story, in houses or in lives. Piles of melting, dirty snow lay alongside the lane, sidewalk, and in the shady parts of the surrounding acreage. Despite his vow, his heart felt like the snow—cold and corrupted. Resentment and despair still hovered in the dark corners of his mind, even though he'd prayed to God to take them away.

Stepping onto the wooden porch, he let the vision of an elderly lady with white hair, glasses, and sensible shoes flit through his mind. The image suited the proprietress of the future Hawthorne Valley Inn of Hawthorne, Massachusetts. Was she the answer to his prayers? Even though he prayed, he still wasn't sure whether God answered prayers.

The floorboards creaked as Kurt stepped toward the door. He wanted to pray that the Lord would help him get this job, but he couldn't bring himself to voice the words. Instead, he released a harsh sigh and rapped his knuckles on the weathered wood of the warped screen door. It rattled in the frame.

Moments later the inside door opened. A tall, slender young woman, dressed in blue jeans and a gray sweatshirt spattered with several colors of paint, answered the door. She stared at him through the screen with wary, pearl-gray eyes. "May I help you?"

Her throaty voice reminded him of a female disc jockey who played love songs on the radio late at night. Curly strawberry-blond hair framed her face and fell to her shoulders. A sprinkling of freckles across her nose made an attractive face strangely youthful, but he sensed she was older than she appeared. He figured she was only a little younger than his thirty-two years. Somehow she seemed familiar, but he didn't know why.

"I'm Kurt Jansen. I'm here to see Molly Finnerty."

"I'm Molly Finnerty." She squinted as she continued to view him through the screen. "Are you the one Steve Barnett sent about the restoration work?"

"Yes." Kurt tried to reconcile his mental image of

Molly Finnerty and the woman standing before him. He had gotten it so wrong. What had Steve said to leave the impression that the woman he was meeting was someone's grandmother rather than a beautiful young woman? This wasn't what he'd expected or wanted. But he needed a better job. "You're the Molly Finnerty who's planning to make this house a bed-and-breakfast?"

"That's me. Were you expecting someone else?" She raised her eyebrows.

"Just someone much older. That's all." Forcing himself to smile, he pulled an envelope from his pocket and held it out. "Steve sent this with me. Did he talk to you?"

"Yes, Steve mentioned that you'd be coming by." She opened the screen door and stepped aside. Taking the envelope, she smiled in return. "Come in and get out of the cold. I suppose Steve's been making me sound like an aging widow again."

"He didn't say you were aging, but I have to admit that his saying you're a widow made me think I'd find you in your rocker with a cane nearby." Kurt walked through the doorway. The smell of fresh paint permeated the room.

"I'm not in the geriatric crowd yet." Closing the door behind them, she laughed.

The pleasant sound of her laughter echoed off the bare walls and floors of the empty rooms and drew Kurt's thoughts away from her and toward the interior of the house. Plank hardwood flooring, in desperate need of refinishing, ran throughout all the rooms within his sight. A staircase rose along the foyer wall. A small round stained-glass window overlooked the landing where the staircase turned at a ninety-degree angle and continued to the second floor. The banister needed work as well. On his right, decorative columns separated the foyer from the living room, and a fireplace stood in the far wall.

"Well, what do you think?" Molly's sultry voice brought his attention back to her.

He looked her directly in the eye. "I'd like the job."

She stared back at him, her gray eyes not giving a clue as to what she was thinking. "And why should I hire you?"

He wanted to blurt out, Because I need this job. But he managed to conceal his desperation. "I've done several restorations of Victorian houses. I have some photos of my previous work. Would you like to see them?"

"Yes."

"Great. They're out in my pickup. I'll get them." As he moved toward the door, he let a sliver of hope settle in his heart.

"While you're gone, I have a phone call to make." She pointed to the deacon's bench sitting near the front door. "You can wait here, if I'm not done when you get back."

"Sure. I'll be back in a few minutes."

Kurt stepped outside. What had Steve told her? Even if she didn't already know his recent history, she would certainly find out. He headed for his pickup and hoped the quality of his work would outweigh his past.

***

Molly stared after Kurt as he left the house. At five

foot eleven, she stood eye-to-eye with most of the men she knew, but she'd had to look up at Kurt with his handsome face and sandy blond hair. His startling blue eyes held a haunted expression when he'd gazed down at her as if she were some kind of apparition. Was it because he'd expected someone much older?

She smiled to herself, thinking that she'd expected the same. A man with decades of woodworking experience. Kurt couldn't be much older than she was. Although she was only thirty, she sometimes felt like the aging widow he had expected. Her life had been filled with more than her share of tragedy.

After going into her office on the left side of the stairway, she closed the double doors. Her oak roll-top desk sat between the two windows with a view of the side porch. She plopped into the chair, ripped open the envelope, and pulled out a single sheet of paper. Steve's scrawled handwriting covered the page. When she took in the meaning of his words, a lightheaded feeling came over her, and the note fell from her hand. She reached for the phone. This time Steve was asking too much.

She punched in Steve's phone number then listened to the ring while she tapped the fingers of her free hand on the arm of the chair. As soon as he said hello, she launched into her speech. "Steve, what do you think you're doing sending this Kurt Jansen over here? I can't have him working for me or living in my carriage house apartment. I just can't."

"It's nice to hear from you, too." She heard the chuckle in Steve's voice and imagined his plump round face sporting a smile.

"I'm sorry, but this note you sent with him doesn't exactly inspire my confidence."

"Moll, you wanted someone who could help you with that house. Kurt seemed like the answer to your prayers."

"With you, everything's an answer to prayer."

"Personally, I think that's a good way to live. Seeing everything that happens as though God's hand is in it somewhere."

"Don't make me feel guilty." Molly twisted a piece of hair around her index finger.

"If you feel guilty, it's not my fault." Steve's voice still held a hint of amusement.

"You should feel guilty for not telling me he went to prison for manslaughter in the death of his wife." Molly took a deep breath. "Please, don't make me do this."

"I'm not making you do anything. Kurt has the skills you need, and you have a job and a place for him to live—two things he needs."

"You're asking me to deal with a violent man—a man responsible for his wife's death. I don't need another one of those in my life."

"I know. At first I hesitated to send him your way…" Steve sighed. "But he'll be able to restore that old house so you can have your bed-and-breakfast, and he can also build your shelter for battered women."

"Isn't that a little ironic? A man with his background working on a shelter for battered women?"

"Maybe, but personally, I think he's telling the truth when he says he's innocent."

"Aren't they all?" Molly couldn't keep the sarcasm from her voice.

"He's served his time, and he deserves a break,

just like a certain young woman who needed help not too long ago."

Molly leaned her head back and stared at the ceiling. How could she say no when some of Steve's friends had been her lifeline at the time of her own arrest? "This is different."

"Yes, but a lot is the same." Steve's voice held a serious note. "Just think it over. Pray about it."

"Okay, but I didn't claim to be innocent."

"But you did claim the same need for help."

"That's true."

"When I found out about his restoration work, I thought you and he were a perfect match. The way I see it, you two need each other. I'm telling you again. I believe his story."

"What makes you so sure?" Molly rubbed her fingers across her forehead in an effort to ward off the headache this conversation triggered.

"I met his mother while he was in prison. Talking with her convinced me his story's true."

"Why doesn't he live with her?" Molly asked in frustration.

"She died early last year after a long battle with cancer and her house was sold to pay medical bills."

"Oh." Molly wasn't sure what else she could say. Was Steve's assessment correct? Over the past few years she had come to know him as a man with a great deal of wisdom and compassion. "I don't know, Steve. Besides my own concerns, I've already heard a few comments in town about my employing parolees even when their crime was petty theft. What will people here say when they find out I have a man convicted of manslaughter working for me?"

Molly knew Steve would be rubbing a hand over

his balding head as he contemplated her question. "If I thought he'd harm you or anyone in that town, I wouldn't have sent him to talk with you."

"I don't know what to think."

Steve cleared his throat. "Listen, Moll, if you ever have any trouble with folks in that town because you're helping parolees and ex-convicts, send them my way. I'll talk to them."

Molly heard the front door open and close. Kurt had returned. "Steve, I've got to go. I'll take everything into consideration before I make a decision. Say a prayer for me."

"I always do."

"Thanks." Molly gently hung up the phone. Heading for the front hall, she prepared to deal with the giant of a man who might have the talent to make this her dream house but a past that alarmed her.

***

Kurt sat on the deacon's bench with the photo albums on his lap. The muffled sound of Molly's voice filtered through the closed doors. Then there was silence. The doors opened, and she stepped into the foyer. The worry in her eyes told him that she knew.

Standing, he wanted to take away her apprehension. Should he bring up his past or wait for her to ask? Waiting would definitely be easier. He hated talking about it. He hated thinking about it. He hated the way it had ruined his life. Besides, what could he say that would ease her concerns?

Kurt offered her the albums. "Well, here they are."

She glanced at them, then back at him. "Let's go into my office. We can look at them there."

He made no reply as he followed her. At least she wasn't sending him away. As he entered the room, he took in the dark oak-paneled walls with a rich patina. Shelves full of books lined two walls. Three leather wingback chairs surrounded an Oriental rug near the fireplace on the wall opposite the door. In sharp contrast to the rest of the house, this room gleamed from floor to ceiling.

"Who did the restoration in here?" Kurt asked.

"The previous owners."

"Why didn't they finish the project?"

"They were a relatively young retired couple who also wanted to make this a bed-and-breakfast, but during the course of the remodeling, the man had a stroke. They decided to sell."

"How long have you been working on this?"

"Since last fall. I've owned the house for about a year, but I needed to tie up some loose ends before I started full time with this. I've done a lot of work myself with help from some of the people Steve has assisted in his prison ministry."

"Is that why Steve sent me your way? Because he knew you'd give me a job?" Kurt asked.

"Just because Steve sent you, doesn't mean you automatically have the job. If I think you're the right person for the project, I'll hire you." A warning glance supplanted the earlier apprehension he'd seen in her eyes. "Steve just sets up the interviews."

Kurt hoped he hadn't overstepped his bounds, but at least she didn't seem afraid of him now. Maybe he had imagined her fear earlier. Paranoia had been his constant companion since he'd been released from prison. He wondered whether he'd ever shake it. Could he go about business as though he was any other craftsman, not one who had been recommended by a man who ministered to prisoners and ex-convicts? "I understand. Let me show you my work."

"All right. Let's sit over here." She motioned to the uncomfortable-looking sofa covered in red velvet.

He loved Victorian houses and their marvelous woodwork, but he hated the furniture that went with them. The sofa seemed more suitable for viewing than for sitting. As he settled his large frame onto the delicate sofa, he hoped it wouldn't break.

After he had opened one of the albums, he glanced up to see Molly still standing. The wary expression in her eyes told him she realized she would have to sit next to him. He hadn't imagined her previous trepidation. He wanted to tell her he wouldn't bite, but he didn't think she'd take kindly to the joke. What could he do to put her at ease?

Even though Steve had helped Kurt turn his life over to God, Kurt still had to tamp down the anger that surfaced whenever he faced the way people would view him for the rest of his life, unless he could find the person who had killed his wife. Where had God been when he'd been sent to prison for something he didn't do? Would he ever know the answer? His mind buzzed with the unfairness of it all, but he couldn't let his thoughts take him to that dark place—the place where hatred and revenge ruled. Each day he struggled to keep his mind focused on something other than the injustice he had suffered.

Maybe he could offer Molly an out. "You can take these and examine them at your leisure, then get back to me."

She continued to watch him, almost as if she was gauging whether he'd attack. "No. No, let's look at them together now. Pictures without a commentary will mean nothing to me."

"Okay." He hated feeling as though he was under a microscope like some specimen in a lab. Would everyone view him this way? He might as well be Hannibal Lecter searching for his next victim. Is that what she saw when she looked at him? The thought sickened him.

"Fine." She sat on the edge of the sofa as if poised to run at any moment.

"These are before-and-after photos of restorations I've done in both Colonial and Victorian houses. I'll answer any questions you have." He pointed to the first page and glanced at her, but her eyes were trained on the album.

She studied the pictures, then turned to the next page. Without warning, she took the album from him and put it on her lap. Her fingers caressed the pages. He noticed the little paint splatters dotting the back of her hand—a sign that she wasn't afraid of hard work.

Wonder crept across her face. "Oh, these are magnificent. The changes are amazing. Will mine come out like this?" She turned to him. For the moment, she seemed to forget that he was a monster.

"Yeah." Hope filled his heart.

"You did these?"

"Uh-huh." Her question and skeptical demeanor shattered his optimism. She couldn't reconcile his work with the criminal she perceived him to be. He wondered about his chances of getting the job when she obviously didn't trust him. Was this the first time she had interviewed someone who had been convicted of a violent crime? He couldn't let negative thoughts take over. He had to fight for what he wanted. "I can do this here, too."

"Let me show you around." She took the album and stood. "I'll tell you what I have in mind."

"Okay." Kurt followed her into the foyer. He wasn't sure what to make of her sudden enthusiasm. His emotions in the past half-hour resembled a roller coaster ride.

She walked over to the stairway and ran her hand along the banister, then looked at him. "What would you do with this stairway? I really like this one you did here." She pointed to a page in the album.

Kurt stepped closer as he gazed at the picture. For the first time, he smelled her perfume or shampoo. The scent reminded him of the lilacs that grew in the yard of his house—the one he used to own. He didn't want to think about the past and all he had lost. He needed to put his mind on something else. Remembering hurt too much.

Trying to forget the past only made him more aware of Molly. The soft curve of her cheek peeked out from behind silken hair that gleamed under the foyer chandelier as she leaned over to study his photo album. For a moment, he had the urge to reach out and touch the reddish-gold strands. The combination of red and gold reminded him of a sunset. He shook the thoughts from his head. He didn't want to feel anything, but her nearness reminded him that he hadn't touched or held a woman in a long time. He didn't need these feelings now. Not ever. The pain ran too deep.

"Well, what do you think?" Her question brought

his thoughts to an abrupt halt.

"I can do whatever you want. We can work with what's here, or I can get new railings and spindles if these are in bad shape. As long as you want to pay the price, the sky's the limit."

She continued to study him as though she was contemplating his response. Putting her free hand to her forehead, she turned abruptly and walked into the living room. She held the album out in front of her as she stood near the fireplace. She tapped the open page. "I want this in here. This one with the mirror."

Kurt went to stand beside her. He studied the fireplace and imagined the possibilities. "Do you also like the detail work in this picture on the mantel and the surround?"

"Yes, that would be wonderful." Her voice held a trace of excitement.

Kurt turned and walked toward the decorative columns that separated the living room from the foyer. Touching them, he glanced at her. "If you like, we can put the same detail in the columns and put rosettes at the corners of all the doorways and windows."

"That sounds lovely. And in here is the dining room." She stepped through a double doorway. "You see the pocket doors?" She pulled one of them out.

"Yeah—"

"I want to keep these." She pointed to the windows on the right side of the room. "And I want to put French doors there instead of a window so I can serve meals on the porch in the summer. Can you do that?"

Kurt smiled inwardly. Her passion for this project

had made her forget everything except her vision for this place. "Like I told you before, I can do just about anything you want as long as you want to spend the money."

Hesitating, she glanced down at the floor, then raised her gaze to meet his. "Can you work up an estimate for me?"

He couldn't mistake the expression in her eyes. She looked as though she had just made a pact with the devil. "Are you sure?"

"I didn't say you had the job. I just want you to give me an estimate as soon as possible."

"Okay. I'll give you a call when I get it done. Then we can go over it."

She handed him the album. "Do you have my phone number?"

"I can get it from Steve."

"Let me give you my card. Then you'll have all of my contact information." She headed toward her office.

Kurt followed, feeling better about the whole situation. Maybe things would work out after all, but at the same time, he had his reservations about working for this woman. He worried that she would always see him with a jaundiced eye. Could he learn to deal with it?

When they reached the office, she opened a drawer and pulled out a card. Turning, she handed it to him. As he took it, their fingers brushed. He didn't miss the awareness that sparked between them. A physical attraction—that was all it was—an appreciation for a good looking woman. But it made him wary.

"Thanks." He quickly stuffed the card into his

shirt pocket as he tried to cover his own unease. "I'll need to do some measuring before I leave."

"I've got a tape measure right here." She reached into a cubbyhole on the desk and laid it on the nearby table. "Measure away."

He took the tape measure and left the room, wondering whether she had purposely not handed it to him in order to avoid further contact. He spent the next half hour measuring and recording the size of each room and all the parts for which he would need to buy materials.

When Kurt finished, he stuck his head around the doorway to Molly's office. She sat bent over at her desk while she went through some papers. The sight of her made his thoughts race. Could he put together a proposal that would satisfy her? Would she always look at him with a hint of fear in her eyes? His insides churned. He wanted this job—the perfect fit for his skills. Did he dare pray about it? He wasn't sure God was listening.

When he finally settled his emotions, he stepped into the doorway. "I'm done, so I'll be on my way. I'll get that estimate to you as soon as I can. Thanks. You won't be sorry if you hire me."

"Just one thing before you go." She got up from the desk and followed him to the front door. "Could you give me the name of someone for whom you've done a restoration? Your pictures are wonderful, but I'd like to have a reference also."

Kurt's heart sank. He wasn't sure anyone would give him a good reference. He slowly shook his head. "I don't know. I've been in prison for six years." He ran his hand across his brow. "When I was convicted most people turned their backs on me. I don't know what they'd say now."

"Won't they give me a straight answer on the work you did for them?" she asked.

"I hope so. I can give you one name. Harold Sullivan. He lives right over the town line in Brookston. I don't know his number, but I'm sure you can find it. That's the best I can do."

"Thank you." She gazed at him with understanding and sympathy. "I'll be waiting to hear from you."

"As soon as I prepare my estimate for the job." He stepped outside.

As he walked to his pickup, he didn't dare look back. Was she watching, or had she simply closed the door behind him? He didn't want to know. After getting into his vehicle, he sat there for a minute and stared at the house. It didn't appear quite as bad now that he'd seen the inside. Maybe his life was like that, too. The hope God put in his heart would make his circumstances look better.

He would get this job.

More money in his pocket meant that he could hire a lawyer and a private investigator to help him find the person who had killed his wife. Getting his kids back depended on it.

CHAPTER TWO

Molly looked out the window of her office as Kurt drove his pickup down the lane toward the highway. Closing her eyes, she released a long, slow breath. When she opened her eyes again, he was gone. She didn't know what to do now. He was a talented craftsman when it came to restorations, but how could she hire him when he was everything she had left in the past?

His handsome face and sky-blue eyes lingered in her mind. Despite her reservations and fears, she knew he could do wonders with her house and make her dream come true. But was he like her deceased husband? Byron had been violent and manipulative, and she had let him make her life a nightmare.

She tried to shake Kurt's image from her mind, but the picture of his eyes remained, filled with emotions. His haunted look mingled with uncertainty, and yet enthusiasm shone through when he talked about his work. Dread gripped her when she thought about those blue eyes turning cold and hard as ice when she said or did something he didn't like. The thought made her shiver, and she wanted to lock away all emotions. The ache in her heart matched the pain pounding in her head.

What was she going to do? She wondered whether she should call Steve again. Maybe he could give her the answers. Then she shook her head. He wouldn't say anything different this time than he had the last. She had to figure this out on her own.

Harold Sullivan's name belonged at the top of her calling list. Maybe he could tell her what she wanted to know about Kurt Jansen.

She returned to her desk and used her tablet to search for a Harold Sullivan who lived in Brookston. After she found his number, she punched it into her phone. On the third ring, a man answered.

"Hello, may I speak to Harold Sullivan?" Molly's heart pounded.

"This is Harold Sullivan."

"Mr. Sullivan, Kurt Jansen gave me your name. He said you could give him a reference concerning restoration work he did for you."

"Kurt Jansen," the man repeated, then paused. "Oh my, I haven't thought about him in years." There was another long pause. "He's outta prison now, huh?"

No beating around the bush with this guy. At least she should get some straight answers from him. "Yes, and he wants to do some work for me. I have a Victorian house built around 1887, and it needs restoration. Would you recommend his work?"

"He did wonderful work for me. I have the before photos. The changes are dramatic. You're welcome to look at what he did here if you want."

"I might do that before I make my final decision. What can you tell me about him personally?"

"You mean about him going to prison?"

Molly hesitated. Harold Sullivan could only tell her about Kurt Jansen's past, and she needed to know about his present. She had so many questions. Can I trust him? Is he safe? "I'm not sure. I just need to get a sense of the kind of person he is. Will he be easy to work with?"

"Well, he did a fine job for me eight years ago, but I can't tell you much more than that. He was a quiet man. Did his work, and that's about it." There was another long pause. "Tragedy what happened in that family, with him being accused of killing his wife and all."

Molly's mouth went dry. Her pulse pounded and she broke out in a sweat. She already knew this about Kurt, but hearing someone actually say it made it more real. Was it true? How could she possibly know? And didn't she need to know before she could hire him?

Harold prattled on. "I never thought he did it, but most folks around here did. The evidence was circumstantial, but it pointed directly to him."

Molly took a deep breath and tried to keep her heart from racing. "Thanks for the information. I'll give you a call if I decide to have a look at your place."

"Give me a call any time. I'd be glad to show you around."

"Okay. Goodbye." Molly let the receiver fall to its cradle. She raced to the kitchen, where she grabbed her coat and purse. She couldn't make up her mind without a face-to-face meeting with Steve.

***

Molly rushed into Steve's office building. She would probably find him doing paper work at his desk. Hurrying across the lobby, she took off her gloves and tried to stuff them into her coat pocket but discovered the flap on the pocket was buttoned shut. With her gaze centered on her pocket, she turned the corner and ran into a solid body coming from the other direction. She let out a cry of surprise and looked up into a familiar pair of blue eyes.

"What are you doing here?" she blurted.

"Checking in with Steve. What are *you* doing here?" The corner of Kurt's mouth tilted with the hint of a smile. "Checking up on me?"

"I see Steve all the time about lots of things." She tried to cover her embarrassment. Her stomach lurched, but she forced herself not to run.

"Steve was getting ready to go home when I left his office. He and his wife have a dinner engagement. But you might catch him if you hurry." Kurt glanced back over his shoulder.

Molly hesitated. If she did catch Steve, he wouldn't have time to talk. But she still wanted to see him. "Thanks for the information." She walked around Kurt then nearly sprinted to the first turn in the corridor. As she turned the corner, Steve was locking his office door.

"Steve, wait." She waved her hand over her head and continued her hurried pace as he looked up and smiled.

He approached her. "Well, this is a pleasant surprise. Came to see me about Kurt?"

"Yeah…I need some answers." She tried to catch her breath.

"I don't have time to talk right now."

"I know you don't, but let me walk out with you."

"Sure. What's your question?" Steve strode down the corridor to a back door that led to the parking lot.

Molly hurried beside him. "What can you tell me about Kurt Jansen?"

"I've told you what I know."

"But it's not enough." Her voice raised in pitch as they crossed the parking lot. The sun, low in the sky, cast long shadows of the trees at the edge of the lot. Molly shivered and wondered whether the shadows made her cold or whether the cold seeping into her bones came from the thought of Kurt's manslaughter conviction. "His killing his wife hits too close to home for me."

Steve unlocked his car, opened the door, and tossed his briefcase on the front seat. "Then don't hire him."

"But he does beautiful restorations, and his reference gave his work a glowing report. I just want to know I'm not dealing with someone who's going to fly off the handle at the slightest provocation." Molly watched while Steve got in his car and rolled down the window.

"You mean like Byron?"

"Yes."

"I can't give you that information. I don't know the answer." Steve looked at his watch. "I'm sorry, Moll, I've got to run. Lindy will have my hide if I'm not home on time."

Molly stepped back. "I'm torn. You know part of the job offer is letting him live in the carriage house apartment. I'm not sure I want to do that."

"Have you prayed about it?"

She shook her head. "I knew you'd say that."

"It's good advice. And you might want to ask Kurt to explain it to you. I think the Lord is offering you the opportunity right now because Kurt's coming this way." Steve partially closed the window. "We'll talk later."

"Sure." She waved as he drove away.

After Steve departed, she scanned the parking lot and saw Kurt walking through the parked cars toward her. Only a few yards separated them. What did he want? She swallowed a lump in her throat and weighed her options. Maybe Steve was right. She should ask Kurt to explain everything. Get it out in the open. Then she could make her decision.

As he drew closer, she saw the reason he had come looking for her.

"You dropped your glove when you ran down the hall." He held the glove out to her.

"Thanks." Taking it, she realized for the first time that her fingers felt like ice. In her eagerness to talk to Steve she had forgotten about the cold. She put on her gloves.

"Did you get to talk to Steve?"

"For a few minutes."

"Did you get your business taken care of?"

"Nosy, aren't you?"

"No, I was trying to make conversation." Kurt shrugged sheepishly.

Molly realized her own insecurity had caused her to be impolite. "I'm sorry. I've been rude."

"Not exactly rude but maybe—"

"Unpleasant?" Molly supplied.

Kurt laughed, then smiled at her. "If you say so. But you did apologize."

"Thanks." Despite all her fears and reservations about this man, his laughter warmed her. His smile made her heart trip, and she found herself smiling in return. She was in big trouble. Her resolve not to like him disappeared, and she wished she could disappear, too. Then maybe she could find her equilibrium and make some sense of her thoughts.

"Does that smile mean I've got the job? Harold gave me a good reference, didn't he?"

"Yes, Mr. Sullivan gave your work a glowing reference." She headed toward her vehicle. "But he couldn't give me the information I need the most."

"What's that?" Kurt fell into step beside her.

Molly stared straight ahead, wondering how she could ask him why he had killed his wife. Had it been in a fit of anger, an accident, or some other tragedy? She couldn't hire him without knowing. She unlocked the door to her SUV, then stood staring at her reflection in the car window. She had run out of time and excuses. "Why did you kill your wife?"

Kurt looked down at the ground for a few seconds then returned his gaze to hers. His blue eyes conveyed a sadness she hadn't expected. He looked directly at her, his gaze never wavering, as he spoke barely above a whisper. "I didn't kill her."

Instead of anger or malice, conviction sounded in his voice. Molly didn't know how to respond, but she needed some answers. While she stood there, Kurt waited for her to speak. "Then why did you go to prison?"

"That's a good question. I wish I could answer it."

"I need you to tell me more than that."

Kurt sighed, and his breath made a cloud in the air. "I don't know about you, but I'm getting cold out here. If you want me to tell you what happened, then let's go someplace warm."

"And where would that be?"

"Your choice."

Molly contemplated her choices. She didn't want to be alone with him. Where was a safe location? A public place would serve the purpose, and the most logical spot at the supper hour was a restaurant. "Okay, I'll treat you to dinner, and you can answer my questions."

"If that's what you want."

"Good." Molly opened her car door. "You can follow me."

"Okay." Kurt sprinted off to his pickup truck.

When she saw Kurt unlock the door of his vehicle, she turned the key. As she drove toward the restaurant, she realized she had never let the burden of this decision rest in God's hands. She kept relying on her own wisdom. She said a silent prayer. *Lord, give me the wisdom to deal fairly with Kurt. Let me see him through your eyes and not my own.*

***

Kurt waited until Molly's blue SUV exited the parking lot. He put his pickup in gear and followed her. This was not the way he wanted to spend the evening, but if it meant getting this job, he would be charming and cooperative. He'd lay all his cards on the table. He would tell her the whole terrible story no matter how much pain it created. Just thinking about it caused pressure in his chest.

Would she believe him? Despite his promise to tell her the story, he feared that after he had spilled his guts to her, she would turn him away. "Lord, please let her believe me."

Kurt followed her to the next town and pulled in beside her as she brought her SUV to a stop in the parking lot of the Riverside Inn.

He joined her at the door and opened it for her. "Do you come here often?"

"No, actually this is my first time here. I'm checking out the competition. My plans include having a restaurant as well as a bed-and-breakfast." Molly looked at the hostess who greeted them. "A table for two."

The hostess seated Kurt and Molly at a small oak table in one of several rooms that had been converted into dining areas in the old house. He unwrapped the napkin and put it in his lap while she appeared to be studying the menu. Praying that this meeting would result in a job, he glanced around the room. Exposed beams in the ceiling and plank flooring evoked the feeling of a bygone era.

He smiled as he studied the building. "Is this place a bed-and-breakfast or just a restaurant?"

She looked up at him almost as if she had forgotten he was there. "Just a restaurant. I'd like to try several different things so I can get a taste of numerous dishes."

"Then you should place the order." Kurt laid his menu on the table and watched her as she continued to study hers. What was she thinking behind her business persona? Was she assessing his reactions, or was he being paranoid?

When the waitress returned, Molly ordered several of the appetizers, then salads, entrees, and desserts for both of them. "I hope you like what I ordered."

"I'm hungry enough to eat anything. Besides, you're paying the bill." Her offer to buy him dinner couldn't have been more welcome even though it forced him to open up the past. The few dollars he had in his pocket wouldn't buy much. He hadn't planned on eating tonight. This meal would probably tide him over until at least tomorrow night. "What kind of menu will you have in your restaurant?"

She tilted her head to the side and gazed at him. "I've thought about doing a seasonal thing, changing the menu with each season. I have lots of time to experiment before we open up. The first thing I did after I bought the house was make the kitchen a chef's dream. It's state of the art."

"I didn't see the kitchen." Kurt wondered how long he could keep Molly talking about her place. Maybe she'd forget all about the reason she had invited him to dinner if he kept her talking about her plans.

"It's a delight, but I've been so busy with all the other aspects of the job that I really haven't had time to use it as much as I'd like. In the following weeks, I'm going to do a mountain of cooking."

Her enthusiasm for the project made Kurt want to be a part of it. In the dim light of the restaurant, her gray eyes sparkled when she talked about her dream. If only his dream could be as attainable as hers. He looked away, not wanting her to know how much her passion for the project affected him. His future lay in her hands. He wanted this job. Would telling his story make that possible? He needed the employment more than he needed to bury the past.

"When do you plan to open?"

"I want to open at the end of the summer, just in time for tourists who come to look at the fall foliage."

"What made you want to own a bed-and-breakfast?"

"I studied hotel management in college. I loved the food preparation part. In fact, I loved it all. So the bed-and-breakfast idea entered my thinking. But it took me almost a year to find the right place."

Before Kurt could inject another question into the conversation, the waitress brought the appetizers. He immediately helped himself. After sampling all the appetizers, he looked up.

Molly stared at him. "Could we give thanks for the food?"

"Yeah. Sorry, I told you I was hungry." Kurt bowed his head, hoping she wouldn't count this against him.

She said a short, simple prayer. When he looked up, she smiled. "So you think the food here is good?"

Kurt shrugged. "I'm so hungry everything tastes good."

She took a bite of the stuffed mushrooms then studied him intently. "Pretty good mushrooms. Okay, now that we've both appeased some of our hunger, I think it's time you tell me about your wife's death."

He released a heavy sigh and gave her a wry smile. "I knew you'd get around to that."

"You didn't think I'd forget, did you?"

"I could always hope. It's not one of my favorite topics." Suddenly the food didn't taste as good. "Where do you want me to start?"

She bit her bottom lip. "Just start where you want. You know the story. I don't."

Kurt popped another mushroom into his mouth and chewed slowly. Where to start? That was a good question. He let his mind wander back to the good times in his marriage and how they had disintegrated right before his wife's death. "I loved Bonnie. We had some problems, but I didn't kill her. The problems were no secret because we argued very publicly the day before she was killed. That's why I was the one and only suspect in her murder."

Molly's brows knit together in a question as she gazed at him. "Why were you the only suspect? Couldn't someone else have killed her?"

"Someone else did, but I was at a loss as to who it could be." Kurt gritted his teeth in order to control the rage that ate at his gut every time he thought of the killer still out there somewhere. "In my mind, as well as the minds of the town and the people who knew her, she had no enemies. Everyone loved her. She worked for charities, helped at the schools, organized the town festivals, and visited the nursing home, all in addition to selling real estate."

"She sounds like a paragon."

"Close to it." Talking about Bonnie was tearing him up inside. And this was the good part. How could he ever get through the rest without breaking down? He hadn't let himself think about that horrible night in so long that he wasn't sure he could tell the story. "The only thing she ever did wrong, at least in her family's eyes, was marry me."

Molly's gaze narrowed as her expressive gray eyes scrutinized him. "Why was that?"

"I wasn't a lawyer or a doctor. Bonnie's mother had higher ambitions for her daughter. I didn't fit in with those plans."

"Is that why they accused you?"

Taking a moment before he answered, he used every ounce of his inner strength to tamp down the bitterness he felt whenever he had to face his unfair treatment. "No. They considered it a crime of passion. The theory was that I hit her while we were arguing and she fell and struck her head."

"Were you angry?"

"I was angry, but I would never hit her. I loved her."

Before Molly could comment, the waitress brought their salads and a loaf of warm bread. He welcomed the diversion as they ate in silence for a few moments. The soft murmur of other diners and the clinking of silverware and glasses provided background noise for his troubled thoughts. He wondered whether he could convince Molly of his innocence.

"I know this is a difficult conversation, but I have to know before I can feel comfortable hiring you," Molly said, breaking the silence. "What did they say when you told them you didn't do it?"

"I was advised to get a lawyer."

"Did you?"

"Yes. When a person is accused of murder, he gets a lawyer." Kurt finished his salad and set his fork on the plate. "I lost everything. I had to pay my legal fees and still wound up in prison."

"Was your lawyer incompetent?"

"Not that I could see. The evidence was stacked against me."

"What was the evidence?"

"Well, like I said, we had argued the night before. We had gone out to eat. While we were eating, she got a phone call from some of her clients. She insisted on meeting these people. I was upset because she would rather do business than spend an evening with me. We argued very loudly right there in the restaurant."

"So you had lots of witnesses to the argument?" Molly asked.

"Right, but that wasn't the end of it. The next afternoon when I got home from work, she was headed out for a meeting when she had promised she'd be home that evening. So I stormed out of the house just as her mother showed up. There was no love lost between her mother and me. She was a very effective witness against me." Rubbing his temple with his fingers, Kurt remembered how terrible he had felt afterwards knowing that the last words he had spoken to the love of his life had been in anger.

"What happened after that?"

Leaning forward in his chair, Kurt tried to keep his voice low. He didn't want nearby diners to hear this story. "I went out and drove around for a while trying to cool off. I didn't go back home until I was sure Bonnie would be back and her mother gone. Consequently, I had no alibi for those critical hours. There was some talk in the beginning about a possible robbery, but nothing was missing, so they said I tried to make it look like a robbery by messing up the house."

"Did the police come looking for you?"

"No, I discovered the tragedy. When I came home, I thought it was strange that lights were burning all over the house. I had expected to find Bonnie in bed. No other cars were around so I knew she didn't have company." Kurt paused for a moment as he steeled himself to talk about the horrible scene he had found. "I walked in and called Bonnie's name, but there was no answer. When I stepped into the living room, I discovered her body lying in a pool of blood. Someone had smashed in her head."

"How awful!" Molly placed her hand over her heart. "What did you do?"

Trying to block the horrible scene from his mind, Kurt released a shaky breath. "I called 911."

"So you called the police?"

Kurt didn't want to provide any more details. What he had already told Molly hurt enough. "Yes. That's what happened. That's my story, the one I told at the trial. The one no one believed. Do you believe me?"

CHAPTER THREE

Molly wondered how she would feel if she were convicted of a crime she didn't commit. Was he innocent? He sounded sincere, but maybe he was a good actor. Pain radiated from his eyes, but he seemed dispassionate as he told the story. Part of her wanted to believe him, but another part was afraid. "I have to be honest. I don't know what to think."

"Why'd you ask me to tell you my story if you can't be sure? You put me through this then shrug your shoulders." His voice resounded in a harsh whisper.

"Until this moment, you seemed too calm."

He laughed halfheartedly. "I've been convicted of a crime of passion, and you want me to show you outrage? Anger?"

"No, not really." She didn't miss the way his hand balled into a fist as it lay on the table. Swallowing hard, she stared at him as he closed his eyes and pressed his fingers to his forehead as if he were trying to calm himself. Her pulse pounding in her head, she wondered if she had released the beast from the cage.

The waitress appeared with their entrees and dispelled the moment. Kurt immediately picked up his fork and started eating. He stabbed at his food and looked everywhere except at her.

"Kurt?"

He stopped eating and glanced up at her. "What?"

"Could we share the entrees?"

"Oh. Sure. I forgot you wanted to try all the food. Can you bring yourself to eat off the same plate as a murderer?" His blue eyes glared at her as he shoved his plate across the table. "Help yourself."

"Thanks."

She couldn't mistake his anger now. Keeping her gaze down, she cut the entrees in half and put some of hers on his plate and took half of his for her own. She stared at the food, but her appetite had disappeared. Everything tasted like cardboard. The whole evening had turned into a disaster.

As Kurt continued to attack his food, she realized she was trying to solve this on her own. She wondered what God was trying to tell her. She wanted to pray as Steve had suggested, but she didn't know what to pray for. Guidance? How would God make his message clear?

"I've spent the past few years in prison learning how to control my temper. That's what sent me to prison, not manslaughter." Kurt's statement shook Molly from her thoughts.

"You want me to believe you don't have a bad temper anymore?"

"Yes, just like I want you to believe I'm innocent. I was sent to prison unjustly. Wouldn't that make you angry?" He set his fork down without taking his gaze from hers.

"Yes, it would."

"Thank you for understanding at least that much." Kurt sighed. "I have a right to be angry. They've stolen six years of my life. I was in prison when my mother died from cancer. I wasn't there to see her through her illness."

"I'm sorry for your loss." Molly remembered what Steve had told her about Kurt's mother.

"People who worked in Steve's prison ministry loaned me a suit. A plain-clothes policeman accompanied me to the funeral. But it was like I wasn't there at all. No one wanted to talk to me or wish me condolences."

For a moment, Molly let her mind drift back in time to her husband's funeral. The circumstances were different, but she understood that feeling of alienation. "That must have been difficult."

"It was."

"Why should I believe your temper is under control?"

"That's a fair question. I have a lot of reasons to be angry, but I attended anger management classes in prison because of the crime I supposedly committed."

"Did they help?"

"I don't know about the classes, but Steve's ministry has helped me deal with all the problems. He's one in a million." A smile crept across Kurt's face. "I grew up in a Christian home. Bonnie and I attended church on a fairly regular basis. But when I was accused of her murder, everyone in the church turned away from me. What faith I had crumbled. Steve led me back to the Lord."

"You're a Christian?"

"Yes, but it's been a struggle. When I first went to prison, my anger escalated. If it weren't for Steve, I'd be a dead man today. Without his help, I'd still hate everyone. I was angry, resentful, and bitter. Some of that still lingers."

"I'm glad to know you're a Christian." Molly wondered whether this information should sway her decision. Was this the sign from God she was looking for? She couldn't help remembering the scripture, I was a stranger and you took me in. "Steve helped me become a Christian, too."

"Does that mean I get the job?"

Sighing, Molly smiled wryly. Already her heart was lighter. "Getting this job is important to you, isn't it?"

"Yes. Do I have it?"

Her earlier tension slipped away, but concern still remained in her mind. Could she deal with having him just yards away in the carriage house? "I still have to see your estimate for the work."

"No problem. I'll have it to you as soon as I can, but I have to work around my current job."

"Take whatever time you need."

"Thanks. Would you like me to call before I bring it over?"

"Sure." Molly tried to concentrate on her food, but guilt gnawed at her. She had made Kurt tell his story while her past was almost as sordid as his. He would surely think her a hypocrite for insisting he reveal his past when she kept hers a secret. But she couldn't share her former life with him. She had been guilty and served no time while he claimed to be innocent yet spent six years in prison. He didn't want to hear her story.

"How did you get involved with Steve's prison ministry?" he asked.

When she looked at him, the blood drain from her face. Kurt's question went right to her troubled thoughts. What could she say without revealing the things she kept hidden from everyone accept a few close friends? Thankful for the dim light, she pasted on a smile and hoped he couldn't tell how his question affected her. "I met Steve through some of his friends. They helped me out when my husband died."

"Is that what prompted you to become a Christian?"

"Yes. For the first time in my life I saw Christians actually making a difference in people's lives. That's why I employ some of the parolees and ex-convicts from Steve's ministry. I want to give back."

Pressing her lips together, Molly hoped this explanation would satisfy Kurt's curiosity. He didn't need to know that she'd had lots of money, a famous name, and an expensive lawyer. She had gotten off with community service. That had brought her in touch with Steve Barnett.

"That's why you're going to employ me, right?"

Shaking her head, Molly chuckled. "Don't push your luck, Kurt."

"Okay, but I'll expect an answer after you've seen my proposal."

"Fair enough." Molly took another bite of food. This time it tasted much better. Steve believed Kurt's story. Could she trust his judgment? What would Kurt say if he knew about her past? Maybe he would understand her fears. But she wasn't ready to share. Her past was just that—the past—and she saw no point in sharing it now.

***

Three days later a clear, cold morning greeted Kurt as he walked out of the halfway house. He rubbed the kink in his neck as he got into his pickup truck. He hoped Molly would offer him this job because it would mean being able to move out of the halfway house. Getting a better bed was only a small part of the reason. Living at the halfway house reminded him too much of prison.

Taking a deep breath then releasing it, he watched the vapor cloud form in the cab. He turned the key and said a silent prayer of thanks when the engine started. He had spent most of his money on this old pickup, and he hoped it would run until he could afford something better. That was a long ways off. He needed his money to hire a lawyer who would help him get his kids back. In the meantime, getting by on as little food as possible would stretch his dollars. He might lose a few pounds, but that wouldn't hurt him.

He headed for the local grocery store to buy a bagel, some paper and pencils, and peruse the deli department for free samples. At the checkout he spied a pay-as-you-go cell phone and added it to his basket. He would need it for the phone calls he'd make writing his proposal. Munching on his bagel, he strolled to his pickup with a good feeling for the first time since he'd been released from prison. Today he had the prospect of getting a good job.

Maneuvering along the quiet street, he headed for the library, where he intended to spend part of his day off writing his proposal for Molly. He had already spent several evenings there doing research, but he needed to look up a few more things before he visited some local suppliers. The prospect of leaving behind the low-paying, mindless warehouse job he had loading and unloading trucks filled him with excitement. Restoring beautiful old houses was in his blood and the job he was meant for.

First, he spread out the list of supplies and materials he had estimated he would need for the job. He spent nearly an hour using a library computer to look up the names and addresses of supply companies in the local area, prices, and phone numbers of non-local companies as he completed his list. When he finished his research, he headed out to an area supplier.

As he drove along the winding, tree-lined road, he couldn't help thinking about the route he would take to his destination. He would travel directly through the town where his children lived with Bonnie's mother. He knew she wouldn't know he was there unless he went to her house and knocked on the door, but he had an irrational fear that her hatred would somehow find him.

He drove through the center of town and made sure he didn't exceed the speed limit. The last thing he wanted to do was get a speeding ticket. When he came to the last traffic light at the edge of the town center, the light turned red. He noticed the street sign. School Street. If he turned left and drove a few blocks, he would drive by the elementary school. His twins, Emily and Eric, would be inside that building. How could he drive through this town without being at least that close to them? When the light changed, he turned left.

His kids wouldn't know him if they saw him. He wondered whether he'd recognize them. They were three years old in the one photo of them he owned.

He slowed his pickup to the twenty-mile-an-hour speed limit as he approached the school. Children of all sizes ran and played in the schoolyard. His heart raced. Going by the school could cause trouble for him. If his former mother-in-law found out that he was anywhere near his kids, she would do everything in her power to send him back to prison. But the desire to see them outweighed the fear of being caught.

Were his kids out there playing, laughing, and having fun? He wanted them to be happy, but he was afraid his efforts to have a part in their lives would upset them. Bonnie's mother would fight him every step of the way unless he could find Bonnie's killer and prove his innocence.

He stopped next to the curb and turned off the engine. He stared through the chain link fence, hoping that he might catch a glimpse of his kids. He didn't like chain link fences. They reminded him of prison, but he still got out and walked closer. The bright afternoon sun warmed the late February day. He searched the faces of the children as they played.

Then he spotted two children, their hands clutching the chain link as they pressed their blond heads against it. He peered across the street to find the object of their rapt interest. A small gray kitten cried softly as it clung to the branch of a large tree.

"Can you save him, mister?" The high pitched voice made Kurt turn around. "Can you get him down?"

Kurt's heart nearly jumped from his chest when he looked into the face of the little girl who had spoken. Blond ringlets framed her face, and freckles dotted her nose. She was the picture of her mother. The blue eyes she had inherited from him stared at him with such hope. How had he ever thought he wouldn't recognize his own daughter? Then he looked closely at the boy standing next to her. A similar freckled face looked back at him. This had to be Eric. An ache filled Kurt's chest.

Resisting the urge to touch the small hands that still clutched the fence, he set out across the street to perform a simple task that would make him a hero in his children's eyes. The kitten had climbed too far up the tree for him to reach standing on the ground. The thick tree trunk had no footholds that would allow him to climb it. Coaxing the kitten down was the best he could do.

"Come on, kitty. Here, kitty, kitty, kitty." He raised his voice a pitch. The kitten meowed more loudly but didn't move. "Come on, kitty. You've got to come down."

"Maybe he wants a treat. Then he'll come down," Eric yelled.

Kurt looked back at his daughter and son. Somehow he had to rescue that kitten. He went back to his pickup truck and searched the floor for some scrap of food, not that any of it would entice the kitten to respond. Finally, he found a stale french fry on the floor lodged between the seat and doorframe.

Feeling slightly foolish, he held the french fry up to the kitten. "Come on, kitty. I've got a treat for you."

When the kitten moved toward Kurt, the sound of small clapping hands filled his ears. Love for his kids overwhelmed him. He continued to call the feline until it had slowly moved within his reach. He grasped the furry ball and pulled it from the tree trunk. Immediately, claws dug into his hand. He grimaced inwardly, but smiled in spite of the pain as he turned to face his children. Emily jumped up and down and continued to clap her hands while Eric looked on with satisfaction. No other accolades could beat these.

As he crossed the street to show them the kitten, the school bell rang. His kids turned and looked toward the building, then back at him. They hesitated as the other children ran by them, and Kurt lowered his gaze as soon as he saw a woman on the playground looking their way. He didn't want anyone to recognize him.

"Come on, Emily and Eric. It's time to go in," the woman called.

The woman's words confirmed the identity of the boy and girl. There was no doubt that they were his kids. As the woman turned away, Kurt glanced up.

The children gave him one last look then ran for the building. Emily stopped, turned around, and waved. "Thanks, mister."

"You're welcome, Emily," Kurt whispered as he held the squirming kitten to his chest. When Emily and Eric had disappeared from sight, Kurt looked down at the tiny creature. "Now what do I do with you? Do you live around here?"

The kitten meowed.

"Was that a yes or a no?" He tried to control the wriggling ball of fur.

He looked across the street and hoped no one noticed he was having a conversation with a cat. Maybe it belonged to the people who lived in the white clapboard house with the big porch. The tree stood in their yard. Did he dare knock on their door? Would these people know him or have some connection with his former mother-in-law? He didn't want to face them if they did, but he couldn't leave the poor kitten by itself.

As he climbed the steps leading up to the porch,

he prayed for anonymity and rang the doorbell.

"Is this your kitten?" he asked when a woman opened the door a crack and peered out at him.

She shook her head. "Is that kitten still hanging around? I thought if I ignored it, it would go away. It doesn't belong to anyone around here. It's a stray."

"Sorry to disturb you. Have a good day." The door closed softly behind him as he went back down the steps and walked to his vehicle. He opened the door and put the kitten on the seat. "Well, it looks like we're two of a kind, kitty. Both of us looking for a place to call home."

He wondered what he was going to do with this cat. How could he feed a kitten when he could barely feed himself? Despite his meager circumstances, this little ball of fur was a connection with his kids that he couldn't toss aside. He had to keep it. Somehow.

He watched the kitten curl up on the passenger seat. Would it stay there when he started driving? Only one way to find out.

He turned the key and the engine churned. The kitten stared at Kurt with green eyes and let out a small meow but didn't move. So far so good. Kurt slowly pulled away from the curb and breathed a sigh of relief when nothing changed. While he drove to the supplier, the kitten continued to lie on the seat. Every time he looked at the little gray ball of fur, his mind filled with images of Eric and Emily as they applauded.

When he came to the traffic light near his destination, he closed his eyes for a moment. He should be able to see Eric and Emily, talk to them, hold them in his arms, and feel their little arms around him. Would that ever happen? Anger threatened to overtake his thoughts, but he managed to push it away.

Just as the light turned green, he opened his eyes and determined to have a positive attitude. He would get this job, find Bonnie's killer, and have his children with him again. He had the truth on his side. This time justice had to prevail. He wasn't sure how he was going to make that happen, but today he had to focus on the job.

***

Molly heard a knock on the door. Getting up from her desk, she frowned. She wasn't expecting visitors. She walked toward the window and peered out. When she recognized Kurt's old pickup parked in the lane near the house, her heart skipped a beat. Did he have her estimate ready so soon? It had only been three days since they had talked. She hadn't expected to hear from him for at least a week, maybe longer. Now she would have to make a decision—a decision she wasn't sure she could make today—or any day.

She squared her shoulders as she opened the door. "Hi. I wasn't expecting to see you again so soon."

"I know I said I'd call, so I hope I'm not disturbing you."

"You're not." She shook her head. "I was going over wallpaper samples."

"Sounds like fun." He gave her a nervous smile.

She shrugged. "It can be. Are you here to give me your estimate?"

"No. I wanted to let you know that I'm not going to get the estimate to you as soon as I hoped. The supplier I thought I would use doesn't carry the kind of materials I need. I'll have to find someone else, and I wanted to make sure you didn't give the job to someone else before I had a chance to give you a bid."

Molly stared up at Kurt. He shifted from foot to foot while he waited for her response. His anxiety made her nervous as well. "I'm under no time pressure, so I won't make any decisions until I have your bid."

"Okay, then. I appreciate it."

"No problem." Molly rejoiced at not having to make a decision about Kurt today. "Just let me know when you've got it done."

"Thanks." Kurt hesitated.

"Is there something else you need?"

"Um...Yeah, I've got one favor to ask you before I go."

"What's that?" What kind of a favor could he want? She hoped it wasn't something she would find difficult to grant.

"I have this kitten in my pickup that I rescued from a tree earlier today. I don't have a place to keep him, but I couldn't let him fend for himself out on the streets. Would you consider taking him?"

Molly's thoughts wrapped around the idea of having a pet. "A cat? I don't know. Strays can pick up all kinds of diseases."

"You think he might have some?"

Molly shrugged. "I would have to take him to a vet to find out."

"Oh...I don't want to cause you any extra work." Kurt lowered his gaze. "I just couldn't leave him."

"I understand." Molly had the urge to touch Kurt's arm to reassure him, but she resisted. "It might not be a bad idea to have a cat around. I do have trouble with field mice from time to time. How old is he?"

Looking up, Kurt shook his head. "I don't have a clue. I'm not even sure it's a 'he.'"

Molly laughed. "Bring it in. I'm sure a vet can tell me."

"Thanks." Relief on his face, he headed for the door.

Molly watched Kurt go to his pickup, her doubts about him slipping away even though she hadn't seen his estimate. Since the moment he'd opened that album and shown her samples of his work, she'd known he was the one she wanted to hire. She had fought her initial reactions because the doubt about his innocence, niggling at the back of her mind, made her wonder about having him in her house day after day. But how could a man who cared about a stray kitten have killed his wife? Was this the answer to her question about hiring Kurt?

CHAPTER FOUR

A week later, Molly shuffled through the papers Kurt had given her as soon as he had walked through her door. The time for a decision had come.

When she looked up, he stepped closer to her desk. "Does it meet your approval?"

She stood. "Walk me through this. I want to make sure I understand everything in this proposal before I give you an answer."

"Sure. What do I need to explain?"

"I wasn't expecting this much detail. I'm impressed." She smiled, hoping the anxious look on his face would disappear, but it wouldn't until she offered him the job.

"I wanted you to know what you were getting for your money."

"I'm still digesting it." A week ago she'd almost decided to give him the job, but her conflicting emotions had returned. Every time she saw the cute gray kitten romping through the house or curled up in her lap she thought of Kurt and his kindness. But then she remembered Byron and how wrong she'd been about him. Could she trust her own judgment? She had to make this a business decision, not an emotional one. She squared her shoulders and turned to face him as she handed him the estimate. "Let's start in the foyer."

"Okay." He flipped through the pages until he

produced the section on the foyer.

As they left the office, a streak of gray flashed through the foyer and skidded around the corner into the living room.

Kurt laughed. "It's my little buddy. Did you ever find out whether it's male or female?"

"Male, and I named him Smoky. I know. Not very original."

"But it suits him."

Kurt spent the next half hour taking her from room to room and showing her exactly what materials he intended to use and how much each would cost. After he finished, he handed her the proposal and gazed at her, waiting for her response. She had no good reason not to give him an answer, but good reason or not, she wasn't ready to make her decision.

The kitten suddenly reappeared. Kurt reached down and scooped him up. "Where have you been hiding?"

Molly chuckled as she shook her head. "He likes to hide. Last night when I was ready to go to bed, I couldn't find him anywhere. Finally, I found him curled up under the desk in my office."

"So he checked out okay at the vet?" Kurt set the kitten back on the floor.

"Yes, he's in good health but a little underweight. Regular meals will solve that, and he certainly likes to eat." Releasing a slow breath, Molly smiled wryly.

"I'm glad he got a clean bill of health."

"Me, too, because I immediately formed an attachment to him." The kitten rubbed up against Molly's legs and purred so loudly that it resonated through the empty room.

"The attachment seems to be mutual."

Kurt bent over and rubbed the kitten's head then straightened as he stared at her, his eyebrows raised. "Do I get the job?"

She chose her words carefully. "I know you're expecting an answer, and I did say I'd give you one today, but I need to look this over one more time."

A muscle in his jaw worked as if he was trying to bite back a caustic reply. "I can wait here or in my pickup."

His message that he wasn't going away until he got an answer settled into Molly's brain. What would he say if she told him she'd call him tonight with her answer? His reaction to that suggestion might give her a clearer idea of his temperament. "Kurt, I know you'd like an immediate answer, but I'm going to need some time to absorb all this information. I promise I will get back to you later this evening. Give me your phone number, and I'll call you later."

"How about I come back in a couple of hours? Will that give you enough time?"

Gazing at him, she wondered whether any amount of time would be enough. His reasonable response gave her no other choice than to go along with his request. "Sure."

He headed for the door, then stopped and turned back. "I hope you understand that I just want to know where I stand with this job."

"I do. Since you're leaving and coming back, I have a favor to ask you. Would you mind stopping at the grocery and picking up a few items for me?"

Surprise registered on his face. "I can do that."

"Good. I have a list in my office." As she hurried through the door, she wondered why she was giving him another test. Would sending him away with her list and her money give her a better idea about his character and make the decision any easier?

When she returned, Kurt paced in the foyer but stopped when he saw her. He didn't say anything, just looked at her with those haunted blue eyes. She wished she knew what caused that look. Guilt or sorrow? She pushed the question away as she handed him the list.

He focused on the piece of paper then looked up, and a small smile curved his mouth. "You need stuff for the cat?"

"Yes, he's making up for all of the meals he missed. I'm about out of cat food." Molly reached into the pocket of her pants. "And here's some money to pay for it."

Kurt didn't take the money right away. As if he was contemplating her motive for this request, he stared at the bills she held in her hand. Finally, he took the money and stuffed it into his jacket pocket. "Thanks. I'll be back in a couple of hours, and I'll expect that answer."

That answer. The words echoed in Molly's mind as she watched Kurt walk away. She had to make a decision. She couldn't put it off any longer. She picked up the proposal she'd laid on the desk. As she fanned the pages with her thumb, the numbers and sketches became a blur. The memories of Kurt's work captured in photos were the only clear images in her thoughts. How could she turn him away when he produced such marvelous work?

She couldn't.

If he returned with the items on her list and the change, the job was his. She had to start trusting her own judgment again.

***

As Kurt stopped his pickup in the lane near Molly's house, he hoped she would finally give him an answer. He hoped he hadn't ruined his chances by pushing her, but he figured he might as well find out one way or another. He gathered his purchases and headed for the front porch. He sensed that she still wasn't comfortable with him, but she had sent him off with a hundred dollars and that list. Her willing acceptance of the kitten was a good sign. She didn't mind taking in a stray. He hoped that boded well for him, too, but he suspected the errand had been a test of his trustworthiness.

Darkness had settled over the landscape. The lights shining through the windows reminded him of the night he had come home to find his wife murdered and his life changed forever. He shook the thoughts from his head as he reached the front door. He lifted a hand to knock, but before he did, it opened. For a moment the past and present collided. His mind played tricks on him, and he expected a petite blonde to greet him. Molly's statuesque figure silhouetted against the light brought him quickly back to the present.

She smiled and pushed open the screen door. "Here, let me help you with that stuff."

"Thanks. I've got an armload of goodies for that cat."

As she reached for the bag of kitten food, their hands touched. The instant awareness between them made Kurt's heart pound. Their gazes met for a moment, then she turned away and walked toward the back of the house.

Just like the time she had given him her card, the slightest touch awakened feelings he thought he'd never have again. He was attracted to this woman. Something about her greeting him at the door had seemed so right, so natural. How could it be, when they barely knew each other? But then, after being isolated from society for six years, why wouldn't he be attracted to a good-looking woman?

Another thought struck him. Would this attraction cause a problem if she gave him the job? He would have to tackle that when the time came.

"Kurt? Are you coming?" Molly's question shook him from his thoughts.

"Yeah, sure." He made his way down a hallway that led to the kitchen.

"You can put everything in the pantry." She walked through an open door and pointed to a basket on the floor. "After he ate, he played himself to sleep."

Kurt set his purchases on the floor and looked down at the furry ball curled inside the towel-lined basket. "He looks right at home."

"He's been a welcome addition."

"I'm glad you could take him." He followed as she went back into the kitchen.

She looked every bit the chef with a bib apron covering most of her green sweater and tan corduroy pants. The only thing she lacked was a chef's hat sitting on her reddish-blond hair. Behind her, the dark oak cabinets matched the hardwood floors. A large three-section sink sat under a window decorated with a fret spandrel. Despite the modern conveniences, the kitchen still managed to have an old fashioned feel.

"This is a great kitchen," he said, "and something smells good."

"I told you my kitchen was fabulous." She took a little bow. Then she picked up a spoon from the large center island workstation, which offered plenty of workspace for any chef. "I've done some cooking since you left."

"I thought you were going to look over my proposal."

"I did." She stirred something in a pot on the commercial stove sitting along one wall then looked back at him. "You've got the job."

He grinned so wide he wasn't sure his face could contain it. He wanted to grab Molly around the waist and twirl her around the room, but he knew that would probably change her mind. Instead, he clutched the ladder-back chair sitting next to a drop-leaf table. "Thanks. You won't be sorry. I'm eager to get started."

"Me, too. I'm eager to see the finished product." She checked another pot then went back to the first one.

Realizing she was busy, Kurt decided it was time to leave. "I'd better be on my way and let you get back to your cooking."

She lifted her head and gazed at him. "I thought you could join us for dinner and give me your opinion of the food. I can always use another taste tester."

His stomach chose that exact moment to rumble. He laughed. "Guess I can't say I'm not hungry."

"Are you afraid to try my cooking?"

"No. I could use a good meal." He wondered

about her use of the word "us." Did that mean the cat and her, or did she have a date of some kind who would show up momentarily? Did he dare ask? Her demeanor had changed from cautious reservation to unguarded readiness to accept him. Did the presence of another person make her less wary?

"Good. Everything's about ready. If you need to wash up, there's a washroom right through there off the mudroom. You can hang your coat on one of the pegs along the wall." She pointed toward a door at the back of the house.

"Thanks." He headed in that direction.

While he washed his hands, he looked at himself in the mirror. His short hair stood up in several directions. He needed a comb. He rubbed his hand over the pale stubble covering his chin. He looked a mess, but he wasn't trying to impress anyone, was he? Not unless it was the beautiful woman in the kitchen. As he finger combed his hair, he couldn't deny that from the moment he'd met Molly there had been an attraction. He'd told himself that it was only natural since he hadn't interacted with a gorgeous woman in a long time or any woman for that matter. Of course, he would appreciate an attractive woman. That's all it was—a recognition that she was beautiful. He didn't need to worry about it. At least, that's what he kept telling himself.

When he returned to the kitchen, a young woman with short dark hair, who was nearly a head shorter than Molly, stood beside her at the stove. They laughed together as they each stirred something in a pan. So Molly's companion was the other part of "us." He was afraid to speak and interrupt their camaraderie. He glanced over at the small table in the corner. Two place settings adorned the blue-checked tablecloth. Why weren't there three?

Just as he was about to ask, Molly turned around. "Oh, you're back. Kurt, I want you to meet Kayla Beaman. She's my assistant. She's learning everything there is to learn about running a B-and-B."

"Hi, Kurt. Molly told me you're going to do the restoration work on her house. I'm so glad she found someone."

"Me, too. I'm ready to get to work." Kurt took in Kayla's exuberance. Obviously, Molly hadn't mentioned his prison record to the other woman. Would the sparkle in her brown eyes disappear if she knew? He had to quit asking himself those kinds of questions. He had to cultivate a positive attitude. Negative thinking would gain him nothing.

Molly touched one of the chairs. "You can sit right here, and I'll join you in a minute."

Settling on the chair, he picked up the blue cloth napkin. "The table is only set for two. Are you sure I'm not intruding?"

Kayla came over and retrieved the two plates. "Molly invited me over to practice. I'm going to serve you and Molly tonight. I was in the pantry when you came into the kitchen, so I guess you didn't know I was here."

Kurt chuckled as he took a seat. "I did wonder where you came from."

Kayla smiled back at him. "Since you're here, I can prepare two plates rather than just one. That works out better. Be prepared to enjoy some fabulous cuisine."

Molly sat down opposite him. "Thanks for helping out."

"I should be the one thanking you—for the meal and for the job." He smiled wryly.

Kayla brought over two plates and with a flourish set them on the table. "Dinner is served."

Kurt nodded. "This looks great."

"Nice job." Molly smiled up at Kayla. "Presentation is always an intrinsic part of food preparation."

He looked at the chicken breast covered in some kind of glaze and what he thought were sliced almonds, sitting on some leafy green stuff. "Presentation?"

"Yeah. You know, how the food is arranged. How it's presented." Molly waved a hand over her plate.

Kurt glanced down, then looked up at Molly. "Oh. I was noticing how good it looked to eat, not how it was arranged on the plate."

"It all works together."

"Did you learn that in chef's school?"

She nodded. "Would you like to say a blessing for the food?"

"Okay." He realized this was the first time someone had asked him to pray out loud in a long, long time.

He bowed his head and said an audible prayer of thanks for the food, then silently thanked the Lord for his new job. When he raised his head, Molly was smiling at him. His heart did a crazy little tap dance. Was he going to have more trouble than he thought curbing that attraction? He wished there was a way he could check his emotions at the door when he came into this house.

"Now be honest and tell me what you think." Molly's gray eyes didn't hold that wary look anymore.

Kurt couldn't help smiling. "If I tell you I don't like it, will you fire me?"

"No. I have to have an honest opinion."

"Tell me what I'm eating here."

"Okay." Molly looked over at Kayla. "I'll let you tell him."

"My pleasure." Kayla grinned as she stepped closer. "You have honey-glazed chicken breasts with sliced almonds on a bed of mixed greens, a potato soufflé and asparagus spears in cream sauce."

Kurt tried his best not to wrinkle his nose. "I've never liked asparagus."

"Give it a try. You don't have to eat it if you don't like it." Molly picked up her knife and fork and cut her chicken.

Kurt did the same. A hungry man in his situation didn't turn down anything, even asparagus. After savoring the chicken, he took a bite of the asparagus. It tasted fine. He didn't know whether he liked it because it was good or because he was famished. When he glanced up, Molly was watching him eat. The expression on her face reminded him of a child waiting to find out a test score in school. He wouldn't keep her in suspense.

"You must be a superior cook, because you can even make asparagus taste good."

She laughed. "I hope you're not just being kind."

"I'm not." He shook his head. "Somehow you made this asparagus palatable."

"That's good to hear."

While they continued to eat, the musical tones of a cell phone trilled through the room. Kurt turned as Kayla grabbed a cell phone from the counter and looked at it. She stepped into the laundry room as she answered. Her muffled voice floated back to them as they ate in silence. When Kayla reappeared, her face had lost all of its color. Kurt glanced at Molly, then back at Kayla as Molly hurried to the younger woman's side.

"Is something wrong?" Molly put her arm around Kayla's shoulders.

Kayla didn't speak for a moment, her throat working as she swallowed. Then she looked up at Molly. "My...my dad's been taken to the hospital. I need to go home."

"Of course, you do." Molly patted Kayla's arm.

Kayla nodded. "I'm sorry to leave before I serve the dessert."

Molly shook her head. "Don't worry about anything here. You just go and spend as much time as you need with your dad. I'll be praying for you."

"Thanks." Kayla hugged Molly.

After the two women ended the embrace, Molly left the kitchen with Kayla. Kurt stared after them, unsure of what he should do. His mind buzzing with memories, he sat there as if glued to the chair. Unexpected trouble always took him back to the horrible scene of Bonnie's death. He tried to push away the images, but they crashed through his resistance. Would he ever shake them?

When Molly returned, he jumped up. The terrible thoughts slowly faded as he forced himself to look at her. "Does she know what's wrong with her father?"

"Heart attack."

Kurt shook his head. "That's how I lost my dad. I hope her dad will be okay."

Molly returned to her seat. "Let's pray for him right now."

Kurt bowed his head and listened to Molly's prayer. Did God really hear their prayers? He'd thanked God tonight for this new job, but deep down Kurt still struggled to find answers. Why had God let his parents die? Why had Bonnie been murdered? Why had he gone to prison for something he didn't do? Kurt didn't have any good answers. Did God?

When Molly finished praying, Kurt lifted his head. "Does Kayla have to travel far?"

"Her dad lives out in Western Mass, so it's not too far." Molly picked up her fork and poked it around in her food. "I hope the food isn't cold."

Kurt took a bite. "It's fine."

They ate in silence for several minutes. Kurt wondered what Molly was thinking. Did she feel uncomfortable around him now that Kayla was gone? Or was he being paranoid again? He wished she'd say something. Anything. "Do you have any new questions about my proposal?"

Molly jerked her head up and blinked as if his question had startled her. "I do. We need to discuss the advance money in your proposal."

"Is that going to be a problem?" He hoped not, because he needed that money to get started. He had to replace the tools he'd sold, along with everything else he'd owned, to pay for a defense lawyer. Most of the profit from this job would go into supplies.

"No, it's not a problem. I understand you need to buy materials and things. I only wanted to know if I could set up accounts for you at the local suppliers you'll be using."

"Yeah, that'll work out great." Relief washed over him. "How soon will you have those set up? I'll need some materials and supplies before I begin the renovation."

"I'll do it tomorrow." She took another bite of chicken.

Kurt thought of all the things he needed to do before starting this project. "How do you want to handle getting materials from non-local sources? I have phone numbers and web sites for those."

"Why don't we go over them together in the morning, and then I can call in the orders."

"Do you have a specific time I should start work? I don't want to get here too early."

"I get up around six o'clock, so any time after that."

"Good. Most mornings I'll probably start working around seven."

"That sounds good." She finished the last bite of her food. "Are you ready for dessert?"

"Yeah. After eating prison food for six years, your cooking is a real treat." He popped the last piece of chicken into his mouth. "That was great. Thanks."

"I'm glad you liked it, especially the asparagus." Standing, she picked up the plates.

"Would you like help?"

She held up a hand. "Not necessary. I use the dishwasher, and we'll load that after we have some of this cake."

While they ate their cake, a small meow broke the quiet. He looked down. Little cat paws padded across the floor and stopped near his foot. Then the kitten rubbed up against his leg and purred so loudly that it sounded like a motor.

"It looks like you've got a pal." Reaching down, Molly gave the kitten a pat on the head.

"Everyone needs a friend." Kurt rubbed the

kitten's head. "Hey, little guy, did the smell of food bring you in here?" The kitten purred even louder and circled Kurt's leg, then finally curled up under the table.

After they finished eating their cake, Molly went to the pantry and brought out a plastic plate. "Let me send some of this food home with you. I can't possibly eat all that's left."

Kurt shook his head. "You don't have to do that."

"I want to."

"I just hope someone else at the halfway house doesn't decide to help themselves. We have a community refrigerator."

"Kurt?"

He heard the sympathy in her voice and hoped he wouldn't see pity in her eyes. Glancing up, he folded his arms across his chest. "Yeah?"

"Did Steve tell you that I could provide a place for you to live if you needed it?" Her brows rose.

Kurt nodded. "Yeah, but I didn't want to be presumptuous. I didn't want to bother you."

"It's not a bother, but I'll tell you the same thing I've told all the people Steve has sent to work for me. If you do anything I find objectionable, you're out of here. This job is your second chance. There won't be another one."

"I understand." His earlier concerns that his conviction for manslaughter might intimidate her fled. She had the upper hand, and she knew it. He wondered whether her warning meant she still had doubts about his innocence.

"Good. Then we should get along fine."

"How much do you charge for the room? I can't afford much. I'm trying to save as much as I can to get my life back in order."

He didn't want to share his real reason for saving his money. Any discussion of his kids was off limits. He feared if he talked about his plans, they would somehow get back to his former mother-in-law, and she would make it impossible for him to ever see them. He knew his fear was irrational, but that didn't change it.

"Nothing. It comes with the job if you want it. I have a small, furnished apartment above the carriage house. You can live there as long as you're working on my house."

"I didn't mean that you shouldn't charge me. I should pay you." He leaned back against the center island. He wanted to save money, but at the same time he didn't want to be a charity case.

"It's not necessary."

"All I can say is thank you." Kurt glanced down at the floor. He was beginning to realize that Molly's Christianity didn't end with lip service. She applied it to her life. He recognized that he had more or less gone through the motions of serving God. Maybe that was why he was having such a struggle relying on God now.

"You can move in tonight if you'd like."

"Okay. I'll be back in about an hour." Grabbing his coat, he headed for the front door. He didn't want to give her a chance to change her mind.

***

After Kurt returned, Molly carried the leftovers she had packed for Kurt as she led the way across the drive toward the carriage house. The yard light cast long shadows as he walked beside her with his duffel bag slung over his shoulder. She glanced at him out of the corner of her eye. He gazed straight ahead. The dim light veiled his expression.

She wondered whether she had done the right thing by offering him this job and a place to live, especially now that Kayla wouldn't be here to serve as a buffer. Maybe she could find someone else to assist her so she wouldn't have to spend each day alone with Kurt.

Why was she having second thoughts now? She had done the right thing, the Christian thing. God had laid it on her heart to help this man. She tried to convince herself she had done this for all the right reasons. There was no turning back.

She could tell he'd been embarrassed to admit he lived in a halfway house. His circumstances touched her. She had wanted to reach out and comfort him, but she knew what would happen if she did. Sparks would fly. She couldn't deny the physical attraction between them, but she wouldn't act on it. She didn't need a man in her life. The whole thing scared her silly.

But, despite all her reservations and fears, she found herself attracted to him anyway. She hadn't been interested in any man since Byron. Now another good-looking man had walked into her life and made her heart beat in double time—something she didn't want to deal with. She would do everything in her power to squelch the slightest progression of this unwanted interest.

After they climbed the stairway to the apartment, Molly unlocked the door and went in. She felt for the switch on the right side of the doorframe. A fluorescent light sprang to life in the kitchenette just inside the door. After she put the leftovers in the nearby refrigerator, she placed her keys on a small rectangular table with two chairs that separated the kitchenette from the living room.

She went directly to the thermostat. "We'll get some heat going in here. It's better than I thought it would be. I guess the sunny day helped keep it from getting too cold."

"This is great." Kurt set his duffel bag on the overstuffed chair covered in a floral fabric that matched the plain blue sofa. "I'm not used to such luxury."

"This isn't exactly luxurious."

"It is to me. Anything's better than a prison cell or the halfway house."

"I'm sure it is."

"If you only knew."

Molly knew about jail cells. She'd spent time in one herself while she'd been waiting for bail, but she'd served no time for her crime, and certainly not six years. Guilt gnawed at her when she remembered the past she kept hidden. She continued to rationalize that his knowing about her past would only serve to remind him of the unfairness of his incarceration.

"If you have toiletries, you can put them in the bath down this hall while I make up the bed back here." She made her way toward the bedroom.

"You don't have to go to that trouble. I can do it myself." He followed her, bringing his duffel bag with him. "You've done enough for me already."

She looked up at him as he entered the room. "It's no trouble. Besides, you don't know where everything is."

"Just tell me, and I can take care of it."

"It won't take me any time at all." She pulled sheets and blankets from the closet. "You can hang your stuff up while I do it."

"Let me help. The work will go faster." He took hold of one side of the sheet she had laid out across the bed.

She wanted to protest, but when she saw his determined expression, she knew she couldn't argue. All of his actions told her what she wanted to believe.

This wasn't a man guilty of murder in any degree.

The simple task of helping to make a bed said a lot to her. She'd never shared that task with anyone. Byron would never have thought to do such a thing. There had been maids to do that kind of work. Everything about the evening had served to show her what kind of man Kurt was. He had praised her cooking, helped with the dishes, and worried about a stray kitten. How was she ever going to keep this attraction under check when Kurt would be around day and night?

"I'm sorry there's no TV here," she said.

"That's all right. I don't watch much TV anyway. A good night's sleep without waking up with a crick in my neck is something I look forward to." He tucked the sheet and blankets in at the bottom of the bed.

After grabbing two pillows and pillow cases from a drawer in the maple chest that sat in the corner, she tossed them on the bed. "I'll let you take care of these. If you need anything, just let me know."

He stuffed a pillow inside a case. "You've done more than enough already. I don't know how I can repay you."

"Make my house a dream come true. That's

payment enough." She turned to go. "Come over around six-thirty in the morning and I'll have breakfast for you. Good night."

"See you then, and we'll start making your dream come true. Good night."

She let herself out and hurried across the yard to her house. She didn't want to think about Kurt's last statement, but it hung in her mind like a promise with too many possibilities. He was thinking about the house, but her heart had her thinking about something she didn't deserve to have. Love and a family. She'd destroyed the one she'd had, and she didn't merit another one. Nothing she could do would make up for the horrible mistakes she had made.

CHAPTER FIVE

Molly washed mushrooms for the omelets she planned to make while she gazed out the kitchen window. Rays of early morning sunshine filtered through the bare-branched trees near the carriage house. She searched for a light in the windows of Kurt's apartment but saw none and wondered whether that meant he wouldn't show for breakfast.

She wasn't sure why she cared as long as he showed up when it was time to start work. She chided herself for her foolish thoughts, but she hadn't been able to stop thinking about him. Her mixed emotions betrayed her better sense. She sliced the mushrooms on a cutting board as if the effort could chop images of him from her mind. She had made a decision, and now she had to live with it. He was going to work for her. She shouldn't have second thoughts.

She shoved the mushrooms off the cutting board into a frying pan containing hot melted butter. As they sizzled in the pan, she heard a knock. Her heart jumped into her throat. She looked around the corner of the mudroom at the window in the back door. Wearing a navy blue parka, Kurt stood on the back porch. She put a smile on her face and waved for him to come in.

"Good morning," she called as he stepped inside. "Hang your coat in the mudroom. You're just in time to tell me what you want in your omelet."

He took off his coat and hung it on the nearby peg. "Mmm, smells good."

He stood in the doorway and looked as though he wasn't quite sure if he should come all the way into the kitchen. His sandy blond hair was damp. A plaid flannel shirt emphasized his broad shoulders and reminded Molly that this handsome man was a temptation she would have to resist. She wondered how he had gotten ready without a light. If she asked, he might think she was spying on him.

"Come on in and help yourself to coffee while I start the omelets." She stirred the blended eggs then slowly poured them into an omelet pan. The bubbling mixture reflected the feelings Kurt's presence generated in her heart and mind.

"I'll live dangerously. Put a little of everything in mine." He grabbed one of the mugs sitting next to the coffee maker and filled it.

"Okay." She was the one who would be living dangerously if she let an attraction to this man override common sense. Any sentiment toward him had to stay in the context of business. She had given him a job and that was all.

"Is there something I can do?"

Shaking her head, she looked away from his brilliant blue eyes toward the task at hand. "No. This will be ready in a couple minutes. Just have a seat on one of the stools by the island."

Kurt sat and watched while she put mushrooms, peppers, onions, spinach, ham, and cheese in his omelet. Taking in his serious expression, she vowed to keep in mind she was dealing with an ex-convict. Although he might be innocent, she had to remember he carried the scars of his unjust treatment. Letting herself have tender thoughts about him was just as foolish as believing Byron's smooth lines. She had let emotions and silly dreams draw her into a relationship with Byron. Now she was older and wiser. She wouldn't let it happen again.

After Molly finished the omelets, she placed them on plates and gave one to Kurt. She set her own plate next to his on the counter, then plucked several biscuits from a warming tray and put them in a basket. She brought the basket over and sat on the stool next to him. "Would you like to give thanks for the food or should I?"

"You can." He put down his coffee cup and bowed his head.

As she bowed her head, she couldn't ignore the flicker of sorrow she had seen his eyes. She gave thanks for the food and said a silent thank you that she hadn't had to endure the horrors of prison that Kurt had seen. She looked up, wondering about his solemn demeanor.

While Kurt carried his plate to the table, Smoky padded into the kitchen with a meow and wove his way around Kurt's legs. He reached down and scratched the kitten behind the ears.

Molly chuckled as she joined Kurt at the table. "He must really like you. He's been hiding since I got up. You come along, and he shows up."

Kurt shrugged. "What can I say? It must be my charming personality."

"Must be." It was nice to joke with Kurt. Sharing breakfast with him was a treat. She just couldn't let it lead to anything else.

While they ate, the kitten purred and wove his way in and out from under the table, then curled up in front of the stove.

After they finished eating, Molly stepped around the kitten as she took her plate to the sink. "Watch your step. I wouldn't want you to start your day by tripping over a cat."

"I'll keep that in mind." Kurt picked up his dishes and joined Molly at the sink. "Thanks for breakfast. This was great. Can I help with the cleanup?"

She shook her head. "No. This will only take me a few minutes. Go ahead into the study. I'll be there shortly, and we can go over the orders you need to make."

"Okay."

Molly smiled but heaved a sigh of relief when he

left the room, the kitten trailing behind him. She rolled her shoulders and tried to relieve the tension his presence had created. She didn't know which was worse. Worrying that he was actually guilty of manslaughter or worrying that she was beginning to like him too much.

Moments later, she found him sitting in one of the chairs near the fireplace and reading her Bible. Her resolve not to care about him melted a little like the snow outside in the warmth of the late winter sunshine.

***

Molly sat at her desk after calling in more orders for Kurt. Over the past three weeks new material for the project had arrived almost daily. He had warned her that the house would look worse before it looked better, and he was right. The inside of the house had become an obstacle course of tools, saw horses, and trim work. The progress seemed slow, but Kurt estimated that he would finish the inside while the weather was still cold.

When the weather warmed, he would start working on the outside. Spring was almost here, and with it came the promise of new beginnings for this project and the people she planned to help— including Kurt.

Looking forward to the outside work, she glanced

through catalogs selling trim work for the porch, windows, and gables, but her mind wasn't on trim. Instead, images of the man who intended to do that work paraded through her mind. His handsome face kept appearing in her mind rather than shutters and spandrels. They shared breakfast most mornings before he started work, and this time together did nothing to mute her initial attraction to him, but she usually managed to focus her mind in another direction. Today was an exception. She couldn't get him out of her thoughts.

While she tried to get her mind trained on the task at hand, the phone rang. She answered, and a female voice sounded in her ear. "Molly, this is Bev Marsh over at the Antique Trader in Oakton. You called some time back inquiring about furniture, and I've gotten several pieces in that I think you might like to see."

"What do you have?

"I have a lyre cocktail table and matching lamp tables. And I've found a goose neck rocker."

"Oh, the rocker. That's definitely one piece I want."

"And I have a couple of room groupings that I'd like to show you. I think they'll be perfect for your house."

"When would you like me to look at the furniture?" Molly asked.

"You can come today, or whenever you'd like. I'm

open from ten to five Monday through Friday."

"Could you give me directions? I've forgotten exactly where you're located." Molly grabbed a pen and pad from the desk.

"Sure." Bev proceeded to give directions.

"Thanks. I'll be over sometime today. Goodbye." Molly let the phone fall into its cradle.

Sighing, she glanced at the catalogs on her desk. Maybe this was a good time to look at the furniture since she wasn't making much progress picking out millwork. Shopping for furniture could go a long way toward taking her mind off Kurt. Being away from the house when he came back with his supplies would give her a chance to clear her mind. She grabbed her coat and purse and went out to her SUV.

Unfortunately, the drive to Oakton did little to keep her mind off Kurt. She kept seeing the look in his eyes when she had handed him the key to her house on the day he started work. Surprise and grateful acceptance had radiated in his gaze when he took it. She could tell he appreciated her trust, but he didn't know she couldn't trust him with the story of her past. What did it matter? He didn't care about her or her past. This was a job for him and nothing more. He wanted a fresh start, and the job provided that.

Molly slowed the SUV as she entered downtown Oakton. A large red brick building with white trim and black shutters sat in the middle of the town square. Large black letters above the door labeled it the Town Hall. Across the street stood a white clapboard church building with a tall steeple, looking out on the small businesses clustered along the streets around the square. The scene before her painted a picture postcard of a small New England town. She had fled to this area of Massachusetts to find peace in its Norman Rockwell towns. She wanted to leave behind the lights and glamor of the big city and the chaos of her former life. Burying the past and all its sorrow remained her mission.

She needed to focus on the present, but the present brought its own dilemma. She was attracted to the first handsome man to cross her path. What had happened to her vow to forget men? Kurt Jansen, with his reserved smile and sparkling blue eyes, had happened. Since Kayla's return was indefinite because she was helping her father, Molly had to deal with Kurt alone. She hadn't counted on that.

Shaking the troubling thoughts from her head, she turned onto School Street. Turning right at the next corner, Molly tried to put Kurt's image out of her mind. When she spied the Victorian house on the corner and the sign in the yard announcing the Antique Trader, she parked her SUV at the curb.

As Molly opened the door to the house, a bell jangled above her head. Immediately, a middle-aged woman with dark brown hair liberally sprinkled with gray appeared in the entry. "May I help you?"

"Yes, I'm Molly Finnerty—"

"Oh, yes, I'm so glad you came." The woman reached out to shake Molly's hand. "Let me show you the furniture I think will be perfect for you."

"Yes." Following the woman, Molly admired the fine woodwork and furniture in the beautifully restored house. "Your house is lovely. I hope mine turns out as well."

"If you have someone who knows their business doing the work, it will. I'd recommend the fellow who did mine, but unfortunately, he died quite a few years ago, just a few years after he did my house. His son took over the business, but he went to prison for killing his wife." Bev shook her head. "Such a terrible, terrible story. His two children live with their grandmother right here in Oakton." She waved her hand in the air as she continued. "But you don't want to hear about that. Let's look at the furniture I promised you."

Rooted to the floor, Molly watched Bev's back as she walked into the next room. Could she possibly be talking about Kurt? Did he have children? Neither he nor Steve had mentioned them, so maybe Bev was talking about someone else. But how many restoration experts in the area could have been sent to prison for killing their wives?

Bev turned and looked at her. "Are you coming, dear?"

"Yes. I was still admiring your house." And thinking about Kurt.

Molly tried to shove those thoughts aside while Bev led her through various rooms displaying more Victorian furniture than Molly had ever hoped to see. After she finished walking the whole house, she went into Bev's office. "I'd like to purchase the lyre cocktail table and matching lamp tables as well as the goose neck rocker."

"Wonderful. Let me write that up for you." Bev picked up her glasses from the desk and seated herself in front of a computer.

"Do you do decorating consultations?" Molly asked. "I need help deciding which pieces to use in the different rooms."

"Oh, definitely. I'd love to see your house. I can help you choose not only the furniture but also things like wallpaper and window treatments. Would you like to set up an appointment? I can come over either tomorrow or Friday, because my assistant comes in on those days."

"Tomorrow morning would be fine. Say around ten o'clock."

Bev nodded. "I'll see you tomorrow at ten."

When Molly arrived home, Kurt's red pickup was parked near the house, its tailgate open. Lumber and other materials lay in the bed of the truck. He emerged from the front door as she stopped her SUV behind his pickup and got out.

He smiled and waved as he approached. "Your front hall is full of building materials. I'd hoped to get it all in and out of your way before you got back."

"That's okay. I've been living with a mess since I moved in. I wouldn't know what to do without it." She walked to the back of her SUV and opened it. "I've got some other things to add to the clutter."

Kurt joined her. "Looks like you've been shopping. Would you like a hand taking that inside?"

"Sure. I'm going to take them up to my apartment until things get done. We can each grab a lamp table, then come back for the other things." She picked up a table and headed for the house.

While she climbed the front steps, she wondered what Kurt would do if she asked him whether he had children. But she couldn't ask directly or he might think she had been spying on him. She entered the house, stepping around the trim pieces lying on the floor just inside the door. "Looks like you're making progress."

"I am." He followed her up the stairs. "I missed doing this kind of thing."

"How did you get involved with restoring and renovating old houses?"

"I worked with my dad. He taught me everything I know. He was a master craftsman, and I wanted to be just like him."

Molly stopped at the top of the stairs and turned to look at Kurt. "You said before your dad died when he had a heart attack, right?"

Kurt shook his head. "Yeah, he died a couple of

years after I graduated from high school, and I took over his business. That's how I met Bonnie. I restored a Colonial house for her aunt."

Molly continued down the hall. "Did your father do restoration work for a woman named Bev Marsh who lives in Oakton?"

A wary look crossed Kurt's face. "Yes. How did you know that?"

"She has an antique gallery in that house now. That's where I got the furniture." Molly opened a door at the end of the hallway then stopped. "She's coming over tomorrow to help me pick out more furniture and give me decorating ideas."

"What time?" Kurt asked, his face somber.

"Around ten. Why?" Molly started up the stairway that led to her apartment.

"I think it'll be best if I'm not around then."

Molly stopped halfway up the stairs to the third story and turned. "Why?"

"It wouldn't be good. Bev Marsh knows me and why I went to prison. Too many people think I should still be there. She's probably one of them."

"Oh. I see." Molly finished climbing the stairway and walked into her living room. Bev had been talking about Kurt. Why hadn't he mentioned his children? Did he not care about them? Surely the man she had come to know in the past few weeks would care about his children. Maybe he was afraid of how they would view him in light of his prison record. She felt a connection with Kurt that he couldn't begin to know. They were both afraid to face the past.

She set her table in the empty space along one wall. "You can put that table next to this one."

Kurt put his beside hers then surveyed the room. "No Victorian furniture up here?"

"My living space is about comfort, not style." She ran her hand along the arm of the tan leather sectional that curved around one corner of the room.

He chuckled. "And I thought I was the only one who looked at Victorian furniture and saw something uncomfortable."

"I didn't say it's uncomfortable, but it's certainly not as comfortable as this." Suddenly, uncomfortable meant being alone with this man. She didn't know why now, after spending so many days alone with him. Maybe her discomfort had to do with his not mentioning his children. If he kept them a secret, could she believe the other things he said?

Trying to shake the troubling thoughts away, she sat down and operated the recliner at one end of the sectional in an effort to divert her own attention away from her uneasiness. "I can sit here in the evenings, relax and watch TV, or read and listen to the stereo." She pointed out the entertainment center containing a TV and other electronic equipment. "And I have my kitchenette. So if I want a midnight snack, I don't have to go down two flights of stairs."

"Seems like you have everything you need."

"Yeah." Pushing the recliner back and getting up, Molly could only think about the things she didn't have. For years she'd had all the material wealth anyone could want, but her life had been an empty shell until she'd found the Lord. Now she yearned for the one thing she thought she would never want again. The love of a good man and a family. "Let's go get that rocker."

"Okay." He headed for the stairway. Molly followed him to the second floor. As they walked down the hallway, he stopped. "Will you give me a tour of this floor?"

Her unease faded at his request. His interest in this project warmed her heart. Byron had never cared about her dreams. He had only cared about her money. "Sure. I still have some work to do up here, but the major renovations were already done when I bought the house."

As she showed Kurt each of the six rooms on the second floor, she couldn't help comparing him to Byron. His charm had captivated her immediately. The same thing was happening with Kurt. The similarities scared her.

She reminded herself that Kurt and Byron were different. Byron's flashy personality had drawn her to him. Now Kurt's quiet reserve made her heart flutter, but the common thread remained. She couldn't deny the instant attraction from the moment she had met each of them. But in this case, Kurt's only interest was doing a job for her while Byron's had been to connect himself with someone rich and famous. She had fit the bill.

"Which room is your favorite?" Kurt's question jarred her from her thoughts.

"The big one at the back of the house that overlooks the woods and the creek. It's such a peaceful view. I have the same view out my bedroom window on the third floor."

"How many acres of land do you have?"

"Twelve."

"Do you have any plans to develop it?"

Molly nodded and pointed toward the window. "For now I'm concentrating on this house, but there's an old farm house and a barn in that grove of trees behind the carriage house. I plan to make them into a shelter for battered women."

Kurt smiled, but sadness radiated from his eyes. "You sound like Bonnie. She was always looking for a good cause. I'm afraid I didn't always appreciate her good causes. They took time away from us. Now I just wish she were here to work on them."

Not knowing how to reply, Molly descended the stairs, opened the front door, and tried to put herself in Kurt's shoes as she went down the front steps. She wondered whether Bonnie was constantly on his mind. This was the second time today that he had mentioned her. Molly wasn't sure she liked being compared to his dead wife. He said he had loved her dearly. He must feel terrible knowing that the person who had killed her was walking around free. How would he feel if he knew Molly had let her own husband die? She didn't want to think about it.

Kurt followed her to the SUV. "If you open the doors, I can carry the rocker by myself." He lifted it out of the back.

"Okay."

After they took the rocker to her apartment, Kurt also carried the cocktail table up to the third floor. When they returned to the main floor, she went out to his pickup with him. "Thanks. That furniture was heavier than I thought. I don't know what I would've done without your help. What can I carry?"

"You're welcome, but I don't expect you to help me with this."

"But if I help, you can continue working sooner."

He sighed. "All right. Carry what you can."

"When I think about the house being finished, I get a fluttery feeling right here." She placed her hand over her heart. "I'm like a kid on Christmas Eve. The anticipation is killing me." Smiling, she picked up several plastic bags containing small items and headed toward the house.

Carrying four long trim pieces, Kurt laughed. "Don't let the anticipation do that. I need the money."

She joined in the laughter. It felt good to laugh with Kurt. She realized, despite her early reservations, that she enjoyed his companionship. She reminded herself that he would probably never understand what she had done. He could never find out. "I promise to live long enough to pay you."

He let out a long, low whistle. "That's a relief. You had me worried."

"Let me get the door." She hurried to open it.

After he set his load on the floor, he glanced at her. "Is it all right if I leave this stuff here?"

"Sure."

"I was planning to put plastic over all your doorways to help keep the dust out. It won't be perfect, but at least it'll help. I'll pick that up tomorrow while your decorator is here. I don't want to be here when she shows up."

"That's fine." When he mentioned Bev, Molly realized he would share a good laugh with her, but he didn't feel comfortable enough to tell her about his children. He talked freely about Bonnie but not his children. Why? Maybe he didn't feel comfortable enough with her yet, even though they had known each other for nearly a month. "Did you spend all your time today getting supplies?"

"Most of it. After I picked up the supplies, I drove around a little and looked at some familiar places. The freedom to come and go as I please is something I'll never take for granted again." Without waiting for her comment, he went back outside.

Molly followed, not daring to quiz him further about his activities. She couldn't ask too much about his past without him wanting to know about hers.

***

The next morning Molly insisted that Kurt taste test her Belgian waffles. After he finished eating, he worked on the stairway banister and spindles. Around nine-thirty, he announced his intentions to pick up some of the specialty tools he had ordered from the nearby lumberyard. Molly knew he was leaving in time to avoid running into Bev Marsh.

When Bev arrived, she inundated Molly with samples of wallpaper, fabrics, and catalogs of furniture, and her mind became totally focused on the house. Thoughts of Kurt faded into the background. After she had picked out wallpaper for every room and fabrics for the window treatments, they made the final decisions about the furniture. Molly pored over catalogs and pictures of beds, chests, and lamps, making choices for each room.

After they finished, Molly stood and stretched her hands over her head. "That was a lot of work. My brain is on overload from making so many decisions."

"You'll be happy with all of them." Bev picked up her sample books. "We've done everything except the outside furniture. We can work on that later. Let me take these books to the car. Then I'll write up the order with the final prices."

After Bev left, Molly's thoughts revolved around

her plans for the bed-and-breakfast. She could almost see the rooms in all their finery and imagined greeting her first guests. A shiver of excitement ran down her spine as the picture formed in her mind. Then reality knocked on her dreams and made her remember that those dreams depended on a man who posed a lot of unanswered questions.

She struggled to focus her thoughts elsewhere as she went to her office, but she couldn't concentrate. Her mind buzzed with questions about Kurt's children. Pacing back and forth in her study, she tried to figure out the most diplomatic way to ask him about his kids.

While she paced, she caught sight of her Bible lying on the desk and realized, once again, she had left God out of the situation. She went immediately to her desk and picked up the Bible. Sitting down, she bowed her head. "Lord, please help me deal with Kurt in a way that would reflect your love. Let your word speak to me."

Letting the pages fall open, she glanced down to see a passage from Ecclesiastes. "Two are better than one, because they have a good return for their work: If one falls down, his friend can help him up. But pity the man who falls and has no one to help him up!"

What could God be trying to tell her with this passage? Was He telling her she shouldn't be afraid to make Kurt her friend? Sighing, Molly wished knowing God's will came easier.

She got up from her desk and looked out the window. Kurt's pickup was coming down the drive. Her stomach churned at the thought of talking with him. He would probably consider her nosy if she asked about his children. Did she have the right to ask about his life outside of work?

When he walked through the door, he laid a large roll of plastic sheeting on the floor then looked up to where she stood in the doorway to her office.

"Hi. Did you get all your decorating done?" he asked with a smile that made her heart do a little flip-flop.

Trying to calm her nerves as well as her jumpy heart, she took a deep breath. "Most of it."

"Good. I hope you're prepared for the dust. I'll get this plastic up before I start this next phase of the renovation."

Molly stepped into the entry. "Before you do anything else, there's something I want to ask you."

"What's that?" He looked at her with a wary expression that probably mirrored the concern on her own face.

Squaring her shoulders, she pushed herself not to chicken out. "When I talked with Bev Marsh, she mentioned that you have two children. Maybe this is none of my business, but why haven't you mentioned them?"

CHAPTER SIX

Kurt stared at Molly while emotions roiled his stomach. He felt the color drain from his face, and his thoughts went on the defensive. Why was she questioning him about his kids? What business was it of hers? He had the illogical fear that his presence at the school would get back to Bonnie's mother. He didn't want that to happen. It could jeopardize all his plans.

"What's it to you?" He rubbed his hand across his chin, wishing he could take back his harsh reply, but it was too late. Someday he would learn to temper his words as well as his actions.

Without acknowledging his tone, she looked at him with gray eyes full of uncertainty. "I was just wondering why you never mentioned them."

He didn't want to face her questions. "There was no reason to talk about them."

"I see." Her gaze didn't waver. Her scrutiny made him feel as though she could see into his soul and gauge the honesty of his answer. "Does that mean it isn't any of my business?"

He lowered his head. All his protective instincts told him that it wasn't her business. She had nothing to gain or lose, but he did. He wasn't sure he could trust her to know his plans. He raised his head. She was still looking at him, only now curiosity colored her eyes instead of doubt. "I'm not sure."

"Then I won't press the issue. I'll let you get on with your work." She turned and walked into her study.

He stared after her. He had gotten what he wanted, but there was no satisfaction in his triumph. While misgivings plagued his thoughts, he began putting plastic sheeting over the doorways leading into the kitchen. Regret over his hasty words continued to eat at him. He wanted her to like him, but he was afraid to let down his guard. Even after working here for several weeks, he still sensed that she had reservations about hiring him. Barking out answers to her questions didn't go very far in soothing her fears.

As he finished with the kitchen doorways, he analyzed his conversation with Molly further. What if she had told Bev Marsh he was working here? That information could get back to Bonnie's mother. He had to know.

Approaching the study in order to cover it with the plastic sheeting, he couldn't help thinking that a frank discussion with Molly about his situation was the best thing for everyone concerned. He released a harsh sigh as he set the plastic on the floor and knocked lightly on the door.

"Come in." The sound of Molly's voice made his heart beat a little faster, and he steeled himself against the interest in her that he didn't want to feel.

Slowly, he opened one of the doors. Hanging onto the door as though it could serve as a shield, he stuck his head into the room and cleared his throat. She looked up from her desk. "I don't mean to disturb you, but I wanted to let you know I'm going to put plastic over the doorway. I didn't want you to run into it."

"Thanks for letting me know." She immediately turned her attention back to the things on her desk.

She had dismissed him without another word. He cleared his throat again. "Molly?"

"Yes?" She didn't bother to look up as she spoke. "Did you want something else?"

"Yeah. I want to apologize for the way I spoke to you earlier."

"Apology accepted." A slight smile curving her lips, she glanced up, then continued her work.

She was dismissing him again. He wondered whether she was angry with him even though she had accepted his apology. She wasn't interested in talking, but he needed to have this conversation with her.

"Thanks." He stepped into the room. "I don't want to do something that will put a wedge between us."

Shrugging, she studied him with a puzzled expression. "I said I accepted your apology. Everything's fine."

"Maybe for you, but not for me. I need to ask you something."

She stuck a pencil in the book she'd been studying and closed it. "What's your question?"

As he gazed at her, he wasn't sure he wanted to know the answer, but this situation called for temerity, not timidity. "Did you tell Bev Marsh that I was working for you?"

"No." Molly shook her head. "I figured, when you told me she didn't think you should be out of prison, that it wouldn't be a very good idea to mention it."

Kurt rubbed his hand across his face as he slowly released the breath that he'd been holding. "That's a relief, but I'm still concerned she might find out."

Molly frowned. "So what if she does? She can't put you back in jail."

"No, but she could cause problems for you."

"Why would she want to hurt her own business?"

Kurt stepped closer to the desk. "Bev Marsh wouldn't, but she's a very good friend of my former mother-in-law, Virginia Spencer, and she would."

"Does this have anything to do with your children and the reason you didn't want to talk about them?"

Looking toward the window, he nodded, unable to speak past the lump in his throat. All the fears, hurt, and pain associated with his kids raced through his mind while he searched for an answer. Whenever he thought about them, it felt as though a large hand was squeezing his heart. Only the memories of Bonnie's death caused more anguish. He wanted Molly to understand, but he didn't trust her or his own emotions. But if he didn't tell her, how could he expect her to be on his side?

Finally, he turned his gaze on her as he swallowed the lump in his throat. "Yes. I have seven-year-old twins. A boy named Eric and a girl named Emily. I've missed over six years of their lives."

"Where are the children now?"

"Bonnie's mother is the children's guardian. She won't let me see them, but I plan to change that."

"How?"

"Hire a lawyer."

"You're going to ask the court to change the original order?"

Kurt shook his head. "I don't know. I'll get a lawyer's advice. At this point, just visitation would be nice."

"Why won't she allow it?"

"She thinks I killed their mother. If she has a choice, she'll never let me near them."

"When was the last time you saw your kids?"

The question stopped Kurt cold. His heart pounded and his stomach sank. Telling the truth could jeopardize his plans. But if he lied about this and Molly found out, she would doubt his truthfulness. He couldn't afford to have her think he was lying when he said that he was innocent in his wife's death. The truth was his only option. If he wanted her to believe him innocent, he had to be honest about this, too.

"Don't you remember?" Molly asked, interrupting his thoughts.

He swallowed hard. "I remember. I'm just not sure I should tell you about it."

She gazed at him as a puzzled expression knit her brow. "Why?"

"Because I want to be truthful, but honesty could cause problems for both of us."

"Now you've really piqued my curiosity. Please tell me."

"If I tell you, will you promise not to say anything to anyone? I have to have your word."

"You have it."

"Okay." He took a deep breath. "When I was getting prices for my job proposal, I drove through Oakton, where my children live. I went by their school. Kids were on the playground, and I wondered whether Eric and Emily were there. So I stopped."

"And you saw them?"

"Yes."

"Is that the problem?"

Kurt nodded. "It could be since Bonnie's mother

is their guardian. She doesn't want me anywhere near my children."

"Then why did you do it?"

"I had to see them." He wondered whether she could truly understand why he had done it. "I couldn't be that close and not take the chance."

Molly eyed him thoughtfully. "What would've happened if you'd been caught?"

"I'm not sure." He shrugged. "But until then, I hadn't seen them since the day I was arrested. They were six months old."

"So they don't know you."

"I'm not sure they even know I exist. I wrote them letters and sent them birthday and Christmas gifts through the years, but I doubt they ever got them." Kurt felt anger boiling up inside him at the unfairness, but he tamped it down. Learning to control his rage was one step in getting his children back. He would have to face Virginia Spencer again in court, and he would have to remain calm and collected no matter what she said. This was a test of his resolve.

"Why do you think that?" Molly asked.

"Because my mother told me when she asked the children about the letters and gifts, they knew nothing about them."

"How awful."

"That's not half of it. When the children asked Bonnie's mother about the gifts, she decided that my mother couldn't see them anymore. Virginia Spencer didn't want them to know me."

"What made you think you'd recognize them?"

"I wasn't sure I would, but I have this picture." He reached into his back pocket and got out his wallet.

He opened it and pulled out a picture with tattered corners. "My mother took this on their third birthday." He handed it to Molly.

She took the fragile picture and studied it. "Oh, they're adorable. Are they still this blond?"

He nodded. "Like Bonnie. Emily looks just like her. That's how I knew her when I rescued the kitten."

"She saw you?"

"Yes," Kurt replied, then related the story of the rescue to Molly. When he finished, he glanced away, not wanting her to see the moisture in his eyes. "But I promised myself I wouldn't see them again until I'm sure I won't jeopardize my chance for visitation rights and hopefully, one day, the chance to have them back for good. But that pretty much depends on proving my innocence. I need two things—a lawyer and a private investigator."

"It must be awful for you not to see them. Do you have a lawyer in mind?

"No."

Molly came up beside him and held out her hand to return his picture. "I can help you find a lawyer, but not a PI."

"That's okay. You don't need to get involved." Kurt turned to face her again. Why was it so hard to accept the help she offered?

"I'm sorry you feel that way." She shook her head. "I want to be your friend as well as your employer. People from the prison ministry want to help. That's why we do what we do."

"I know that, but at this point in my life, I want to depend on myself."

"What about depending on God?"

"I'm working on that."

"Me, too." She gave him a wry smile. "I didn't mean to lecture."

"That's okay. I need to be reminded from time to time that God's in control even when it doesn't seem like it."

"Speaking of God, I'd like you to attend church with me on Sunday."

Shaking his head, Kurt rubbed his hand across his chin. "I don't know. I'm not sure I'd fit in there."

"Just give it a try."

"Is this a requirement to keep my job?"

"No, but where have you been attending?"

"I've been going with Steve. I feel comfortable with that group. They know me."

"Do you like going back to the prison?"

"Not really, but—"

"Then go with me," Molly interrupted.

"I'll think about it," Kurt replied, eager to get back to work in order to avoid any further discussion about church attendance. Fear of being seen only as an ex-convict and not as a regular person made him reluctant to accept her invitation. He didn't want people to look down at him from their pious perches and judge him. He'd had enough of that to last a lifetime.

"Okay. I'll let you get back to work."

"Thanks for listening without judging. I appreciate all you're doing for me."

"No need for thanks. You're helping me as much as I'm helping you," Molly called after him when he walked toward the door.

Turning back to her, he smiled. "I'm glad you feel that way."

***

Molly opened the cookbook she had been reading before Kurt interrupted. She picked up the pencil that marked her place and tapped it on the desk as she tried to get a pair of sky-blue eyes out of her thoughts. When she managed that, the image of two little blond children filled her mind.

Her first reaction when she'd heard Kurt's desire to see his children had been one of sympathy and a desire to help. But those troublesome doubts crept back into her thinking. Was he really innocent? She understood why he had surreptitiously seen his children, but would helping him allow a murderer near kids? Her intuition told her he was innocent, but she'd been wrong before. Byron had fooled her with his effervescent charisma and wit. Now Kurt's quiet charm drew her in and made her like and trust him. Was his charm insidious or sincere? Closing her eyes, she laid her head back on the chair and let the pencil fall to the desk.

As she let Kurt's story roll through her brain, she wondered what she should do. Maybe the best thing was to leave well enough alone as he had requested. But if she did, it would be months before he could hire a lawyer. If he was innocent, he deserved to be with his children. She had the means to hire the best lawyer money could buy, and she wanted to do it if it helped an innocent man. That was the catch. How did she know for sure that he was innocent?

God, why aren't the answers easy?

She opened her eyes and stared at the ceiling. Slowly lowering her gaze, she saw her Bible lying next to the cookbook on her desk. She picked up the Bible and let the pages fall open. So many times in recent days she had turned to the Bible in just this fashion. What would the scripture say to her today? The words from the fourth chapter of First Peter stared back at her.

Above all, love each other deeply, because love covers over a multitude of sins. Offer hospitality to one another without grumbling. Each one should use whatever gift he has received to serve others, faithfully administering God's grace in its various forms. If anyone speaks, he should do it with the strength God provides, so that in all things God may be praised through Jesus Christ. To him be the glory and the power for ever and ever. Amen.

God's word cut straight to her heart. Helping Kurt in every way possible was her way to serve. If that meant giving him a place to live or finding him a lawyer, she would do it. His innocence or guilt didn't matter. God was reminding her that He had forgiven Kurt's sins as surely as He had forgiven hers. And she had been guilty. She wanted to believe Kurt was innocent for her own peace of mind, but she knew, no matter what, God had given him a clean slate, and she had to do likewise.

The phone rang, making her jump. She released a loud sigh before she picked up the receiver. "Hello."

"Moll, how are things going?" Steve's question came over the wire.

How could she answer that? God's word had given her the direction, but she felt as though that decision caused her to swim against the tide in so many emotional ways. "My house is full of plastic."

"What?"

"Kurt has put plastic sheeting over the doors."

"So the work is progressing. Good. I just wanted to make sure you're feeling comfortable with the situation. I know you had your reservations."

"I still do, but I'm working through them."

There was a pause from Steve's end. "You don't have to do this if it's making you worry."

"I'm fine. He's over three weeks into this project. There's no going back." She contemplated asking Steve about her plan to get a lawyer for Kurt. Surely Steve knew about Kurt's kids, but if he didn't, she would betray Kurt's confidence. Shaking her head, she recognized that a direct and honest approach was the best way. "What do you know about Kurt's children?" She bit her lower lip as she waited for Steve's reply.

"Not much except that his former mother-in-law is their guardian, and he's not allowed to see them. He wouldn't talk about them much. I think it was too painful, especially after his mother wasn't allowed to see them anymore. Did he tell you about them?" Steve asked.

"Not voluntarily. I found out indirectly and asked him about them."

"And what did he tell you?"

"About the same thing you just told me." Molly tapped her fingers on the desk and wondered how she could broach the subject of a lawyer. "Did Kurt ever mention what his plans are concerning his kids now that he's out of prison?"

"No, he keeps things pretty close to the vest."

"You can say that again." Rubbing her temple with her free hand, Molly couldn't bring herself to tell Steve about Kurt's plan. Instead, she decided to change the subject. "I invited Kurt to attend church with me, but he says he'd rather go back with you."

"He did?" Incredulity colored Steve's voice. "I thought he'd jump at the chance to be finished with anything that has to do with prison."

"Well, he said he was more comfortable meeting with your group."

"I like having his help, but he needs to get on with his life. Do what you can to encourage him to go with you."

"I will, but he's sensitive about other people knowing he's been in prison."

"Nobody has to introduce him as an ex-con."

"I know that. But I gathered from our conversation that he knows they'll eventually find out, and I think he's afraid of their reaction."

"He has to face the rest of the world sometime. Help him do it."

"I'll try my best." Molly sighed. "If you don't see him Sunday, you'll know I succeeded."

"Let's ask the Lord for a little help."

"It'll be the first thing on my prayer list. I'll talk to you later." Molly hung up the phone.

She wondered about her inability to mention the thing she wanted to talk about the most—getting Kurt a lawyer. She feared betraying his trust. If she did that, she would have no standing with him and have no chance to help him at all. When she remembered the way he had handed her that tattered picture of his children as if it were his most priceless possession, she knew she had to find a way to get him to accept a little assist in the game of life. She didn't know how to overcome the dilemma, but she was determined to find someone to help Kurt see his children.

Molly scrolled through the contacts on her cell

phone until she came to Nick Rinaldi's name. If anyone could help Kurt, Nick or someone in his law firm would do it. Inviting Nick to Sunday dinner might open the door.

***

On Sunday morning Kurt glanced toward Molly's house as he made his way down the steps of his apartment. The sun, glinting off the windows, gave the drab exterior a surprisingly cheery look. Or maybe the fact that a lovely woman with a giving heart occupied the place made her house appear in a better light. His breath created a cloud in the air as he released a sigh. He had to quit thinking of Molly in terms other than his employer. Such thinking would only lead him down a path where neither of them could go.

Despite the sun, the cold morning air nipped at his unprotected ears. As he approached his pickup, he realized the windows were covered with frost and retrieved a scraper from under the front seat. While he watched the white film disappear under the careful guidance of the scraper, he wished he could eliminate all the horrors of his past just as easily. The simple act of attending church had him torn between the past and the present. Going back to the prison for church to help Steve with his ministry meant revisiting the part of his life he'd like to forget, but going with Molly meant facing the present while he still dragged the shackles of his unjust imprisonment. Neither choice was appealing. He tried to remind himself that going to church wasn't about himself but about worshipping God.

Kurt got into his pickup with that thought firmly in mind. He put the key in the ignition and turned it. An anemic sputter emanated from the engine, then ceased. He turned the key again. Nothing. He slammed the heel of his hand against the steering wheel. Closing his eyes, he released a long slow breath. Sensing another test of his self-control, he turned the key again. The same silence greeted him. He wasn't going anywhere in a vehicle that didn't start.

The morning air seemed even colder as he headed to Molly's house. He hoped she had jumper cables, though they might not be the answer to his problem. Before he reached the back door, Molly stepped outside, closing the door behind her. Despite her black wool coat, she looked like an angel as her strawberry-blond hair gleamed in the morning sunshine.

She glanced up as she stepped off the porch. "Well, good morning. Does this mean you're going to church with me?"

Kurt shook his head. "I was planning to go with Steve to the prison, but my pickup won't start. Do you have jumper cables? I think it might be the battery."

She gave him a wry smile. "Have you considered that it won't start because the Lord wants you to go to church with me?"

Seeing her smile and hearing her words made all the frustration and anger at his circumstances fade into the background. "No, I can't say I have."

"Well, let's look at it that way. A sign from heaven." She pointed upward.

"If you say so."

"I do." She headed for the carriage house. "I

should've let you clear out some of the junk in the carriage house so you could put your pickup in there along with my car."

"That's something I can work on tomorrow." Kurt fell into step beside her.

"Oh, no. I can't let you do that." She turned to look at him as she kept walking. "You keep working on the house. I can clear out the carriage house and see if there's anything in there I can use. I should've done it earlier, but I've been waiting for warmer weather."

"This week we're supposed to have some temperatures in the sixties. Even though the calendar says its spring, we're sure to get one more snow before winter leaves for good," he said, thinking that his emotions, like the weather, ran hot and cold. One minute he contemplated seeing where his attraction to Molly might go, and the next he realized the complete lunacy of any such action.

"You're probably right. I'd better make good use of the warm days."

"And I'd better get things done inside, so I'll be ready to do the outside work once the weather changes for good." He headed for his pickup.

"Where are you going?" Molly called after him. "I thought you were going with me."

He turned to look back at her. "I am, but first I need to get my Bible."

"Good. I also want you to come over for dinner after church. I have company coming."

"Someone from church?" Kurt wished his pickup had started after all. Going to church was hard enough without having to socialize afterwards.

"No. It's a friend of mine from Boston. He and I

share the plans for that women's shelter I mentioned, if you remember."

"I do. That's fine." While Kurt retrieved his Bible from the front seat of his pickup, he couldn't help the sinking feeling that captured his heart when he thought about Molly being involved with someone. How stupid he'd been to think that a beautiful woman like her didn't have a love interest.

"You don't mind?" She asked as she waited for him.

"I never mind free food." He tamped down his disappointment but reminded himself that this would help remove the temptation to act on his fascination with her.

Molly laughed as she slid behind the wheel of her SUV. "Good. You'll like Nick."

Kurt buckled his seatbelt. "I'm sure I will."

When Molly stopped her vehicle in the church parking lot, Kurt said a silent prayer that he'd remember the purpose for being here. Despite his trepidation, the white clapboard building with a tall steeple had a welcoming effect on him. As they entered the building, several folks greeted them, and Molly introduced Kurt to her friends. Gratitude filled his heart when her introduction only included the fact that he was restoring her house. He noticed the speculative glances that followed them as they settled on one of the dark oak pews near the front.

He surveyed the building and took in the stained-glass windows that depicted various Bible stories. It reminded him of the church building where he had attended services as a child. The image of his parents rolled through his mind. Those were happy times, but those times were gone. He wondered whether he'd ever have happiness like that with his own children. He closed his eyes and prayed that God would somehow make things right in his life.

When he opened his eyes, Molly was looking at him.

She touched his arm. "Are you all right?"

Smiling wryly, he nodded despite the rapid beating of his heart. He shouldn't let a friendly gesture affect him like this. Remembering her friend Nick, Kurt vowed that he would keep his relationship with Molly where it belonged.

Before he could respond, a choir filed into the pews at the back of the platform. In addition, several guitarists, a drummer, and other musicians with various instruments found their places. A screen lowered from the ceiling as a group of singers picked up microphones and began to sing. Soon the congregation joined in the festive singing. Kurt realized all resemblance to the church experiences of his childhood stopped with the likeness of the building. Not only was this a far cry from his youthful memories, but it sure beat anything he had experienced at the prison.

The music spoke straight to his heart. Lifting praises to God, he joined his voice with Molly's as she sang harmony. Although these songs were more modern, singing them reminded him of the times he had sung hymns with Bonnie. Even thoughts of his deceased wife didn't make him sad today. God's presence filled his heart, and Kurt silently gave a prayer of thanks for a vehicle that wouldn't start.

He was thankful for that dead battery until the minister's sermon about forgiveness made Kurt examine his feelings. As he listened to the scriptures and sermon about the need to forgive the people who have wronged us, he admitted that he didn't want to forgive. He clung to a log of unforgiveness in a sea of self-pity. Letting go meant forgiving those people who had turned away from him when he needed help the most. Forgiving meant changing his attitude toward Bonnie's mother. Despite all the joy he had experienced during the song service, his heart was heavy with the realization that he had a long way to go in letting God lead his life. At this point, Kurt wondered whether he would ever feel the forgiveness God wanted him to experience.

When the sermon ended, tension from the guilt worked its way through Kurt's whole body. He rolled his shoulders as he tried to work out the tightness. While he tried to figure out how to deal with his troubled thoughts, the choir softly sang a hymn he remembered from his childhood, "Just as I Am." The words, "tossed about with many a conflict, many a doubt," spoke directly about his life. Even with all his shortcomings, he recognized that God would take him. As the choir finished the song, Kurt prayed, thanking God for his forgiveness and asked God to give him the strength to forgive as well.

After the final prayer, Molly turned to him. "Well, what do you think?"

Kurt smiled. "It was good. Thanks for insisting that I come."

Molly returned his smile. "I'm glad you liked it." She picked up her purse from the pew, then turned back to him. "I'm sorry we have to rush off before I can introduce you to some more people, but I want to get back so I can have everything ready when Nick gets there."

"Sure." Kurt was just as glad to bypass the after-church chitchat. Her eagerness to see this Nick didn't make him feel any better, but meeting him would serve as a reminder that a personal interest in Molly was out of the question. He etched that thought permanently on his mind as they got into her SUV.

Kurt breathed a sigh of relief when they pulled into Molly's drive and he didn't see another car. Her company had yet to arrive. When she stopped her SUV, he glanced her way. "Do you have those jumper cables I asked you about earlier?"

Molly chuckled. "I sure do. They're in the back under the seat. Nick gave them to me last Christmas. He thought I might need them."

Nick certainly didn't give romantic gifts. Kurt smiled inwardly as he waited for Molly to open the back of the SUV. "A very practical gift."

"Yes, Nick is very practical." She held out the keys. "Here. You can try to get your pickup started. If a dead battery is your problem, there's a battery charger in the carriage house, but you'll have to look for it. I'm not sure where it is. I've got to run. I have to get busy with the meal preparations."

"I can do this later if you need help." Kurt pushed the hatch closed.

"You go ahead. I've got everything cooking in the oven. I just need to check on it and do all that last minute stuff. Come up to the house when you're done. Nick should be along any time."

"Thanks," he called after her as she hurried toward the house. Turning back to the SUV, he released a harsh breath. Even though he tried to keep things in perspective, thinking of her in business terms remained a difficult task.

***

Molly watched out the window as Kurt hooked the jumper cables from his truck to her SUV. She hated to spy on him, but she loved watching him work. Even from a distance his movements made her heart trip. She shook her head as she turned from the window and forced herself to finish the meal preparation. While she prepared the sauce for the vegetables, she heard an engine start. A few minutes later another one sputtered to life. She glanced out the window just in time to see Kurt sprinting toward the house.

She greeted him at the back door. "You're in a hurry."

He gave her a lopsided grin. "Looks like my problem was a dead battery. Will I mess up your dinner plans if I run into town to give the battery a little charge?"

"No, in fact, I just discovered I'm out of an ingredient for my salad. I was sure I bought some sliced almonds when I went to the store this week, but I can't find them anywhere. I'd appreciate it if you'd stop at the store and get some for me."

"Your wish is my command." He waved as he raced down the back steps.

Wondering what she really wished for where he was concerned, she watched him drive toward the main road. With each passing day, her feelings had changed from a wary attraction to a growing fascination. She tried to tell herself these thoughts were crazy, wrong-headed, and impossible, but they wouldn't go away. Somehow he reminded her of

Smoky the stray kitten. The kitten liked to stay nearby in the kitchen, but on his own terms. Kurt approached her in the same way.

While she woolgathered at the kitchen window, Nick's Jag turned into the lane. When he emerged from the car, she couldn't help comparing him with Kurt. Nick had a slight build in contrast to Kurt's large frame. With a tan overcoat slung over one arm, Nick looked every bit the high-priced lawyer in his expensive navy blue suit and coordinating tie. His wealthy clients were glad to pay his fees because he won most of his cases. While Kurt's nearly blond hair had the earmarks of a prison barber, Nick's black hair showed the latest stylish cut of one Boston's trendiest salons. Despite their many differences, both men shared one thing. A love of the Lord.

When Nick stepped through the back door, Molly hurried to greet him with a hug. "It's so good to see you. I wish you could've brought Allison."

She says hi and hopes to see you next time. Anyway, it's good to see you." He embraced Molly, then stepped back, glancing around the kitchen. "Lots of changes here since my last visit."

"That tells me you've been away too long."

Nodding, he smiled. "Do I get a tour?"

"There isn't much to tour. The kitchen was a long time getting done, and the rest of the place is a construction mess, but I've finally found someone to finish the rest. You'll get to meet him as soon as he gets back from the store."

"Yeah. Steve told me you had hired a guy from the prison ministry. That means our plans can move forward."

"Yes. That's why I've invited you here for dinner."

"And here I thought you wanted to see me." Nick stepped further into the kitchen.

"I do, but I have ulterior motives. Did Steve tell you anything about the man I've hired?"

"He told me that he's a talented carpenter, and that he might be able to start the other part of our project."

"Steve didn't mention that to me." Molly busied herself at the stove, stirring a simmering pot of sauce. She couldn't help wondering whether Steve was using Nick to allay her worries about Kurt. "Can he handle all that by himself?"

"I don't know. Steve thought it would be a good idea for me to show him the other property and see what he says."

"I wasn't expecting that." Molly wasn't sure what to think.

"You sound a little hesitant about working with this guy. Is there a problem?"

"No. No, not really." Molly didn't dare tell Nick about the real problem—her growing attraction for an ex-convict. Having him work on the other houses meant he would be around longer and make it more difficult to resist his quiet charm. She turned from the stove and wiped her hands on her apron. Looking directly at Nick, she hesitated before she spoke. How could she let Nick know about Kurt's need for a lawyer without betraying his confidence? Nothing came to mind. Somehow this meeting had to conclude with Nick finding a lawyer for Kurt.

"I...I want...I wish..." She threw her hands in the air.

Nick chuckled. "Having a tough time expressing yourself?"

Molly laughed half-heartedly. "Yes. I just want you to be Kurt's friend."

"And I take it that Kurt is the fellow you've hired?"

Molly nodded. "I'd like to tell you everything I know about him, but I promised to keep some things I know to myself. But I was hoping somehow you could gain his trust and learn these things, too."

Chuckling again, Nick stepped closer and put his arm around her shoulders. "You should see the pained expression on your face. Is it that hard to keep a confidence?"

"In this case, yes. He needs your help. That's all I can say."

"Does he know about you?"

Gazing at the floor, Molly shook her head. "No."

"Why not?"

"Because I haven't told him." She held up her hand to ward off Nick's anticipated advice. "And there's a very good reason. He was sent to prison for a crime he didn't commit. He doesn't need to know about a rich model who got off without serving any prison time when she was guilty. Very guilty."

"Don't you think he'd understand?"

"No. I doubt my two years of community service would compare with six years in prison. Think about it, Nick."

Nick gave her a skeptical look. "I hope you don't live to see the day you regret not telling this man about your past."

Before Molly could reply, a furry gray ball jumped from beneath the kitchen table and attacked the belt dangling from the coat Nick still had slung over his arm.

"What's this?" Nick scooped the kitten off the

floor.

"Smoky, my newest house guest." Molly scratched Smoky behind one ear, glad that the kitten had interrupted the conversation. "He's letting you know that it's okay to hang up your coat."

"And where did Smoky come from?" Nick put his coat on a mudroom hook.

"Kurt found him. I said I'd take him to keep the mice away." Molly stood next to Nick and stroked Smoky as he purred, nestled against Nick's shoulder.

"I see you're taking in all kinds of strays. Human and otherwise. That's one of the reasons I like you so much." Nick leaned over and gave Molly a peck on the cheek.

A knock on the back door made Molly look up. Kurt stood outside. She stepped away from Nick and hurried into the laundry room to open the door for Kurt. "Come in. That was a quick trip. Did your pickup do okay?"

"Fine, but I'm still going to need that battery charger." He held out a plastic grocery sack. "Here are your almonds."

"Thanks." She took the bag. "Come into the kitchen."

Kurt hung up his coat. "I see your company has arrived."

"Yes, come and meet Nick." She went into the kitchen where she made the introductions and prayed that this meeting would accomplish what she hoped.

After the introductions, Molly urged the two men to make themselves at home in her study while she put the finishing touches on her meal. As they departed, she noticed how ill at ease Kurt looked. She hoped Nick would be able to break through his barriers.

CHAPTER SEVEN

Kurt followed the man in the expensive suit toward the study. What could he say to this guy? As far as he could see, they had nothing in common other than their interest in Molly. Envy had crept into Kurt's heart when he had seen Nick kissing her earlier even though it had only been a peck on the cheek. Kurt knew he didn't have the right or a reason to be jealous, but he was anyway. He wanted to be in Nick's place. Maybe God was reminding him that he didn't need the distractions of a woman. He should concentrate on the job and getting his kids back. That was the first priority.

When they reached the study, Nick sat in one of the chairs around the Oriental rug. Reluctantly, Kurt eased his large frame into the other. Not even the sunlight cascading through the windows made Kurt's thoughts any brighter. His mind buzzed with ways to start a conversation, but all of them seemed lame so he said nothing.

Nick broke the silence. "Molly tells me you're going to restore the rest of her house. Are you responsible for all the plastic?"

"Yeah," Kurt replied, glad that Nick hadn't asked him about being in prison. "It helps keep the dust from the rest of the house."

"How long will it take you to finish?"

"If all the supplies come in when I need them, the house should be ready to go by the end of August.

Molly told me she hoped to open about that time."

Nick got up, walked over to one of the windows, and looked out. "Has she explained her plans for the place?"

"It's going to be a bed-and-breakfast."

Nick turned. "Yes, and she intends to employ the women who live in the women's shelter. Did she mention that we're working together on the shelter?"

"Yes. Is that how you met her?"

Shoving his hands into the pockets of his pants, Nick hesitated. He turned away again. "Not exactly. We met through some mutual acquaintances and found we had a common interest in helping abused women. The shelter rose out of our shared concern."

Kurt wondered about the other man's lack of eye contact and hesitation in answering the question. Did he have something to hide? Maybe he had been one of Molly's charity cases at one time and had spent time in prison as well. But whatever the man did now paid well. His Jaguar, suit, and shoes spoke of money. "What's your line of work?"

"I'm an attorney. I specialize in family law."

Warning signs flashed through Kurt's mind. Had Molly told Nick about Eric and Emily and his need for a lawyer? Is that why she had invited Nick here today? Kurt stood, knowing his height gave him at least one advantage over this man. "What has Molly told you about me?"

"Other than that you're working on her house?"

"Yes."

"She said you'd been in prison and that Steve Barnett's prison ministry recommended you for the job."

"And that's all?"

"No, she said you weren't guilty of the crime."

Kurt couldn't help feeling pleased that Molly believed him. "Nothing else?"

"That's all she told me. Is there more I should know?"

Relief flooding his mind, Kurt slowly released the breath he'd been holding. Why had he doubted her? He had forgotten how to trust people. Maybe it was time to start, but not with a stranger. "Not that you'd be interested in."

"You never know."

"Well, I doubt you came out here today to hear about my problems."

Nick smiled. "You're right. I came out here to see how Molly and her project are coming. You happen to be part of that process. So I'm interested in you, too."

Kurt studied the man standing on the other side of the room. Was Nick's concern for Molly's safety because she had hired an ex-con, or was he worried that some other man might steal his girlfriend? What woman in her right mind would choose an ex-con over a wealthy lawyer? He should take a few boards, a hammer, and nails then box up his thoughts before they got any crazier. "I can promise you this. You won't be disappointed in my work."

"Good." Nick walked across the room and stood next to Kurt. "After dinner today, I'd like to show you the other part of the project. The part that Molly and I share. Are you interested?"

"Sure." Kurt nodded, realizing that Nick wasn't intimidated by anything.

The rustling of plastic captured Kurt's attention. He turned and saw Molly standing in the doorway.

He hated the way the sight of her made his heart race even in the presence of the man she cared about.

She smiled. "Everything's ready."

During the meal, Kurt listened to Nick and Molly as they discussed their mutual friends and projects. Even though they tried to include him in their conversation, Kurt felt like an outsider. He didn't belong. Even if he had never spent a day in prison, he came from a different world than they did. They were part of the rich and famous with their fundraisers and charity projects. For the first time, he realized Molly came from a privileged life similar to Bonnie's. He didn't need another woman like Bonnie to remind him that he was a poor kid who didn't measure up. He hated feeling like one of their charity cases. He tried to remind himself that he wasn't taking charity here. He was earning a living by working hard at an honest job. But coming from the prison ministry made him feel as though he was somehow inferior. Would he always feel this way?

"What do you think, Kurt?" Molly asked.

A sinking sensation hit Kurt's stomach. He didn't have the slightest idea what she was asking him about. His reverie had completely taken him away from their conversation. Shaking his head and gritting his teeth, he grinned sheepishly. "I'm sorry. I wasn't paying attention to what you were saying. I was thinking about work."

"That's what I was asking you about. We were talking about adding a gazebo. What do you think?"

Kurt shrugged. "You can do whatever you want."

"Can you build one?" Molly looked at him with expectation.

"Sure. I can show you several designs. When

would you like to look at them?"

"Tomorrow would be fine."

"Speaking of building something, I'd like to show Kurt the site for the women's shelter." Nick glanced at Molly. "Do you still have those old clothes I left here the last time I visited?"

A thoughtful look crossed Molly's face. "Yeah, I think they're in the laundry room closet. As I recall, I had to wash them. You got them a little muddy."

"Probably will do that again today." Nick turned to Kurt. "I'd advise you to change into something old before we take a trek out to the site."

"That's no problem. My clothes are made for getting dirty."

"You guys can go now, and we'll have dessert when you get back." Molly stacked plates as she cleared the table.

"Sounds like a plan." Nick got up and pushed in his chair.

"Okay." Kurt picked up his dishes and carried them to the sink.

When Kurt turned back toward the table, he saw Nick lean over and give Molly a kiss on the cheek. "Thanks for a great meal. We'll see you in a little bit." Then Nick glanced in Kurt's direction. "You can change, and I'll meet you out by the carriage house in five minutes."

"All right." Kurt wished he'd complimented her on the meal. He could still do it, but it wouldn't mean as much since Nick had wisely beaten him to it. Shaking himself mentally, he tried to hammer home the thought that this was no contest for her attention. She wasn't his kind of woman, and he wasn't her kind of man. This was business. When was his brain going to absorb that message?

Five minutes later, Kurt stood in the yard near the carriage house. The afternoon sun warmed the late March day to near sixty degrees. The warmth of the last few days had melted all the snow, leaving behind soft muddy ground. When Nick emerged from the house, he wore a pair of faded jeans and an old jean jacket over a gray sweatshirt sporting a large maroon *U Mass* across the front. Even in these clothes, he looked like someone important. Or maybe Kurt felt that way because he knew what Nick did for a living.

Nick motioned toward the nearby stand of bare-branched trees. "Ready for a trek through the woods?"

Kurt nodded and fell into step beside the other man. "How far away is it?"

"It's only about a quarter of a mile, but the lane has deteriorated over the years. Before we do any construction out here, we'll have to fix the road."

"Why not build closer to Molly's house?"

"You'll see why when we get there."

Kurt's work boots squished in the muddy lane. He looked ahead through the trees and wondered why Nick wanted him to see the building site. "What are your plans?"

"Molly wants to establish a place where women who are down on their luck can learn a skill and make something of their lives. She sees the bed-and-breakfast as a place where they can work. She has the vision, and I have the fundraising job."

"Why does Molly do this? And don't give me the pat answer that it's the Christian thing to do."

Nick stopped and put his hands in the pockets of his jacket. This seemed to be his thinking mode. Kurt wondered whether Nick did that in the courtroom as well.

"Are you worried that she has some ulterior motive?"

Kurt shook his head, feeling ungrateful because he was questioning her motives. "I just want to understand why she's willing to do so much."

"She's got a big heart."

"I've seen that. But why the prison ministry and the women's shelter?"

Nick trudged ahead with his hands still in his pockets. Appearing to be in deep thought as though he was searching for just the right answer, he looked over at Kurt. "Molly worked for several years at a women's shelter in Boston. She didn't want to leave that ministry behind when she decided to follow her dream of owning this bed-and-breakfast. And Steve knew there would be opportunities for her to help people from his ministry also. You could ask her why she does all this."

Kurt laughed half-heartedly. "I didn't figure I should question the boss's rationale."

Nick laughed out loud. "So Molly intimidates you?"

"No, not exactly." Kurt frowned. "I just figured it wasn't my place."

"My advice. Put her on the spot."

"Easy for you to say. Your job wouldn't be on the line."

"Neither is yours. She needs you to finish this project."

"What makes you so sure?" Kurt followed the lane as it wound its way through the pine and hardwood forest. The sunlight filtered through the branches, casting beams of light across their path.

"Maybe I shouldn't tell you this, but she's been looking for someone to do this project for months. Everyone she found was booked until sometime next year. You are the answer to her prayers."

"I've never been the answer to anyone's prayers."

"You are now. Don't blow it."

Before Kurt could comment, they walked into a clearing. Two buildings occupied the open space surrounded by forest. A two-story, white clapboard house stood closest to them. Broken windows and a missing door gave the place a forlorn appearance. At the back of the clearing, not far from the house, an old barn sported a coat of graffiti. Kurt remembered the conversation he'd had with Molly when she talked about the barn and farmhouse. He never imagined they were in such bad shape.

Kurt let out a low whistle. "And I thought Molly's house was bad when I first saw it. Hers looks well-kept next to these."

"Well, this is the next project on the list. We plan to make these two buildings into living quarters for the women." Nick stepped through the open doorway and kicked an empty beer can. He turned to Kurt. "Unfortunately, before Molly bought the place, it was used by some of the area high schoolers for drinking and sex parties. At least with Molly living here, those activities have come to an end. Have a look around."

Kurt let his eyes adjust to the dim light inside the house. Dirt and leaves covered the hardwood floors. A musty smell emanated from the soiled brown sofa that sat in the middle of the room surrounded by empty beer cans and liquor bottles. "Are the buildings structurally sound?"

"Yes, we had a building inspector check them out

before Molly bought the property but as you can see they're in bad repair. This is what is meant by a 'fixer-upper.'"

"Good to know the structure is sound." Kurt surveyed the other rooms on the main floor, all littered with the same garbage.

As he climbed the stairs, he noticed the curse words spelled out in various colors of spray paint. The upstairs rooms contained filthy mattresses that produced a putrid odor. Inspecting the rest of the old farmhouse, he pictured how it had looked before the neglect. He couldn't help thinking about the day he had first seen Molly's house and the comparison he had made to his own life. The carpenter in him imagined the possibilities for its restoration. Was this the way God viewed his creation?

"Let's take a look at the barn." Nick's statement brought Kurt's thoughts back to the project at hand.

"Sure." Kurt made his way down the stairs. "Why haven't you been working on these places, too? You'll have the bed-and-breakfast done and no place for the women to live."

Nick loped across the yard toward the barn. "We've been waiting for warmer weather to fix this lane, and we needed someone who could handle the job of making these buildings into a home."

Kurt's boots sank into the soft, wet ground as he walked gingerly across the yard. "Looks like you'll have to wait until this ground dries up before you can bring any heavy equipment back here."

Nick nodded. "Hopefully, we'll have a few more warm days, and this muddy mess will be gone."

Kurt walked into the barn and gazed up at the beams of light filtering in through the roof. "A good roof job is the first thing this place needs."

"How would you like the job?"

Quickly turning in Nick's direction, Kurt knit his brows together in a frown. "Are you asking me whether I can fix up these buildings?"

"Yeah. Can you handle both projects?"

Kurt rubbed his hand over his face. More work. It was what he needed, but he couldn't do this alone. This required other people. He didn't have the connections he used to have. He didn't want to do a haphazard job, especially with Molly's house. Releasing a long, slow breath, he studied Nick. "What do you want done with the house?"

"We aren't looking for restoration like Molly's. We just want to make it livable. This barn is another matter."

"That's for sure." Kurt walked the length of the barn and inspected the exterior walls. "I'd like the work, but managing both projects at the same time could be tricky. Just what do you have in mind for the barn?"

"I have plans for the barn in my car. An architect friend of mine drew them up gratis. Would you like to look at them?" Nick returned Kurt's gaze with a speculative look.

"Yeah. I would."

"Good." Nick clapped Kurt on the back. "Let's go back to the house, and we can look them over while we get some of that dessert Molly promised us."

When they got back to the house, Molly greeted each of them with a big piece of coconut cake. They ate the cake while Kurt studied the blueprints. The project excited him as much as Molly's house, but the work involved overwhelmed him. He wondered whether taking on this project would be more than he could handle. He wanted the work. He needed the work. Getting this kind of job would mean having money to hire a lawyer.

"Well, what do you think?" Nick asked.

Kurt glanced at Molly, who hovered in the background, almost as if she was afraid to intrude. Her expression was emotionless. He wanted to ask her how she felt about it, but he didn't want to be seen as someone who couldn't make a decision. Finally, he looked at Nick. "I'd love to do this project, but I'll have to think it over. Do you want me to make a bid?"

"You want the job and give me a reasonable bid, the project is yours." Nick stood and rolled up the blueprints and secured them with a rubber band. "I'd better get going, but I need to change first. I'm supposed to take Allison to dinner after I pick her up at the Worchester airport. Jeans and work boots aren't suitable attire for the place where we have reservations."

"You can leave the clothes for your next visit," Molly called after him as he went into the laundry room to change.

"Who's Allison?" Kurt asked when Molly turned around.

"Nick's wife."

"His wife?" Kurt tried to reconcile the day's events with this new information. "Does she know he goes around kissing you?"

Molly smiled. "Yes, sometimes we even kiss in front of her."

As Kurt stood rooted to the floor that he hoped would open up and swallow him, chagrin overtook him. He should have known better than to open his mouth. He wondered whether she would know that jealousy had prompted the question. He hoped not. "Forgive me. It was none of my business."

"That's okay." She stepped closer to him. "I want you to understand about Nick and me. We're like this." She held up two fingers side by side. "He's one of my best friends. We've shared a lot of things, including a love for his wife. I introduced them. Ours is a once-in-a-lifetime friendship. I love him like a brother."

"I see. I'm sorry. I misunderstood." Kurt wondered why he felt no satisfaction in the fact that Nick wasn't Molly's love interest.

Nick's exit from the laundry room brought Kurt and Molly's conversation to a halt. "I left those clothes in the laundry room. I don't think you'll have to wash them. I stayed pretty clean this time out."

"Thanks for saving me some work." Molly chuckled as she gave Nick a hug. "Have a safe trip and give Allison a hug for me."

Nick gave Molly a quick peck on the cheek before grabbing his coat from the hook in the mudroom. Then he reached in the pocket of his suit coat. "Here's one of my cards." He handed the card to Kurt. "Give me a call when you have your bid ready."

Kurt took it and studied it for a moment before shoving it in his pocket. "Thanks. I'll call you sometime this week."

"Great." Nick exited with a wave.

Standing in the mudroom, Kurt wished he didn't have to turn around and face Molly. Surely she thought he had been way out of line. What could he do to make it right? After church today, he was finally

"Yes, that's what I want."

"Okay, you can start by telling me whether you told Nick about my kids, or if it's just a coincidence that he's an attorney specializing in family law."

"I didn't say one thing to Nick about you needing a lawyer to get your kids back. I will admit I invited him out today in hopes that somehow the two of you would connect in a way that would lead to his helping you with that effort." She jutted out her chin.

"He offered me a chance to earn more money so I can hire a lawyer. That's a start."

"But wouldn't you like to start right now?"

"Sure, but without the money, that's not possible." Leaning back against the center island, Kurt crossed his arms.

"If you told him about it, maybe he could work something out for you."

"Like what?"

"I don't know. Maybe you could barter with him. Your building expertise for his legal expertise. Sounds like a fair trade to me."

"What makes you think he'd go for something like that?"

"You'd have to ask him. Don't be afraid to reach out and ask for help."

CHAPTER EIGHT

Kurt woke and lay in bed for a few moments as he contemplated the day ahead. Today was his thirty-third birthday, but there would be no celebration. He was another year older and no one cared. His kids might if they knew him and knew he was innocent of any crime.

He didn't have time to lie in bed and feel sorry for himself. He had a job to do so he could hire a lawyer.

Then there was the problem of finding the person who had murdered Bonnie. At the beginning of his prison term, his anger had kept him from thinking clearly. Bitterness had consumed him, and he'd let his hatred fester. He was no use to himself or anyone else. Finally, after Steve had helped him conquer his misguided thoughts, Kurt had compiled a list of possible suspects. The list was short and flawed because Bonnie didn't have any enemies.

After getting this job, he had forced himself not to dwell on finding Bonnie's killer. He had thought getting his kids back was more important, but deep down, he knew they were all tied together. He had to prove his innocence if he wanted to get his children back. Now that he was out of prison, was it possible to do something about that list of suspects? Could Nick help him with that, too?

Over a week had passed since Molly had introduced him to Nick. Throughout the preceding day, Kurt had wrestled with Molly's suggestion that he ask Nick for help—to bargain with him for his services. Maybe it was time to quit being stubborn and distrustful and ask for what he wanted. He wasn't getting anywhere on his own.

Kurt got out of bed and walked across the room. He picked up Nick's card from the dresser where he had laid it, where it had reminded him daily of the opportunity he might be passing up. He studied the card. He doubted lawyers were in their offices at six in the morning, but he could make the call later. He stuffed the card into his wallet, then grabbed his jacket and headed for Molly's house.

While he ate breakfast, his mind roiled with the ideas he had considered proposing for the work on the women's shelters. Molly never mentioned their discussion or Nick's visit, and Kurt was hesitant to bring up the subject. He let the breakfast conversation revolve around his plans for the day to start on the woodwork in the living room.

Midmorning he stopped to get a drink. He walked back to the kitchen and filled a glass with ice and water. Taking a couple of big gulps, he contemplated making that call to Nick. He set down the glass and reached into his pocket for his wallet.

When he pulled out Nick's card, he spied the picture of his kids. As he studied the picture, he realized how much they had changed since that picture was taken. Every day they were growing up, and he was missing it. He couldn't let another day go by without doing something about it.

Getting his kids back was going to take a fight. He was ready.

Nick's card in hand, Kurt marched to Molly's

office. He pushed aside the plastic and knocked on the door.

"Come in," she called out.

He stepped into the room and prayed he wouldn't lose his nerve. "Do you have time to talk?"

She turned away from the computer. A curious expression crossed her face as she nodded. "Sure. Is there some problem?"

"No. I want your help and maybe some advice."

She smiled. "I'll try to do my best. What can I help you with?"

"I have a problem."

"With the house?"

"No, with my proposal to Nick."

"What kind of a problem?"

Kurt released a heavy sigh. "The only way I can finish your house and do the women's shelters at the same time is to become the general contractor for the shelters. I can take bids and hire the subs to do the work over there while I do my work here. I'll supervise the work over there, but most of my time will be spent here."

"Sounds like a good plan to me. What's the hang-up?"

"I'm afraid when the sub-contractors find out I'm an ex-con, they'll turn away. Or we might have trouble getting the best bids." Kurt rubbed his hand across his chin. "I have a bad feeling about it."

"Are you going to let that stop you from doing a good job and helping yourself as well?"

"No, that's where I'd like your help."

"What can I do?"

"You could be the general contractor."

Her brows knit in a frown. "I've never done

anything like that before."

"In a sense you've done it here. I'd help you find the sub-contractors to contact, but you would be the one to deal with them. You'd be my front man. I mean, woman."

Molly laughed. Kurt drank in the pleasant sound. It made him want more than he knew was wise out of this relationship. He shook away the thought.

"I'm glad you have that straight." She grinned.

"Me, too. As I was saying, I'd remain in the background. I'd be your project superintendent. What do you think?" He held his breath as he waited for her answer.

She shrugged. "I suppose that would work. Have you talked to Nick about this?"

"No." Kurt shook his head. "I wanted to run it by you first."

"Then I say it's time to run the plan by Nick." She picked up her phone and held it out to Kurt. "Call him and also mention the barter offer. The legal system works slowly enough without having to wait to get a lawyer."

Kurt hesitated to take the phone. "You should talk with him so he knows you agree."

"Okay. Let's call him, but chances are we'll have to leave a message." Molly placed the phone on her desk and punched in the number as she put the phone on speaker. The ringing sounded throughout Molly's office. When it finally stopped, they had reached Nick's voicemail. Molly motioned for Kurt to leave a message.

After Kurt left his message, he looked up at Molly. "How long do you suppose it'll be before he returns our call?"

"I wouldn't sit around and wait. He's probably in court or with a client. He'll get around to us eventually."

"I'll get back to work. Thanks for your help."

"Don't mention it. I'm helping myself as well as you."

Kurt went back to work, but he kept listening for the phone to ring. Each time the musical tones of Molly's phone sounded through the house, he waited for her to appear to tell him Nick was on the phone, but the day came to an end without a call from Molly's friend. Kurt knew he shouldn't have gotten his hopes up. The thought of seeing his kids again had made him forget the need for patience. After all, Nick was a busy lawyer.

While Kurt swept sawdust from the floor, Molly came into the living room. She leaned against the columns separating the living room from the front hall. "You've made a lot of progress in here today. It's looking good. I get excited when I think about how it's all going to look when it's finished."

"You'll like it even more in the next couple of days. Your mirror and mantel are here. Check out the box."

Molly went to the large box next to the fireplace. She opened the flaps and looked inside. "Oh, it's even more beautiful than the pictures. When will you put that in?"

"Tomorrow. After I get it installed in the morning, I'll spend the afternoon doing stain and varnish. You might consider finding something to do away from the house. The smell can get overwhelming at times."

"The weather's supposed to be nice tomorrow. You'll be able to open the windows, won't you?"

"Yeah, but even with the windows open the smell can get to you after a while."

"Are you ready for some dinner? I've got a dish I want to try on you."

"You know you don't have to feed me. That wasn't part of the deal. A place to sleep, but not room and board." Kurt stopped sweeping and gazed at Molly.

She gave him a lopsided grin. "But I like feeding you. You're my built-in guinea pig. Who else could I get on the spur of the moment to taste my culinary efforts?"

Shaking his head, he smiled and continued sweeping the floor. "At least I know I won't go hungry living next door to you."

"Come to the kitchen when you're done," she called over her shoulder as she left.

While Kurt finished his clean up, he contemplated how he was going to deal with Molly. The constant invitations to eat her delicious food not only expanded his waistline but also expanded his desire to share life with a woman again. That just wasn't possible under his current circumstances. How could he even think about a romantic relationship when people considered him guilty of a heinous crime? He hated the thought that Bonnie's killer was still out there somewhere. What could he possibly do to find the real killer, even with Nick's help?

And the time he spent with Molly made him remember his life with Bonnie. Bonnie wasn't a cook, but Bonnie had a loving and giving nature just like Molly. He hurt for the loss of his wife, and he hurt for the future he would have to have without a woman in it. He couldn't bear the thought of having a future without his kids.

He shoved aside the negative thoughts along with the sawdust he shoved into the dustpan. He vowed to think positive things. Nick would call. He would agree to Kurt's offer, and he would have a lawyer. With those thoughts permeating his mind, he made his way toward the kitchen. Wonderful smells greeted him as he walked through the dining room. He pushed open the door leading from the dining room to the kitchen and spied Molly arranging food on four plates. Did she have other guests?

When he stepped into the room, an out-of-tune rendition of "Happy Birthday" greeted him. Besides Molly, Nick and a petite brunette with dark chocolate eyes clapped as they finished singing.

Kurt glanced at Molly. "How did you know it was my birthday?"

She grinned from ear to ear. "Steve told me. He called early this morning and gave me the heads up."

"So how did you get through to Nick when I couldn't?" Kurt glanced from one to the other.

Molly gave him a sheepish grin. "Oh, he called back. I just didn't tell you. I wanted this to be a surprise. And I want you to meet Allison, Nick's wife."

Allison stepped forward and held out her hand. "It's nice to meet you, Kurt."

"It's nice to meet you, too." Kurt wondered if his face was red as he remembered his shock at learning that Nick had a wife.

"Let's eat." Molly set the plates on the kitchen table.

After giving a blessing for the meal, Nick looked at Kurt. "Molly tells me you have a proposal for me."

"I do. We can discuss it after we eat." Kurt didn't want to discuss this during the meal. Even though

Molly knew about his kids, he didn't want to share the whole story with the group. He wanted a one-on-one with Nick.

Nick picked up his fork and paused in midair. "That sounds good to me. We can go over your proposal and then celebrate with some cake."

This meal wasn't like the one on that Sunday when he'd first met Nick. Kurt didn't feel out of place today. The laughter around the table included him. And maybe knowing Molly's relationship with Nick was only friendship made the situation more comfortable. Kurt reminded himself that friendship was all he could share with Molly as well. All his thoughts had to be centered on the job and his kids.

After they finished eating, Molly took Allison to show her the rest of the house and the furnishings she had ordered. When the two women left the room, Nick eyed Kurt and leaned back in the chair until the front legs came off the floor. "So what's your plan?"

This was the time to lay it all on the line. "I've decided the best way to handle the work on the women's shelter is for me to act as general contractor. I can't do the work over there and the work here at the same time."

"I can see that." Nick let the front chair legs down to the floor and leaned forward. "Explain the process."

Kurt told Nick basically what he had told Molly. When Kurt finished, Nick didn't say anything for a few moments. He steepled his hands in front of him while he rested his elbows on the table. "So you'll identify the subs, and Molly will do the face-to-face? Won't you eventually have to work with these people if you're the superintendent?"

Kurt nodded. "Yes, but by that time they'll be contracted and doing the work. I didn't want my prison record to be a problem in finding the contractors. Many of them may never have any idea about my record. I just didn't want to take the chance that it could interfere."

"That sounds reasonable to me." Nick settled back in his chair again. "What's it going to cost for your services?"

Kurt braced himself before he made his barter proposal. This was going to be the hard part. Nick might ask more questions than Kurt wanted to answer, but there was no turning back now. "Would you be interested in bartering?"

Nick raised his brows as he leaned forward again. "Are you asking for me to trade my legal services for your construction services?"

"That's what I had in mind."

"You've served your time. Why do you need my legal services?"

Kurt took a deep breath and released it slowly. "I have two children. Twins, a boy and a girl. Their maternal grandmother is their guardian. I want to have my children back, but I'm willing to start with just visitation. Can you help me?"

Nick let out a low whistle. "So that's what Molly meant when she told me you needed my help. That's why I offered you the job."

"Then you really don't want to hire me?"

"Oh, no. I think you're the person we need. The job's yours, but I'll have to know a little more about the circumstances surrounding your kids before I know whether I can help you there."

"What do you need to know?" Kurt braced himself

for the inevitable answer.

"Everything. Starting with why you went to prison."

Kurt looked toward the kitchen window. Nothing was fair about this process. He had to go through the story again with all its pain and sorrow. But the image of his children's faces smiling at him after he rescued Smoky gave him the courage to tell Nick the awful truth. He slowly recounted the events that led up to his arrest.

"Wow!" Nick rubbed his fingers across his brow. "That's tough. Where were the kids while all of this was going on?"

Kurt closed his eyes for a moment. He wanted to see the faces of his children as they were today, not the terrible scene he had just described. "They were there in the house asleep in their cribs. After I discovered Bonnie's body, I rushed into their room to see if they were okay. They were sleeping peacefully." He released a harsh breath. "I shudder every time I think about them being there while their mother was being brutally murdered."

"Why do you suppose a jury didn't believe you?"

"Don't you think I'd like the answer to that question?" Drumming his fingers on the table, Kurt made a mental effort to tamp down the anger he felt toward those twelve men and women who had found him guilty. "The only thing I can figure is the police were focused on me from the beginning. There were no signs of a break-in so they assumed Bonnie knew her murderer. The investigators never found any other physical evidence like fingerprints or hairs that weren't mine."

Nick tapped his fingers together as he

contemplated what Kurt had told him. "I'll have to be frank with you, Kurt. This could be an uphill battle, especially if your former mother-in-law opposes this."

"There's no doubt in my mind she'll do that. She hates me."

"If you're ready for a fight, I'll take your case because Molly believes in you. You couldn't have a better advocate." Nick extended his hand.

"Thanks. I appreciate your taking my side." Shaking Nick's hand, Kurt breathed a mental sigh of relief. His initial reaction to Molly's interference had been irritation, but he was glad she had decided to ignore his resistance. "How long will this process take?"

"Much longer than you'd like." Nick grimaced. "Let me explain the likely scenario. First, you're probably looking at a year before any decision will be made."

Kurt's heart plummeted. "A year? Does it have to be that long?"

"Yes, unless you know of something the grandmother has done that will harm the children."

Kurt shrugged as he slowly shook his head. "I don't know of a thing."

"Well, then, I will file a petition for modification of the original order. You and the children's grandmother will have to meet with family relations, and they will try to mediate an agreement."

"Mediating with Virginia Spencer? That's a laugh." Kurt interrupted Nick's explanation. "She'll do anything in her power to keep me away from my kids."

"It's not unusual for the parties to resist an

agreement. So the court will appoint counsel for the children. Family relations will do a full-blown study of the case. The children will receive therapy. This could take months. When the study is complete, the court will assign the case for trial. The bad news is the lengthy process. The good news is family law in Massachusetts is very pro-parent."

Kurt sighed. "I had no idea the process would take so long."

"Yeah, you should be glad Molly decided to continue her annoying habit of sticking her nose into other people's business." Nick smiled. "She hounded me until I finally went out with Allison. And you see where that led."

"I'm glad she has that habit. Annoying or not."

"Me, too." Nick went to the mudroom and brought back a legal pad and pen. "Let me take some notes. Then I can draw up some papers when I get to work tomorrow."

When Nick finally quit asking questions, he leaned back and put his pencil down. "That should be a good start."

"Only a start?" A big knot formed in Kurt's stomach. "What if I try to prove my innocence? Wouldn't that help?"

Nick narrowed his gaze. "By doing what? Finding the real killer?"

Kurt nodded. "I have this list I made of possible suspects."

"What do you plan to do with it?"

"That's just it. I don't know."

"I could ask one of our private investigators to look into it, but I don't think that will shorten the timeframe. Going back over old trial records and checking into people's backgrounds is time-consuming, too. My advice is to let it go for now."

"But how will I ever prove my innocence?"

Nick grimaced. "I think you have a better chance of seeing your kids if you work hard and show everyone that you're now an upstanding citizen."

"But I've always been one. I'm innocent, and everyone should know that." Kurt gritted his teeth to keep himself from saying something he might regret. Maybe Nick didn't think he was innocent.

"I know you don't want to hear this, but the odds are against you finding the guilty person. If the police with all their resources were unable to find the right person, how can you expect to find the guilty party? Concentrate on this job, and I will do my best to help you see your kids."

"You said this was going to be a battle, but what do you really think my chances are?"

Nick shook his head. "I can't make any predictions. My best suggestion is for you to do a lot of praying."

Kurt nodded, but he secretly wondered how God could answer this prayer when He hadn't kept Kurt out of prison. God was there, but sometimes he seemed too far away.

CHAPTER NINE

Molly led Allison into the living room. Molly hated leaving the men behind because she was afraid Kurt might not ask the question she had suggested. As she left the room, she knew the only thing she could do was pray that God would give Kurt the strength to reach out and ask for help. The best way to keep her mind off of what was happening in the kitchen was to get involved in showing Allison the house.

"Come look at this." Molly opened the flaps on the box containing the mantel and mirror.

"Gorgeous. It will make this room."

"I know. I get goose bumps every time I imagine the finished project." Molly turned toward the stairs. "Let's go up to my apartment, and I'll show you the furniture I have up there and the stuff I have ordered."

"Is the house the only thing that gives you goose bumps?" Allison asked as they climbed the stairs.

"What do you mean by that?"

"Oh, I was just observing the way you looked at Kurt tonight while we were eating."

"And how was I looking at Kurt?" Molly opened the door of her apartment.

"I don't know. It just seemed like you couldn't take your eyes off him." Allison followed Molly into the apartment and made herself at home on the couch. "You can't deny you think he's wicked handsome."

"Allison, are you trying to push another man at me?"

"You ignored my question."

"You made a statement. You didn't ask a question." Molly stood on the other side of the room with her hands on her hips.

"Okay. How about this? You can't deny you think he's wicked handsome, can you?"

"Yes, I can. Quit matchmaking."

"I'm only trying to return the favor. After all, you got Nick and me together."

"Yeah, but that was different."

Allison shook her head. "I don't think so."

"This conversation is going nowhere." Molly joined Allison on the couch and picked up some books and papers from the coffee table. "Let me show you the stuff I ordered."

"Okay, but I know I'm right, otherwise you wouldn't be so afraid to talk about it."

Molly ignored Allison's comment and proceeded to show her the purchases for the house. She rued the fact that her attraction for Kurt was so transparent. She hoped he had no clue. He could never know that her interest went beyond friendship.

After Molly showed Allison the books, she pointed out the rocker and tables she had stored in her bedroom. Despite her efforts to forget what was going on in the kitchen, Molly's mind kept reliving the way Kurt looked when she and Allison had left. He had that abandoned-puppy look on his face.

"Should we head back downstairs?" Allison asked as they exited the bedroom.

"I don't know. I don't want to interrupt the negotiations," Molly replied even though she was dying to know what was happening two floors below. "I think we should wait a few more minutes."

Before Allison could make a reply, there was a knock at the door. She scurried across the room and opened the door.

"Hi, beautiful." Nick looked at his wife as he entered the room. He held the birthday cake. "We brought the birthday celebration to you. And we're going to celebrate Kurt's and my new relationship. Attorney and client."

Kurt carried the plates and utensils as he followed Nick. "What should I do with these?"

"Here. I'll take them." Molly resisted the urge to hug the two men. Instead, she took the plates and forks from Kurt and put them on the table in her kitchenette. "So it's all worked out?"

Nick set the cake on the table. "Yeah, I'm going to start on the paperwork tomorrow and get it filed with the court as soon as possible."

"That's good news." Molly glanced at Kurt and wondered what he thought about the role she had played in introducing him to Nick. Maybe the question was better left unasked.

After they finished eating cake, they all went downstairs. Molly and Kurt walked out to Nick and Allison's car with them. The yard light cast long shadows. Molly stood beside Kurt while they watched the car disappear up the lane.

When the car was out of sight, Molly turned to Kurt. "Before you go back to your place, I have something I want to give you."

"Okay, what is it?" Kurt followed Molly back into the house.

"You'll see when we get inside."

As she opened the door going into the mudroom, she hoped Kurt would accept the birthday gift she had selected for him. She knew from their conversations that he disliked taking help from others. Her goal in inviting Nick to meet Kurt was to break down the barrier that he had erected against accepting other people's help. Now she hoped her gift would work in the same way.

After they entered the kitchen, Molly went to a cupboard and pulled an envelope off the shelf. She turned and found Kurt standing near the mudroom with his arms crossed over his lower torso. His eyes narrowed with distrust. How could she change his attitude? Clutching the envelope, she feared he would reject her gift.

"Is that something I need to do for the house?" He unfolded his arms and extended one hand for the envelope.

"No, this is something I got you for your birthday."

Shaking his head, he dropped his hand. "I can't take anything more from you. You've done enough already."

She continued to hold out the envelope. "You'll have to take this. I can't use it myself. And I can't take it back."

He sighed and took the envelope. "You shouldn't have done this. You've done enough already."

"Go ahead and open it. I thought it was something you could use as you look forward to going to court."

He eyed her suspiciously. "How did you know I'd be going to court? You had no idea whether I would even ask Nick to represent me."

"I've been praying about it. I believe God answers

prayer. So I was prepared when He granted my request."

Kurt ripped open the envelope and pulled out a piece of paper. He read it. Slowly shaking his head, he glanced up at her and waved the paper in the air. "This is way too much. What will I do with a gift certificate to an exclusive men's shop? I wear jeans and flannel shirts."

"Buy a new suit. You'll need one for your court appearances."

"I don't need your charity." His voice held a defiant edge. "Besides, Nick said it could be a year before they even hear the case."

"Well, even if you don't need this suit until a year from now, it still isn't charity. This is a gift from one friend to another. You can return the favor when it's my birthday. Mine is August twenty-fifth."

His expression softened as he looked at her. "Okay. I'll remember that. August twenty-fifth. From one friend to another."

"Thank you for accepting my gift." Molly smiled.

"Thanks is what I owe you, not the other way around. You've done so much for me. I'll never be able to repay you."

"I'm not looking for repayment. Friends do things for each other. The kindest thing you can do for me is accept my friendship."

Kurt gave her a lopsided grin. "I'm trying. My friends from the past turned away from me when I needed them the most. That's why I have a little trouble with the whole friendship deal now. Be patient with me."

"I will. That's what friends are for."

***

The following week Molly sat at her desk and thought about how well things were going. Kurt had installed the mantel and mirror in the living room, and the look was everything she had hoped it would be. Besides the excellent progress Kurt was making on the house, she and Kurt had established a tentative understanding of their new friendship. All her dreams were falling into place.

Molly looked up the number of the gravel company and punched out the number on the phone. After the first ring, she heard a knock on the front door. Holding her phone to her ear, she quickly walked to the door of her office and looked out toward the living room where Kurt was working. "Kurt, could you see who's at the front door? I'm on the phone."

"Sure." He glanced at her with a smile as he put down his hammer. "I'll take care of it."

"Thanks." She retreated into her office.

While Molly talked to a contractor about putting gravel on the lane leading back to the old farmhouse, she overheard what she thought was an argument coming from the front hall. A shrill female voice penetrated the closed doors to her office, and the low rumble of Kurt's voice followed. Molly tried to concentrate on her own conversation, but she was having trouble ignoring the commotion. Before she could tell the contractor that she would call him back, Bev Marsh burst into the room. Kurt followed with a helpless expression on his face.

Bev marched over to Molly's desk and pointed at Kurt. "What is this man doing here?"

Molly turned away from the angry woman and ended her conversation with the contractor. After she put the phone on her desk, she turned around. Staring at Bev, Molly walked out from behind her desk. "He's working for me. Do you have a problem with that?"

Bev's eyebrows knit in a frown as she took a step back. "Yes! He killed my friend's daughter. How could you have him working for you?"

Molly glanced at Kurt, who stood in the corner. A pained expression crossed his face while his shoulders slumped. She wanted to close her eyes and block out this whole scene. This just couldn't be happening. He had warned her about Bev's reaction, if she knew he was working here. Nothing she said would appease the woman.

"Well? I'm waiting for an answer." Bev stood with her hands on her hips, the frown still creasing her face.

"Bev." Molly took a deep breath and tried to keep her voice calm. "He works for me because he does an excellent job restoring houses. And I don't believe he is a murderer."

The older woman waved one of her arms in the air. "But he was convicted and went to prison. He should still be there."

"He's served his time—"

"But it wasn't enough," Bev interrupted.

Before Molly could reply, Kurt stepped in front of Bev. "Ms. Marsh, please don't take this out on Molly. Your argument isn't with her. She hired me out of the kindness of her heart to help with a prison ministry. She doesn't deserve your anger."

Molly watched Kurt's Adam's apple bob as he

finished speaking. His defense of her made a lump rise in her own throat. He didn't deserve Bev's anger either. What could she do to diffuse the situation?

Squaring her shoulders, she stepped around Kurt. "Bev, I'm glad you stopped by. Has my order come in? I'm eager to hang the wallpaper in the upstairs rooms."

Bev didn't speak immediately. She looked as if she didn't understand what had just happened. "Didn't you hear what I said?"

"Yes, I heard." Molly's gaze didn't waver as she stared at Bev. "If you aren't here to talk about my order, then there isn't much else to say."

Again, Bev was silent. She appeared to be thinking about how to respond. Finally, she placed one hand on her forehead. "I don't believe this is happening. I...I just can't work with you now."

"I understand." Molly approached Bev. "Would you like to talk alone?"

The older woman nodded. "Yes."

Molly glanced at Kurt.

Before she could say anything, he walked toward the doors. "I'll go back to work. We'll talk later."

"Okay." Molly turned back to Bev as the door closed softly behind Kurt. The rustle of plastic accompanied his exit. "Do I understand that you don't want to complete the order I've placed?"

Bev sank into a nearby chair and placed her head in her hands. "I don't know."

Molly knelt down next to the chair. "Are you all right?"

Bev looked up at Molly. "How could I be all right when I've come face-to-face with a murderer?"

Molly bit back a nasty retort. "Please let's talk

about my order. Do you want to deliver the items, or would you like to cancel our agreement?"

Tears welled up in the older woman's eyes. "I don't know how I can go through with it. I'll betray my friend if I do."

For the first time, Molly began to understand the woman's dilemma. This order meant a lot to her business, but filling it would mean associating with the man she thought had murdered her friend's daughter. "I understand. I'll agree to whatever you decide."

Bev removed her glasses and wiped her eyes. "Why are you being so nice when I barged in here like a crazy woman?"

Molly contemplated her reply. Would this woman want to know that God had put the gentle response in Molly's heart? Maybe this explanation would help Bev understand why Molly had hired Kurt. "Bev," Molly hesitated. "I try to live by Christian principles. God's word says that 'a gentle answer turns away wrath.'"

Bev looked at Molly with skepticism written all over her face. "Are you trying to make me feel guilty by parading your Christianity in front of me?"

Molly shook her head. "No, just trying to explain what motivates me."

"Well, as far as I'm concerned, if you were a Christian you wouldn't harbor a murderer."

Molly pressed her lips together as she wondered how long she could continue to keep her cool. Every time she thought she was making some progress with Bev, she began berating Kurt again. She couldn't let it go. Molly hated to think of losing all the lovely things she had ordered for the house, but it seemed that was what this would come to. She would have to start all over finding her furnishings. The prospect made her sick inside.

Standing, Molly walked to the door. "Well, I guess you'll be going because we're at an impasse here, Bev. I'm not going to get rid of Kurt, and you don't want to deal with me if I don't. So it appears that I have my answer. I'll expect a return on my deposit."

A stricken look crossed Bev's face as she stood. "But I have wallpaper in my car for you."

"Okay," Molly replied, completely taken aback by Bev's sudden change in attitude. Then she realized the older woman was trembling. Molly rushed to her side. "Are you okay?"

"No. I'm so sorry. This encounter has really shaken me up. Please help me out to my car."

Molly held Bev by the arm as they walked out of her office. With her free hand, Molly waved at Kurt as she went out the front door. He nodded in understanding. When Molly reached Bev's car, she opened the driver's side door and helped Bev inside.

Bev sat in the car and laid her head back against the seat. She closed her eyes. Molly glanced in the back seat of the car where she saw the packages of wallpaper. Would it ever find its way into her house? She didn't know what to think about this whole bizarre incident.

Finally, Bev opened her eyes. "I don't think I can drive."

"I was thinking the same thing. Would you like me to drive you home?" Molly asked.

Bev nodded. "If you don't mind."

"I'll be back in a minute. I need to get my purse." Molly sprinted toward the house to tell Kurt where she was going.

When she opened the door, she found him standing in the front hall. "What's happening?"

She grabbed her purse from the desk then looked up at Kurt, who had followed her into the office. "She wants me to drive her home."

"How will you get back?"

"You can follow us in my SUV." She handed him the keys.

He took the keys as he gave her a quizzical glance. "Do you think that's a wise idea considering how she feels about me?"

"I think the poor woman's in shock. If you don't get out of the car, she won't even know you're there."

"If you say so." He shrugged. "Are you taking her to her business or home?"

"I'll take her home. If I don't I'm not sure she could get herself home from there. But I don't know where she lives."

"I do. She lives next door to my former mother-in-law."

Letting out a low whistle, Molly headed for the front door. "I guess that poses a problem. I don't think we should go there."

"My thoughts exactly, although it could give me a chance to see my kids."

"And get you in trouble as well. You don't want to blow it now that you're seeking visitation rights."

"Yeah, a year from now if I'm lucky. We don't know what chance I have in the eyes of the court." Kurt stared at Molly, his expression grim.

"A better chance than if you do something crazy like try to see them now." Molly put her hand on the doorknob as she looked back at Kurt.

"I know." He released a harsh breath. "I'll meet

you at the Antique Trader in Oakton."

"Okay. I'll wait until you get my SUV out of the carriage house before I leave."

***

Kurt followed Bev's Cadillac at a distance. The afternoon sun glinted off the windows of Bev's car so he couldn't see inside. He wondered what Molly might be saying to Bev or whether they were talking at all. Would Bev tell Virginia Spencer about seeing him? His former mother-in-law could be more of a problem for Molly than Bev Marsh ever thought of being.

He didn't want to bring his problems into Molly's life. Maybe he should leave. She could find someone else to finish the house. But that would help no one. He remembered what Nick had told him about how much trouble she'd had finding someone to work on her house. She needed him as much as he needed her. He couldn't give up the chance to go to court and see his kids again.

Molly drove through the center of Oakton and turned onto School Street. Kurt braced himself as he made that same turn. Going by his children's school would only remind him of the day he saw them. His mind's eye saw the delight on Emily's face when he'd rescued the kitten. He wanted to see that face again. He wanted to hold his little girl in his arms and play catch with his son. He couldn't let anything get in his way now.

Up ahead, Molly parked Bev's car at the curb at the Antique Trader behind a black Lincoln Town Car. He pulled the SUV to a stop about half a block away.

He watched while Molly helped Bev out of the car and up the front walk. They disappeared inside. He released a long, slow breath and wondered how long she would be.

While he waited, he found a local weekly paper on the floor of the passenger side of the SUV. He began reading the area news about town meetings, church socials, and school sports. As he closed the last section a picture on the back page caught his eye. The photo featured eight children holding tennis rackets. The caption read, "Oakton Tennis Club Awards Beginner Certificates." Eric and Emily stood on the front row. Kurt studied the picture as his heart swelled with pride.

Kurt read the story that accompanied the picture. His children had completed beginning tennis lessons at the club where Bonnie used to play. He wondered if Molly knew she'd been riding around with a picture of his children in her car. Surely she would have mentioned it if she'd known.

While he studied the picture again, the high shrill laughter and chatter of children caught his attention. He glanced up as a number of school children carrying backpacks skipped, sauntered, or meandered down the sidewalk. He wondered whether Eric and Emily were also walking home from school. It took all his inner strength not to get out and watch for his children. He wanted to see them so badly that he ached inside. He closed his eyes. *Lord, keep me from doing something I'll regret.*

When he opened his eyes, Eric and Emily were walking down the sidewalk only a few feet away from where he sat in Molly's SUV. He blinked twice to make sure what he saw was real. Emily's blond curls bobbed as she skipped down the walk, her blue backpack bouncing against her back. Eric moseyed a little ways behind and kicked a stone along the walk. It bounded ahead of Emily. She raced to get it and kicked it forward. Eric chased after it.

As Kurt watched, everything within him wanted to get out of the car so he could join in their game. He wanted to embrace them and tell them that he loved them. But that wasn't possible now. He could only hope that it would be possible in the future. Wondering why they were walking down this street to go home, he closed his eyes again and willed himself to stay where he was.

He opened his eyes just in time to see them cut across the lawn at the Antique Trader. They were headed to the front door. He knit his eyebrows together as he puzzled over their presence until Virginia Spencer came out the door. She hadn't changed in six years. Her silver-gray hair was coiffed to perfection, not a hair out of place. She wore a tailored, navy blue pantsuit that made her look more like a businesswoman than someone who was picking up her grandchildren.

Instinctively, he grabbed the paper he had been reading and held it up in front of him just in case she looked his way. He wished he could poke holes in the paper so he could see what was happening, but he was afraid she might see him. Then he remembered that Molly was still inside the Antique Trader. Had she met Bonnie's mother?

Kurt slowly lowered the paper until he could just see over the upper edge. The children ran to meet their grandmother. She took their hands and led them into the house. Molly was in the house with his children. He wanted to be there, too.

He drummed his fingers on the steering wheel as he trained his eyes on the front walk. Five minutes passed, but it seemed like five hours. There was no sign of Molly. He knew they weren't having cookies and tea. Maybe Bev and Virginia were telling Molly that if she didn't get rid of him, they would ruin her business. But they wouldn't tell her that in front of the children, would they? He was tying himself in knots trying to figure out what was keeping her.

Another fifteen minutes passed. His concern escalated with every passing minute. He tried to calm himself by imagining they were having cookies and tea. With the children. That was the key. The children's presence would keep anything terrible from happening. Molly was charming them with her ready smile and easygoing manner. Surely her willingness to help Bev would weigh in Molly's favor. He reassured himself with that thought.

Finally, when he thought he couldn't wait any longer, Eric and Emily came charging out of the house. They raced to the black Town Car and got in. Moments later, Virginia and Molly came down the walk together. They appeared to be engaged in a congenial conversation. When Virginia walked around to the driver's side of the car, he expected Molly to step away. Instead, she opened the front passenger door and got in at the same time Virginia got in on the driver's side. Bev was nowhere in sight. What was going on?

Virginia's car engine roared to life. Stunned, Kurt watched the car pull away from the curb and drive down the block. Shaking himself out of his shock, he punched the button to start Molly's SUV and slowly followed the Town Car. He couldn't let them out of his sight, but he had to make sure Virginia didn't think she was being followed.

He wondered whether Molly knew he was not far away. Where were they going? He didn't want Virginia's hatred of him to affect Molly's life, but he was afraid he couldn't do anything to stop it.

CHAPTER TEN

Glancing in the passenger side-view mirror, Molly noticed her SUV following at a distance. Kurt must surely think she was crazy for getting into a car with Virginia Spencer. Grateful that he wasn't close enough for Virginia to figure out who was in the car behind them, Molly listened to the chatter of the children in the back seat.

His children were delightful. Her heart ached that they didn't know their father. But with the Lord's help that would change. She had already witnessed a miracle back at the Antique Trader. She could hardly wait to tell Kurt about it.

"Grandma, are we there yet?" Emily asked as they drove out of Oakton toward Hawthorne.

Virginia chuckled. "Emily, dear, we just started the trip. It will take us about twenty minutes to get there. Do you know how long twenty minutes is?"

"A long time."

"It's not that long," Eric interjected. "What will we do when we get there?"

Molly smiled. "You can look at the farmhouse. It has a secret passage. Would you like to see it?"

"It does?" Eric looked impressed. "What's it for?"

"I'm not sure. Possibly it was used in the Underground Railroad. Do you know what that is?" Molly asked.

Emily waved her hand in the air as if she was in the classroom trying to get the teacher's attention. "I do. I do. We studied about that during Black History Month. People used to help slaves escape."

"That's right."

"I knew that, too," Eric said.

Molly recognized a little sibling rivalry in that comment. When she looked at Eric, there was no doubt in her mind that he was Kurt's son. Even if she hadn't known, she would have guessed. The little boy was his father in miniature. The resemblance was incredible.

"Do you have kids?" Emily asked.

"No." Molly shook her head. "I have a kitten. His name is Smoky."

"I want a kitten, but Grandma won't let us." Emily wrinkled her nose.

"Emily, you know we can't have a cat in the house because Grandma is allergic to them."

Emily's voice held a note of resignation. "I know."

"Well, you can play with mine while you're visiting if your grandmother gives permission." Suddenly, Molly remembered how she came to have the kitten. She wondered if the children would recognize Smoky. Small chance. There were thousands upon thousands of gray cats in the world.

"Grandma, can we play with the cat?" Emily asked.

"I don't think so, dear. You probably won't have time."

"Maybe another time," Molly said, knowing that Virginia Spencer wouldn't let the children come if she knew about Kurt.

"We'll see," the older woman replied.

"You'll need to turn left at the next intersection. My house is about a mile down the road from there." Molly glanced in the rearview mirror again. Her SUV still followed in the distance. She hoped Kurt knew enough not to drive in behind them. As they neared her lane, she took another look in the rearview mirror. Her SUV wasn't in sight.

Virginia parked near the house. "Oh, this will be a magnificent house when it's finished."

"I certainly hope so. It'll mean a lot to me and the women I hope to employ here." Molly got out of the car.

Eric and Emily jumped from the car and followed Molly.

Eric looked up at Molly as he walked beside her. "I want to see the secret passage."

"I want to see the kitten." Emily tugged at Molly's arm.

"Children, Ms. Finnerty is going to talk to Grandma first, then you can see the passage and the kitten, if there is extra time."

While they climbed the steps to the front porch, both children gazed up at Molly for confirmation. Smiling, Molly looked at them. She saw very little of their father's reticence in these two little firecrackers. They must have gotten their exuberance from their mother.

Molly unlocked the front door then turned to Virginia. "As you can see, the outside of the house is in bad repair. We're going to start working on that as soon as the weather is consistently warm. Meanwhile, we are making great progress on the inside."

"This is lovely." Virginia stepped into the front hall and looked around. She walked over to the newly installed mantel and ran her hand along the dark wood. "Oh my, this is wonderful workmanship. Who's doing your restoration?"

Molly's heart sank. How could she answer this question without telling Virginia that her former son-in-law was doing the work? "He came from the western part of the state. A friend of mine recommended him. So far I'm pleased with his work." Molly hoped her explanation would suffice.

"I would be, too."

"Let's go into my office, and I'll give you the information you're looking for." Molly pushed aside the plastic and opened the double doors going into her office. "This should come down soon."

"This kind of work always has its inconveniences, but it's worth it in the end." Virginia followed Molly into the room. The children tagged along, looking bored. "Children, sit there on the window seat while I talk with Ms. Finnerty."

Molly went to the bookshelf on the other side of the room and pulled a couple of books from a shelf. "I've got some books the children can look at while we talk." Molly handed the books to Eric and Emily. "And if you don't mind, you and the children should call me Molly."

"Thanks, Molly." Emily emphasized Molly's name and took the book.

"You're welcome, Emily."

Eric followed suit when Molly gave him the other book. As she turned to her desk, she glanced out the window just in time to see her SUV come down the lane and pull into the carriage house. She pretended to look for something on her desk until Kurt got out and disappeared up the stairs to his apartment. When she looked up, she was relieved to see that Virginia was watching the children and hadn't seen the vehicle.

Molly picked up the papers from her desk and walked toward Virginia. "This is the information on our foundation. This is my partner's card. He's a lawyer and lives in Boston. Sometimes he's difficult to get a hold of because of his schedule, but he'll get back to you if you give him a call. He can answer all the questions that I can't. He handles all the fundraising while I do all the things here on the property."

"Thanks." Virginia studied the card, then folded the papers and put the card and the papers in her very large purse. "I'll have my attorney, Benton Turley, contact Mr. Rinaldi."

"Good. I'm sure they can work out the details, and if I can answer any other questions, I'll be glad to try."

Virginia patted her purse. "I'm sure the information you gave me will be good for the time being. But right now, I'd really like to see the other part of the property. I heard you mention to Eric and Emily that you think the house may have been a part of the Underground Railroad. You know, I'm well connected with the historical societies in the area. I'm sure they could help you find out."

"Thanks, but I don't think I want to know. I'm afraid someone might try to keep me from using it as I plan if it turns out to be a historical house."

Virginia nodded. "I understand. Let's take a look."

"It's a bit of a hike, but we can't drive back there yet. I made arrangements today for some work to be done on the road. Luckily, the mud has dried up so we can walk." Molly looked at the children. "Are you ready to see that secret passage?"

"Yeah," Eric and Emily chorused, jumping up from the window seat.

"Good. Let's go." Molly picked up a flashlight as they left her office.

"Do I get to see the kitten out there, too?" Emily asked.

"No, the kitten is somewhere in this house. He likes to hide. Maybe you won't get to see him this time. You'll have to come back."

Emily looked up at her grandmother. "Can we, Grandma?"

"We'll see." Virginia took Emily's hand.

While they walked past the carriage house, Molly hoped Kurt was looking out at his children.

When they reached the old farmhouse, Molly stopped before they went inside. "Let me warn you. This place is a real mess. Luckily, we did clean out some of the garbage and removed the graffiti a few days ago, or I wouldn't have brought the children back here."

"You're right." Virginia followed Molly through the doorless entry. "Children, watch your step. This place will require a lot of restoration work."

"I don't want to restore it. I only plan to make it livable. That's why I didn't seek any information about its historic nature because I was afraid they might make me restore it. We just want to house the women here." Turning on her flashlight, Molly opened a door that went into the basement, then turned to the children. "Watch your step as we go down here."

"Grandma, are you coming?" Emily asked.

"No, I'm going to wait right here."

"Okay, kids, follow me. Stay close behind me." Molly wasn't surprised that the proper Virginia Spencer didn't want to walk through an underground passage.

"Is that the door to the secret passage?" Eric pointed to the door on the opposite side of the basement from the stairs.

"Yes, that's it." Molly shined the flashlight on the door. "Eric, you can open it."

"I want to open it," Emily protested.

"Emily, you can open the door on the other end." Molly took the little girl's hand.

"Okay." Emily grasped Molly's hand tightly.

After Eric opened the door, they walked into the dark tunnel. Molly shined the light ahead of them.

"Do you think this is haunted?" Eric asked.

"I don't think so." Molly felt Emily's hand tighten around hers.

"Is this very long?" Emily asked.

"We'll be out in no time. But we can imagine what it was like to be a slave and have to hide down here until it was safe to come out."

"Cool," Eric said.

Emily was silent.

A musty smell permeated the air as they walked along the dirt floor. Cobwebs hung from the crude rafters in the tunnel. The other end of the tunnel opened into a small room with dirt walls.

Molly motioned toward the shelves that lined the walls of the room. "This was used as a root cellar where they kept vegetables from the garden during the winter."

"I see the door to get out." Emily pointed across the little room. "Can I open it now?"

Molly recognized Emily's eagerness to get out of the passageway. "Sure. Let's go out."

Emily tugged on the door. It opened and light

poured down a set of stairs and illuminated the little room. Eric and Emily scrambled up the stairs, and Molly followed them out into the sunlight in the yard between the house and the barn.

"I bet some of the slaves hid in the barn." Eric pointed across the yard.

"You're probably right." Molly nodded. "Let's find your Grandmother and tell her about the passage."

"Okay." Eric jogged toward the house.

Emily stayed behind, seemingly content to walk with Molly. "Do you know why we live with our grandma?"

Molly found Emily's question intriguing. "Why?"

"Because our parents are dead."

"I'm sorry, Emily." Molly took Emily's hand and puzzled over her statement. "Do you remember them?

Emily shook her head. "No. They died when I was too young to remember, and Grandma doesn't like to talk about it."

"That's too bad." Molly slowed her pace so she could talk to Emily before they got back to the farmhouse. "Have you seen pictures?"

"Just of our mother. Grandma doesn't have any of our dad."

"I bet you look like your mother." Molly watched Eric reach his grandmother's side, then turn and wave.

Emily smiled shyly and looked up at Molly. "That's what grandma says, too." Then Emily dropped Molly's hand and took off in a sprint to join her brother.

On the way back to Molly's house, the children regaled their grandmother with their insights into how the slaves might have used the secret passage. Molly pondered Emily's pronouncement that both her parents were dead. Would Virginia's lying to the children have an impact on Kurt's wish to get his children back? Molly would encourage him to pass this information along to Nick.

Molly watched the children with their grandmother. Despite Virginia's lies, Molly realized the children loved this woman and she loved them. A court battle would cause pain for Virginia as well as Kurt. If only there could be an easy way for Kurt and his former mother-in-law to come to terms over the children. When Molly thought about the impending court case, she could only see heartache ahead for everyone.

***

Kurt watched out the window of his apartment for Molly and the children to return. Virginia would be there, too, but he didn't mind seeing her as long as she didn't see him. Curiosity had nearly driven him crazy while he waited. He couldn't imagine how his former mother-in-law could be on friendly terms with Molly after the scene he had witnessed between Bev and Molly earlier in the afternoon. He could hardly wait to talk with Molly.

When Eric and Emily finally came into view, Kurt stood to the side of the window. He observed them through the partially open blinds. His children chased each other around the car while Molly and Virginia talked. Finally, Virginia turned to the children. She said something, and they got into the car. Molly and Virginia shook hands. Then Virginia slipped behind the wheel of her vehicle and drove away.

Molly stood in the yard until the car reached the main road. After the car turned onto the road, she dashed toward the carriage house. Kurt didn't wait for her to come to him. He raced to the door and down the stairs. He met her on the bottom step.

As Kurt's gaze roamed Molly's face, he realized that his heart was racing. Emotions overwhelmed him. Love for his children. Hatred for Virginia Spencer. And an undefined feeling for Molly that scared him. He didn't want to explore it further. Fear made him shove it aside. He needed to think of one thing and one thing only.

His children.

"Molly—"

"Kurt—"

They both spoke at once, then stopped.

"You go first." Kurt's heart raced.

Molly put a hand to the side of her head. "I'm not sure where to begin. You're probably wondering what happened."

"That's an understatement."

"Let's go up to the house, and we can talk." Molly headed across the yard.

Kurt fell into step beside her. He wanted to know about his kids. Jealousy ate at him because Molly had been so close to them and had talked with them. But he couldn't express those feelings. "What are my kids like?"

Molly looked over at him. Her eyes conveyed a sympathy he hadn't expected. "They are precious. They're well-behaved and polite. You would be proud of them."

"And I suppose I have Virginia Spencer to thank

for that." He couldn't keep the bitterness out of his voice.

"Yes, I think you do. I know you don't want to hear that, but it's true. She's raised your children."

"Only because she helped send me to prison." Kurt kicked at the dusty ground as he walked ahead of Molly. He didn't want to hear anything good about his former mother-in-law.

"Listen to me, Kurt." Molly caught up to him and touched his arm.

Her touch made him stop mid-step while his heart pounded. He gazed at her. A lump rose in his throat, and he couldn't talk for a moment. Lucky for him and her. Otherwise he would have yelled at her.

Swallowing the lump, he took a deep breath. Calm settled over him, but it didn't take away the bitterness. "Don't lecture me. You have no idea what it's like to go to prison for a crime you didn't commit."

She glanced away. Then without saying anything she walked away from him toward the house. He chased after her. "Molly."

She quickened her pace.

He called after her again. "Molly."

She still didn't stop. She took the back steps two at a time and disappeared into the house. Sprinting after her, he almost expected to find the door locked, but it wasn't. He let himself in and found her standing in the kitchen looking out the window. She turned when he entered the room. "What are you doing here? I thought you didn't want to listen to me."

He sat down at the kitchen table. "I want to hear what happened."

"I'm not sure you do, because I might say some things you don't want to hear." Her eyes narrowed as she talked.

"I said I'd listen."

"Okay, but be forewarned I'm going to lecture."

Kurt sighed heavily. "I deserve it."

"I don't know what you deserve." Molly sat down at the table across from him. Again he saw the sympathy in her eyes. "But I do know this. You've got to get over the past. One day you are going to be in the court room with Virginia Spencer, and your bitterness will not help you. I understand that you feel cheated and that life has been unfair to you. Get over it."

Looking away, Kurt clenched his fist under the table and gritted his teeth. He didn't want to get over it. She didn't understand. How could she? She and Nick came from a world of privilege. Kurt figured people like her did charity work to ease their consciences because of their guilt over all they had. Virginia Spencer was a woman like that, and she had trained her daughter Bonnie in the same vein. Maybe Virginia had seen that in Molly.

Kurt unclenched his fist. He placed his elbow on the table and rubbed his hand on his forehead. He hated feeling this way. Pushing away someone who had done so much to help him made him an ungrateful bum. His bull-headed thoughts about her charity work were misplaced. She was nothing like his former mother-in-law. Everything Molly said was right. He should agree with her and move on. But he couldn't admit it to her.

He glanced up. Molly sat on the other side of the table. She stared at him. No sympathy shone in her eyes now. Her somber expression told him her patience with him would soon run out. She wasn't interested in how he felt about the past.

"Okay, I'm ready to listen. I want to know what happened."

"Good." Nodding, Molly gave him a little smile. "I want you to take note of the extraordinary happenings because I see God's hand in this."

Kurt wrinkled his brow in a frown. "How?"

"Just listen." Molly waved her finger at him as if he were a bad schoolboy. "When I left here with Bev, she immediately got on her cell phone and called Virginia Spencer. I heard her tell Virginia to meet her at the Antique Trader. I could tell there was some problem having to do with the children. Then Bev told her to have the children meet her at the Antique Trader rather than going home."

"What did you think?" Kurt leaned forward in his chair.

"I didn't know what to think. Bev suddenly seemed quite capable of taking care of herself. She didn't seem like the disoriented woman I helped to the car, especially when Virginia called her back and confirmed the meeting."

"What did you do then?" Kurt tried to put himself in Molly's place and wondered what he would have done.

"I prayed."

"I should have expected that of you."

Molly gave him a curious glance. "Why do you say that?"

"Because you always seem to rely on God."

Molly chuckled. "I wish that were true. I usually find it easy to turn to God when I feel vulnerable. And I certainly felt that way as I drove Bev home. I had images of these two women ganging up on me and doing who knows what."

"My talk about Virginia Spencer probably didn't help."

"Yeah." Molly's lips curved in a wry smile. "Anyway, when we got to the Antique Trader, Virginia was there waiting for us."

"Did Bev go ballistic again like she did here?"

"I didn't give Bev time to do anything. As soon as I came into the house, I immediately went up to Virginia and introduced myself and began telling her about my house and the proposed women's shelter. She took me in like a long lost friend."

"Why?" Kurt frowned.

"Because she's been looking for a women's shelter in this area to support. She's going to donate money to the foundation Nick and I set up for this shelter. That's why I said that only God could have caused these events."

"Didn't Bev tell her about me?"

Molly shook her head. "No. Once she realized Virginia's supreme interest in my project, Bev didn't seem to have the nerve to ruin the whole thing. I also think she realized she could keep my business now and wouldn't feel guilty about it."

Kurt let out a long, low whistle. "Incredible."

"God's doing," Molly said.

"I wish I had your faith." Kurt was still learning to trust God.

"Don't put me on any kind of pedestal when it comes to faith in God. I have as many struggles as the next person. I just saw how He helped today."

"But what happens when we go to court, and she finds out I'm working for you?" Kurt had a sinking feeling in his gut.

"By that time, her name and donation will have been connected to the project for months. Nick will have made a big announcement about her donation, and she'll look pretty bad if she tries to take it back."

"You're sure that'll be the case? You don't know Virginia Spencer like I do." Kurt couldn't get rid of the bad feeling. When it came to his former mother-in-law, he couldn't generate much positive thought. He needed to think about something else. "Tell me about my kids."

"Okay." Molly reached across the table and touched his arm.

Kurt steeled himself against this familiar, friendly gesture. He should be thankful that she didn't shrink away from him anymore. But when she touched him, he found himself thinking about her in terms other than friendship. That kind of thinking had to stop. "I want to know every detail."

She gazed at him for a moment before she spoke as if she was trying to find the right words to say. "I learned something today that you'll find interesting. I think it's something you need to tell Nick."

"What's that?" Kurt asked.

"Virginia has told the children that you're dead."

"She what?"

"Emily told me today that she and Eric live with their grandma because both her parents are dead."

Kurt sat there for a moment and let Molly's statement sink in. At first, anger bubbled up inside him, but he silently asked God to help him overcome it. As the anger subsided, a calming peace came in its place. "Maybe it's better to be dead in their eyes than alive and painted as a murderer."

Molly shrugged. "Could be, but you've got to tell

Nick as soon as possible. This could mean something for your petition."

"I'll do it tomorrow." Kurt nodded. "Tell me more about my kids."

"Okay." Smiling, Molly proceeded to indulge all of his questions and gave him every detail she could remember until there was nothing else to tell.

Kurt relished every bit of information and tucked it away in his mind. He didn't want to forget one thing. The image of his children playing in the yard made him more determined than ever to make them his again.

CHAPTER ELEVEN

"I want you to see what's in the newspaper today."
Molly handed Kurt the paper as soon as he
walked into her office. "Nick works fast. It's only
been four days since I talked with Virginia about the
women's shelter. Everyone in this part of the state
now knows about Virginia Spencer's donation."

Kurt studied the news article then held it up so
she could see it. "It's a good picture of Nick and
Virginia. Why aren't you in it?"

Molly gazed out the window. She didn't want Kurt
to read anything in her eyes when she answered. She
feared he might guess there was more to her
reluctance to have her picture taken than she was
willing to tell. "I like to keep in the background. Nick
likes all that publicity stuff. I don't."

Kurt chuckled as he laid the paper on her desk. "I
know what you mean. I was never fond of cameras
and reporters myself. I had enough of that when I was
on trial."

Me, too, Molly wanted to say, but she caught
herself. Every time she thought about telling Kurt her
story, she could hear his words. *You wouldn't
understand.* But in reality, he was the one who
wouldn't understand. He had put her on such a
spiritual pedestal, despite her protests, that she was
afraid to let him know about her past. Nick's words of
warning, *You'll be sorry if you don't tell him*, haunted
her, too. The two statements battled in her mind like

wrestlers. But in the end it was easier to let things ride as they were. "Unwanted publicity is tough, but this is the kind we need."

"Especially when Virginia finds out that Nick filed that emergency petition regarding my request to see Eric and Emily. He said it would probably be only weeks now rather than months before the hearing takes place." Kurt released a harsh breath. "My stomach gets tied in knots whenever I think about it."

"You'll do fine. After all, you have the best attorney in Boston." Molly knew how much Nick had helped her. "What does Nick think?"

Kurt shrugged. "He thinks her lying will give me a better chance at getting, at the least, supervised visitation. The whole thing hinges on the best interest of the children. That's what the judge goes by."

"I'd say it's in their best interest to know their father." Molly wished she could make that come true.

"Too bad you're not the judge." Kurt smiled wryly. "Well, I'd better get busy so my great lawyer thinks I'm holding up my end of our bargain." Kurt turned toward the door then stopped. Turning back, he looked at her. "I forgot to tell you I took a newspaper out of your car that day I followed you back from Oakton. It had a picture of Eric and Emily in it. I hope you don't mind that I took it. Seeing the picture of Virginia in the paper reminded me of it."

"No, I don't mind. Why was their picture in the paper?"

Kurt explained the picture he had seen. "I cut it out and put it in my wallet with the other picture. I'm glad I have a more up-to-date photo of them, but I wish it was more than a newspaper clipping."

"I wish it were, too." Molly's heart hurt for this

man who didn't know his own children. She remembered holding Emily's hand while they went through the secret passage. Emily should have been holding her father's hand.

"Sometimes, I think pictures are the only thing I'll ever have." Kurt shook his head. "I don't have a good feeling about facing Virginia in court. In the long run, the only way I'm going to get my kids back is to find the person who killed Bonnie."

"And how could you possibly do that?"

"I don't know. When I mentioned it to Nick, he didn't encourage the idea, although he did say he'd have one of the PIs at his firm look into it. But I don't think that's a top priority with him. He thinks I'm better off concentrating on being a productive citizen, but I can't stop thinking about finding the real killer. I've decided to do a little research."

"What kind of research?"

"I'm going to the library to go back through the newspapers from that time period and see if they could give me any clues."

A sinking feeling hit her gut. What if Kurt's mission led him to newspapers that contained the story of her arrest? She couldn't let that happen. "Are you sure, since Nick didn't encourage that idea?"

Kurt let out a heavy sigh. "I hate sitting around doing nothing, but, at the same time, I don't want to jeopardize the chance to see my kids."

"Let me do it."

"But you've done so much already."

"No, I insist. I want to help. In fact, I'm running a few errands this morning. I could look today while I'm out." Hoping he would agree, Molly raised her eyebrows as she waited for his answer.

Kurt finally nodded. "You're right. I should let you do the research. That way I won't be going against my lawyer's advice."

"That's the smart thing to do." Molly smiled. "Do you have any idea what I should look for?"

"I wish I did, but maybe this can be a starting place." He reached into his back pocket and brought out his wallet. He took out a folded piece of paper and held it out to her. "These are the people I put on my suspect list."

Molly took the paper and read the three names. "Who are these people?"

"Connor Drake was Bonnie's boss. Dan McNeil was one of Bonnie's coworkers, and Jerry Malone was a guy who used to do odd jobs for us from time to time."

Molly wrinkled her brow. "Why are they suspects?"

"Bonnie didn't have any enemies. Everyone loved her, but I tried to think of who could, on the remotest chance, have a motive to kill her. It had to be someone she knew because there was no sign of a break-in. With the two coworkers, I thought it might be a disagreement or jealousy about work. With Malone, it might have been an argument that turned into an accidental death." Kurt shook his head. "I know I'm probably manufacturing scenarios, but there's someone out there somewhere who killed my wife and let me take the blame. I have to come up with something."

Molly stared at the fists Kurt held by his sides. What could she say—that she knew how he felt? Not really. But she knew about seeing her husband shoot himself and doing nothing to help him until it was too late. What would Kurt say if he knew? Would he sympathize or think she was a terrible person? "Maybe my research will help."

"I hope I'm not sending you on a doomed mission." Kurt gave her a wry smile, then turned again to go. "I'm headed to the other site to check on things over there this morning. I'll be back in a while to work on the dining room. When the dining room's done, I'll be ready to start on the outside."

"You're making great progress on the house. You keep working, and I'll do your research for you."

"Thanks."

"My pleasure." Nothing suited her better.

***

With the help of the reference librarian at the local library, Molly brought up the online files of the area newspapers. Before she started poring over the news from the past, she did an online search of Kurt's suspects to see what she might find. She found information about Connor Drake and Dan McNeil mostly related to their work in the real estate business and their involvement in some local charity events— nothing that would tie them to Bonnie's death. Jerry Malone was a very popular name, and Molly had difficulty pinpointing just one. She needed more information to find the Jerry Malone that Kurt had talked about.

Finally, she decided to look at the police reports and the main headlines in state and local news. What would she find in the news from Worcester County the year preceding Kurt's incarceration? She wondered what kind of things she should look for.

After reading for an hour, Molly stood and stretched her arms over her head. She rolled her shoulders to ease the tension, then closed her eyes and breathed deeply. So far she had seen nothing that might lead anywhere. The police records were full of arrests for drunk driving, petty theft, burglaries, assaults, drug possession, and drug dealing.

Molly wondered whether Bonnie's death could be somehow connected with drugs. Could she have been dealing drugs without Kurt's knowledge? After all, he had indicated Bonnie had unexpected meetings that took her away from home. Maybe she had used her real estate job as a front for selling illegal substances. Could that be the explanation for why a well-liked woman was murdered?

Rubbing her forehead, Molly sat down again and continued her hunt. She did a search for Bonnie's name then spent an hour reading through articles about her. Kurt's wife had been involved in more activities than should be humanly possible for one woman. How had she found the time, especially with two babies at home? Molly recalled the things that Kurt had said about his wife and her charitable functions.

Could any of those be the answer to her death? Could someone in one of the charities have embezzled money? If so, maybe Bonnie had found out and confronted them, and they killed her and tore up the house looking for any evidence she had against them. Molly let this scenario roll through her mind while she perused more news articles. She found a number of stories about a big real estate development, which contained references to Connor Drake and Dan McNeil, as well as Bonnie, in connection with the development, but that was no surprise considering their jobs in real estate.

More research only made for more questions. How could she begin to narrow it down? Could Bonnie have had a secret life that involved an affair rather than drugs? After all, Kurt said they were at odds over her busy schedule. Bonnie and her lover could have had an argument that resulted in her death. Molly shook her head. She was coming up with more theories, but were any of them believable? Not so much. No wonder the police had found Kurt the most likely suspect.

Molly sighed. If she didn't come up with some meaningful information to give Kurt, he would insist on coming to look for himself. Somewhere in all these news stories there was bound to be at least one article about Mary Finn. Would Kurt make the connection between a blond, rail-thin model named Mary Finn who was arrested for drug possession and one Molly Finnerty? She didn't want to think about the possibility.

Molly wondered whether anyone could see a resemblance between the way she looked now and how she had looked back then. She weighed at least fifteen pounds more, and yet people still considered her thin. Her hair was now its natural color, not the blond that had come from a bottle. The only thing that remained the same were the freckles that were more often than not airbrushed out of her photos. She had been born Molly Finnerty, and Molly Finnerty was the person she wanted to be. She liked to think Mary Finn was dead and gone. But one newspaper story could resurrect her.

The hours skipped by like minutes as Molly

continued to pore over newspaper article after newspaper article. Eventually, the picture she dreaded seeing came into view. There she stood in handcuffs flanked by two police officers. Her disheveled appearance reflected her debauched state. SUPER MODEL ARRESTED ON SUSPICION OF DRUG POSSESSION, the headline screamed at her. Even now her face flushed with shame.

Wondering if there were more articles about her, she continued her search. If she could get through all the news stories about her, then she wouldn't have to worry about Kurt finding them. Hopefully, he would continue to let her do the research.

"Molly." Kurt's voice came from behind her.

She shut down the computer page she'd been viewing and turned, her pulse pounding. Her hand over her heart, she stared at him. "You startled me. What are you doing here? How long have you been here?"

He smiled. "Just walked in. I came to get you. Do you realize what time it is?"

She glanced down at her phone that lay nearby. "Six o'clock. I completely lost track of the time."

"Obviously." Kurt stepped closer and glanced at the computer monitor in front of her. "Did you find anything?"

"No." She clicked back to the login page. "At least I don't think so."

Kurt sat in the chair next to her. "Maybe I should do some research, too, since I'm here."

"But I just logged out." She couldn't let Kurt find any articles about her. "I thought you were going to follow Nick's advice and let me do this."

"Even though Nick told me to let it go, I can't. I

want to help you. I don't see what it would hurt." Kurt turned on the computer. "We can do another hour of research, then go out to eat. I'll treat."

"That's not necessary."

He grinned. "Sure it is. I have to pay you back for all this work you've done."

"I certainly don't expect payment."

"I know, but it would make me feel better."

Molly sighed. "Okay, you win. Another hour, then we eat."

"Where do I start?" Kurt turned to the monitor in front of the chair where he sat.

She looked over at him as the monitor flickered to life and resigned herself to the situation. He wasn't going away. "I'll show you where I left off. No need to go over information twice."

"That's true."

Relieved, Molly logged onto the computer she'd been using. She wrote the file name and a date on a slip of paper and handed it to Kurt. "Start with this. I've already done the preceding issues."

"And you said you didn't find anything? What did you look for?" Kurt gave her a sideways glance as the file appeared on the screen.

"I searched the police reports and the main stories. I didn't see anything substantive." Did she dare bring up all the crazy scenarios that had crossed her mind during the search? They wouldn't paint Bonnie in a good light. Molly wasn't sure Kurt would take kindly to the ideas she had about his beloved wife. Maybe discussing them while they ate was a better plan.

Trying not to tie herself in knots over what Kurt might see during his search, Molly looked through the papers from the time nearer Kurt's arrest. No stories about her appeared. She surreptitiously glanced at the stories Kurt was reading, but she couldn't tell what they were. "Let me know if you come across anything."

After another hour of searching, Molly looked over at Kurt, whose concentration was intent. She wondered whether she dared ask him about the article he was reading. As if he sensed her scrutiny, he looked up. "Did you find something?"

She shook her head. "No, but you look like you might have."

"No." His disheartened tone matched the grimace on his face. "I was reading about the big land development that Bonnie worked on. I should've remembered it was a big news item back then."

"I know. I read several articles about it. Connor Drake and Dan McNeil were mentioned in conjunction with that deal. Is it that one near the lake with the golf course?"

"Yeah, all the people at Bonnie's office worked on it." Kurt's eyes conveyed a troubled sadness. "Bonnie also worked on it a lot. It brings back unpleasant memories. I thought she spent too much time on that project. That was one of the sources of tension between us. It makes me sad to think I let something like that ruin all the good times. Everything ended on such a sour note..." His voice trailed away almost as if he was trying to hold back tears.

Again, she found herself aching for his loss, but she didn't know what to say. If she were honest with herself, she would admit that she cared for Kurt more than she ever thought possible. Everything she did these days, she did with him in mind. How could she have let this happen? He obviously hadn't gotten over his wife's death, and getting his children back was his main concern.

Molly knew he didn't think of her as anything other than his boss. He never asked her about her past or her family. He didn't care enough to find out about those things. At this point, she was just as glad he didn't, but it was a telling sign that he made no effort to get to know her beyond their working relationship. "I'm sorry this is bringing back bad memories. It's hard losing a spouse."

He turned from the computer and gazed at her as though he was seeing her for the first time. "Molly, I've been incredibly insensitive. I've been wallowing in self-pity as though I'm the only one who has ever suffered the loss of a loved one. I'm forgetting that you lost your husband, too. And I've never asked about it."

She smiled slightly. It was almost as if he had read her mind. But she let his concern wash over her like a warm spring breeze, taking away the chill of winter. "That's okay. I don't like to talk about it. It's better left in the past."

"I understand. Sometimes it's hard to relive those old hurts." He stretched his hands over his head. "Let's call it quits. Okay?"

"Are you sure? We haven't made much progress in our search."

"I'm sure." He nodded toward the clock on the wall as he logged off the computer. "Our hour is up. It was a long shot anyway."

"I can look another day." Molly stood and pushed in her chair.

Kurt shrugged, a frown puckering his brow as he

joined her. "I don't know. It's probably like trying to find your way in a dark room. You don't have a clue where you're going."

"What would you do if you found the person you suspect might have killed Bonnie?" Molly gave Kurt a pointed look while they walked toward the door.

"Good question." Kurt stared back. "Go to the police?"

"Would they believe you?"

"I don't know." Sighing, Kurt opened the door and waited for Molly to go through before he followed. "I haven't thought this through very well."

"Maybe that's why Nick didn't encourage you to do this."

"Yeah, I suppose you're right."

"We can talk it over while we eat. Where should we go?"

"I'd like to take you to one of the places where I used to eat." Kurt stopped next to her SUV. "I hope it's still there. If not, we'll find something else."

As Molly followed Kurt's pickup out of the parking lot, a multitude of thoughts tumbled through her mind. She tried not to think of this dinner invitation as anything other than coworkers going out for a bite to eat, but deep down, she wanted it to be more. The burden of her secret past weighed heavily on her mind, as well, but she couldn't consider divulging any of it to Kurt. Then there were the theories as to why Bonnie was murdered—one more thing she was reluctant to talk about.

The setting sun cast a myriad of reds, yellows, and oranges across the western sky. The colorful sky in weather lore signaled a good day ahead, and she wished the sign also meant a good day ahead for both

Kurt and her. She wondered whether that was ever possible.

Kurt's pickup turned off the highway onto a road that headed toward one of the nearby lakes. About half a mile down the road, she saw a building near the shore. From a distance, the dilapidated place had little appeal, and she guessed that Kurt's choice for the evening was probably closed. But as they drew nearer, she spotted numerous vehicles in the parking lot and light coming from inside the building. The words Lobster Shed were spelled out in a bright neon sign that illuminated the window by the door. She pulled her SUV up beside Kurt's pickup and got out.

Kurt came around to meet her. "Looks like the place is still going strong. I should've warned you. It's a ramshackle of a place. It doesn't look like much, but the food's great."

"I'll take your word for it." Molly followed him into the dimly lit interior.

A hostess seated them by a window in a booth with dark wooden benches on either side of a table made of the same wooden planks. A small lantern sitting in the middle of the table provided the only light. A country western tune played on the brightly lit jukebox sitting in the far corner.

Molly glanced out the window. The water reflected the colorful sky. The sun glowed like a large orange ball as it slipped behind the hills on the other side of the lake. "This is a beautiful view."

"You're right. It doesn't get much better than this." Kurt picked up one of the menus the hostess had left on the table. "If the menu's still the same, the lobster feast is terrific. If you like lobster."

"I do." Molly picked up her menu and looked it

over. "It's still there."

"That's my recommendation." Kurt closed his menu and eased back.

"Okay, I'll go with that." Molly gazed at Kurt in the dim light.

In a minute a waitress took their order then just as quickly returned with their drinks. After she left, Kurt gave Molly a wry smile. "It's good to be free, so I can come here again."

Molly didn't want to think about freedom because she wasn't free. The prison of her own making—the prison of her past—held her captive. She had to think about something else. "How did you find this place?"

"Actually, Bonnie brought me here when we were dating. It was one of her favorite places. We used to come here a lot when we first got married, too. As time passed, we came here less often. I guess we were too busy to make the trip." Sadness painted his blue eyes.

"Life has a way of getting in the way of doing things we like." Changing the topic hadn't helped. Now Molly's heart twisted with a knot of jealousy. Bonnie again. He was always talking about Bonnie. Molly chided herself for forgetting that this wasn't a date. She had asked to be his friend and that was what this was. But when she looked at the handsome man sitting across from her, she wanted it to be different. The reality of her feelings for him hit her hard as she sat there. She didn't want to feel this way, but against her better judgment, she had let herself care too much.

"Is that what you've done?"

Molly puzzled over Kurt's question. "Do you think I don't do anything for fun?"

Shrugging, Kurt shook his head. "Just an observation. You spend all your time on that house."

"It's a mission."

"I know it's a good work. You're doing something to help others, but you should take some time for yourself."

"Is that what you told your wife when you thought she was working too hard?"

Kurt looked thoughtful. "It didn't do any good. She enjoyed her work. That was her fun."

"It's like that for me, too. I enjoy what I'm doing. Working on that house is fun to me. Cooking is fun. As far as I'm concerned, it is time for myself."

"You sound just like Bonnie."

Molly wasn't sure she wanted to sound like Bonnie. She wanted Kurt to look at her in her own light, not in the light of his deceased wife. "Is that good?"

Kurt nodded. "Yeah, but you're single and you never go out. A pretty young woman should be going out and doing things."

"Are you trying to flatter me or give me advice?" Molly wondered where this conversation was leading. He couldn't possibly be hinting for a date. That was wishful thinking on her part. In light of all the things she couldn't share with him, where had her crazy thoughts come from?

"Take it however you want. I'm just being honest."

Molly couldn't help smiling. "Thanks for your honesty."

The waitress came with their order. After a prayer of thanksgiving for the food, they ate in silence for several minutes. The whole time Molly kept thinking about her feelings—the ones she'd been hiding from herself as well as from Kurt. She did want to be his friend and help him see his children again, but in the midst of all this helping, he had slipped around her defenses and captured a little corner of her heart. She feared that even that tiny part meant heartache.

He was still too tied up in memories of Bonnie. Maybe if she brought up the scenarios about Bonnie, she could distance herself from these troubling emotions.

Molly opened her mouth to bring up her thoughts but quickly snapped it shut. She didn't know how to start. She didn't want to alienate Kurt, and she was afraid that would happen.

"You looked like you were about to say something." Kurt set his ear of corn on the plate. "I hope I didn't offend you."

Molly stared at him. Was this the opening she needed? She took a deep breath. "You didn't offend me, but I've been putting off telling you something that might offend you."

"You don't like my work?"

"Your work is wonderful. This has to do with the research I did this afternoon."

"You found something you didn't mention to me?" He frowned.

She shook her head. "I didn't find anything concrete, but I did come up with a few reasons why someone would want to kill Bonnie."

"You didn't tell me? Why?" His frown grew deeper.

"Because you won't like what I have to say." Molly looked him right in the eye.

He didn't speak immediately, just stared back, a muscle working in his jaw. "I want to know. Don't keep it from me."

"You're sure? I don't want you to be angry with me."

He turned toward the window and appeared to be looking out toward the water where moonlight shimmered on the ripples. When he finally looked back at her, his eyes narrowed. "I've grown accustomed to hearing bad news. You might as well tell me."

Drugs or an affair—which one would Kurt find the least objectionable? What did it matter? He certainly didn't want to hear either one of them. Afraid to look him in the eye, she stared at her half-eaten meal. "I was reading about drug busts and wondered if there was any possibility that Bonnie might have been involved in some kind of drug trade."

Kurt made no response. Was he scowling? Or was he simply weighing her statement? At first, she didn't dare to look at him, but curiosity simmered around the edges of her mind like a pot ready to boil. She had to look. She slowly raised her head to catch a glimpse of his response.

As soon as she met his gaze, he shook his head, his face expressionless. "What gave you that crazy idea?"

"I told you. The police logs in the newspaper." Molly grimaced. "You said she went out on business a lot—maybe it was for more than real estate."

"Impossible." His voice was low and controlled.

The scowl that now dominated his features made Molly consider forgetting her other thoughts, but she might as well get them all out in the open. "You're probably right about the drugs."

"Thanks for that much." His expression softened.

"Are your other suggestions just as ludicrous?"

"One of them. The other not so much. Do you want to hear them?"

Kurt looked away then nodded as he returned his gaze to hers. "Might as well."

"Was it possible that Bonnie was having an affair, and a lovers' quarrel resulted in her death?" Molly didn't breathe as Kurt looked at her wide-eyed.

"Are you thinking this because I told you we argued—that we hadn't been getting along?"

Molly shook her head. "I'm telling you this because I was trying to come up with some explanation for why a well-liked woman would wind up dead. I know it's not stuff you want to hear, but I thought you should explore all possibilities."

"I'm not sure I can get my head around Bonnie having an affair." Shaking his head, Kurt released a harsh breath. "Even though we were at odds a lot after the twins were born, I can't see her having an affair. No. It's not possible. Just not possible."

Molly wondered whether he was trying to convince her or himself that Bonnie hadn't had an affair as he continued to shake his head. She couldn't begin to relate. Her marriage had been a mess, but she had never considered having an affair. Kurt was probably correct in saying it wasn't possible. "Then there's one more thing."

"And that would be?"

"I noticed there were several articles about Bonnie's involvement in charitable fundraisers. Could someone have been embezzling funds?"

"Are you suggesting that Bonnie was an embezzler in addition to all the other accusations you've made about her?" His voice low and harsh,

Kurt frowned again as he leaned forward.

"No. I didn't mean she was doing the embezzling. I was thinking that she might have found out someone else was embezzling funds, and they killed her to keep her quiet."

"Wow!" Kurt rubbed his chin, his shoulders relaxing. "That never occurred to me."

"So is that a possibility?"

"More so than anything else you've mentioned."

"Then maybe we should pursue that angle."

"How?" Kurt took another bite of his food.

"I could go back and look more closely at the articles and see what other people were involved. Maybe you know some of them."

"Let me look."

Molly's heart sank at the thought. She shook her head. "You work on my house, and I'll do the looking."

"This really isn't your problem, so why are you so eager to help?"

"I think you're innocent, and the real killer shouldn't be free." The half-truth fell from her lips with ease. Kurt shouldn't have to take the blame for something he hadn't done. He didn't need to know the other half of her reason.

"Thanks for your vote of confidence. Thanks for being my friend as well as my employer."

"You're welcome." Trying not to wish for something more than friendship between her and Kurt, Molly turned her attention back to her meal. Maybe she should be grateful that he was still willing to be her friend after she had practically accused his deceased wife of drug dealing and adultery. She pushed the troubling thoughts away as they continued their meal in silence.

"Tell me what you did for fun before you started on this house."

At the sound of Kurt's voice, Molly glanced up. He had finished eating. He leaned back in his seat, his arms crossed. Why was he bringing up that subject again? "Why are you so worried about what I do for fun?"

"I think you work too much."

"Maybe I do, but that's okay. I've had my share of fun."

"Like what?"

Molly thought back over the years. There had been lots of times when she'd had fun. Yet, when she dissected all those times, she realized they were all related to work or her charity missions. She hadn't done anything fun just for the sake of fun since she was a kid. She began working as a model when she was fifteen. There had never been any high school homecomings or proms. No high school graduation. She had grown up too fast. She had married at twenty and let Byron suck all of the fun out of her life. She had turned to drugs to elude the madness of her marriage and work. In the beginning, the modeling had been fun and a great adventure. She had seen the world, but her life had become a roller coaster ride that wouldn't end. She wanted off and the only way to accomplish that was to escape into the "never-never land" of drugs.

"Either you've had too much fun to tell me about, or you're having a hard time thinking of something. Which is it?" Kurt leaned forward and put his elbows on the table.

Kurt's question brought her back to the present.

She wondered how she could answer it. "I think your idea of fun and my idea of fun are different. You'd probably think my idea wasn't fun at all."

"Try me."

"All right. I can't think of a thing that I've done that hasn't been somehow related to my work. People can have enjoyment when they work. Like the time I went to see the Tall Ships at Boston Harbor when I was working at the women's shelter there. Is that fun enough for you?"

Kurt laughed. "You don't have to get defensive. You and Bonnie would have been great soul mates. She loved to have fun at work, too."

Molly forced herself to smile. Kurt's constant references to Bonnie made her want to bang her fist on the table and tell him to get over the past. But she didn't have any place telling him to forget the past when she couldn't get over her own. "Some of us like our work."

"I do, too, but I also like to have fun in other ways. And it's been a long time since I've been able to do that."

"I hope you're not telling me this because you think I've been making you work on the weekends." Molly grimaced. "I thought you wanted to."

"No. No, I've been working just like you because I've enjoyed watching the changes in your house. I like seeing what I've accomplished. It gives me a sense of pride."

"You should be proud. I'm sorry I haven't taken the time to tell you what a marvelous job you've done."

"Thanks. So now I'm going to take a day and enjoy some entertainment."

Molly nodded. "You should. You deserve it."

"I will, but I'll enjoy it more if I can share it with someone. Can I convince you to go with me?" The expectation in his expression was hard to ignore.

Molly's heart jumped into her throat. She glanced away. She couldn't let him see the excitement in her eyes. How did she take this invitation? She couldn't allow herself to read anything into this. He was probably lonely. If she were honest with herself, she was lonely, too. But was that a good combination? Two lonely people sharing some fun. A day spent with Kurt could make her act on her desire for more than the friendship he offered. She already cared too much, and that was dangerous.

When she glanced back at him, a worried look knit his brow. "I didn't mean to put you on the spot. I should have remembered that you're my boss. I can go by myself."

"Oh, no. I don't mind your asking. As you said, we're friends, too. I just wasn't sure what you had in mind." Molly hoped her response didn't indicate a reaction one way or another.

"You don't like surprises?"

Molly found herself smiling despite the nervous pounding of her heart. "Not much."

"Why don't you live dangerously and let me surprise you?"

Molly wondered what he would think if he knew how dangerously she had lived in the past. She doubted he would understand how she had nearly thrown her life away, let alone the life of her husband and unborn child. She couldn't let herself get too close to him. But one day of fun couldn't hurt anything. Could it?

CHAPTER TWELVE

Kurt combed his hair, then glanced in the mirror. His hair didn't comb very well. Before today it didn't matter. Even though he saw Molly every day with his bad haircut, now it made a difference. He wanted to look good. He kept reminding himself that this wasn't a date, but he couldn't help himself. Molly intrigued him. He couldn't help thinking of her in terms of romance.

Ever since the day he'd learned that Nick was only Molly's friend, Kurt couldn't shake the idea of a relationship with her. He knew it was folly and had told himself over and over again not to let his mind run in that direction. Sitting with her in church for the past two Sundays hadn't taken away that idea either.

He liked spending time with her. From the moment he'd met Molly, he'd been attracted to her. In the beginning, it had only been a physical attraction to a good looking woman, but now it was so much more. He admired her for the charitable work she did, for the way she went out of her way to help others. He was tired of fighting his growing feelings for her. But he had to remember that getting his children back had to be his first priority. He couldn't lose focus of that goal. He'd reminded himself of these facts before, but the reminders didn't change his thinking.

After he had put on his best jeans and a long-sleeved, blue and white striped shirt, he grabbed his jacket and headed out the door. His nerves zinged as he walked toward Molly's house. He hadn't been this nervous or excited about going out with a woman since he'd been a sophomore in high school. Even his first date with Bonnie hadn't made him feel like this. He had to remember that today's excursion wasn't a date.

As he raised his hand to knock, Molly appeared in the mudroom and opened the door. "I'm ready." She took a tan jacket from the peg on the wall. She looked him over from head to toe. "When are you going to tell me the agenda for the day?"

"As soon as we get into your car. You're driving."

"I am?"

"Yeah, you have a better knowledge of the terrain than I do." He couldn't help watching her as they crossed the yard toward the carriage house. Her strawberry-blond hair glowed in the early morning sunlight as it swished around her shoulders. Her brisk walk emphasized her long legs. He took a deep breath. Maybe this wasn't such a good idea after all. He was going to have to summon all his willpower to keep his hands to himself. Teenage nerves weren't the only thing he was feeling. "I'm glad to see you followed my instructions on the appropriate dress for the day."

"Me, too. Jeans for comfort." She got into her SUV. As she drove onto the main road, she looked over at him. "Where are we going?"

"Take me to Boston."

"And what are we going to do in Boston?"

Kurt grinned. "I can only divulge so much

information at one time."

"Does this mean I'll be part of a constant guessing game all day?"

Kurt laughed at her consternation. "No. This is your mission if you wish to accept it: Find an all-day parking spot somewhere near Newberry Street."

"I accept. Does this mean shopping? I thought men didn't like to shop."

He grinned. "You'll find out when we get there."

They rode for a while without talking. The silence gave him time to reflect on his feelings. Calmer now that they were on their way, he looked forward to this visit to Boston. He hadn't been there in over six years. The weather forecast for sixty-five degrees and sunny was perfect for a day in mid-April. As Molly drove toward the city, she turned the CD player on and Christian music filled the silence.

When they finally arrived in the city just a little before noon, Molly took the Prudential Center exit off the Mass Pike. "I used to live around here in college. There's a street near the Fens where you can park without having a residents' sticker. If we're lucky we might find a free parking spot. If not, we'll have to park in a parking garage."

"Do whatever you like. You know the city better than I do."

Molly turned onto a street that bordered a park. They drove a couple of blocks without seeing an empty parking space. Just as they entered the third block, she looked over at him and pointed ahead. "Looks like our lucky day. Someone's pulling out of a spot up ahead. If I can maneuver this tank into it, we're set for the day."

Kurt helped direct her as she managed to get her

SUV into the tight parking space.

After she parked, she hopped out of the car. "Now what?"

Kurt glanced around. Nothing in the immediate area looked familiar. "I hope you don't mind walking."

"No. When I lived down here, that's about all I did. I didn't own a car because trying to find a parking spot can be tough." Molly slung her purse over her shoulder. "Lead the way."

Kurt tried again to figure out which direction he wanted to go. In the distance the John Hancock Building and the Prudential Center rose high into the bright, blue April sky. He figured Fenway Park must be somewhere in the other direction, but he wasn't sure.

"Do you need some help?"

Kurt gave her a wry smile. "I guess I should have stuck with Newberry Street. I'm not sure how to get to Fenway from here."

"Are we going to a baseball game?"

Kurt nodded. "I hope you like baseball."

"And if I don't?"

"Then you aren't going to enjoy the first part of our day." He held up two tickets. "Please tell me you aren't one of those women who hates sports."

She laughed. "I'm not, but I had you worried there for a moment, didn't I?"

"Not worried, just concerned that you wouldn't have as much fun as I'm going to have."

"So you were going to have fun regardless?"

Kurt nodded. "That's what this day is for. Fun."

"Let the fun begin. Follow me."

Kurt resisted the urge to grab Molly's hand as they

walked along the edge of the park. Maybe if he pretended she was his sister, he might make it through the day without embarrassing himself.

In the top of the ninth inning, Kurt stood alongside Molly and cheered the last out and a win for the Red Sox. Full of hot dogs, peanuts, and soda, they followed the crowd to the exit. Kurt took in the jostling fans, the smell of popcorn and hotdogs, and the sounds of laughter as they left the ballpark. He would never take those things for granted again. One thing being in prison had taught him was to savor everything, even the little things in life. Having his kids with him was the only thing that would have made the day better.

"Did you have fun?" Kurt asked when they reached the street outside the stadium.

"Do you really have to ask that question?"

"No." He chuckled. "I think you enjoyed this more than I did."

"I'd call it a draw." She looked over at him. "What's next?"

Kurt glanced down at his watch. "We have lots of time before our dinner reservation."

"Where do we have reservations?" She looked at him, a smile tugging at the corner of her mouth.

"At a place on Newberry Street."

Kurt wanted her to have a great time so she wouldn't forget this day. Even though she had told him she believed he was innocent, he couldn't purge his worry that she still might harbor some doubt. He hoped the past two months in her employ had worked toward erasing that doubt, but his conviction hung over him like a circling vulture. He needed to find Bonnie's killer. How could he do that? He didn't want to believe that Bonnie had sold drugs or committed adultery. He especially didn't want to believe the latter, but had the animosity that hung between them in those last few months driven her into the arms of another man? He couldn't dismiss that thought even though he questioned its veracity. He wanted to concentrate on Molly's other theory about the embezzlement. Would that lead him to the killer?

"So that's why you were so tied to Newberry Street." Molly's statement shook him from his thoughts.

"I only knew how to get where I was going from there. Whenever we came into Boston, we always came to Newberry Street because Bonnie liked to shop."

Molly made no comment as they continued to walk with the crowd leaving Fenway Park. Her stiff posture signaled her irritation at something, but he couldn't figure out what. Maybe she didn't like to shop and didn't like being compared to the typical woman. Could he bring it up without annoying her more? Sometimes women were hard to figure out. He'd made his share of mistakes with Bonnie, and he didn't want to start wrong with Molly.

He released a heavy sigh. "We have two hours to kill until our dinner reservation at six-thirty. What do you want to do?"

"Let's walk down to the Public Garden and the Common and hang out for a while." She looked at him, her eyebrows raised with anticipation.

With relief washing over him, he nodded. "Sure."

They walked toward the Boston Common on Boylston Street. When they reached the Public

Garden, Molly insisted that they look at the bronze sculptures of the ducks inspired by the book, *Make Way for Ducklings*.

As they drew near, Molly pointed to the sculptures. "Every time I see this it makes me want to be a kid again."

"What were you like as a kid?"

She looked at him as though he had asked a question she couldn't answer, but the look quickly disappeared as she shrugged. "I was just a kid like everyone else."

"Not like everyone else. We're all different."

"I know. I guess you could say I grew up too fast. My dad died when I was twelve, and my mother wanted the best for me so she pushed. I did what she wanted even when it wasn't for the best. Judging from what you've told me, I think my mother was a lot like Bonnie's mother."

"I doubt it. No one's as hateful as Virginia Spencer." As soon as the words were out of his mouth, he wished he hadn't injected his dislike of his former mother-in-law into the conversation. Despite Molly's confession about her mother, Kurt got the feeling she was skirting his question. He wondered why. Maybe she knew about abuse first hand. That would explain why she was involved with the women's shelter. He'd like to ask, but it wasn't any of his business.

"Let's wander over to the Common." Molly headed that direction without waiting for him.

He strode after her. Obviously, she didn't want to talk about her mother or listen to him complain about Virginia Spencer. They stood in silence as they waited for the light to change so they could cross Charles Street. What should he talk about now? He couldn't help thinking about how much he'd like to bring Eric and Emily here to see the ducklings, but he didn't want to talk about that either. Talking about his kids only made him sad. He didn't want to be sad today.

They left the Common and walked back through the Public Garden. As they meandered along Newberry Street, Kurt again drank in the laughter and conversation that surrounded him. Even the honking of car horns signified freedom. Yet, he could never be completely free until he cleared his name. Despite his physical freedom, his unfair conviction still held him hostage. About a block from the restaurant, Molly stopped in front of a store window full of stuffed Easter toys and baskets. "Look at the bunny. How precious."

"Yeah." The image of Emily holding that fluffy white rabbit with the pink ears flashed through his mind. If only he could give it to her. He wished they could move on so he didn't have to think about what he couldn't have. "You're a little old for stuffed animals, aren't you?"

"Hardly." She looked at him. "Would you like to give this to Emily?"

"How?"

"I could give each of the kids an Easter basket. Let's go in and see what we can find. You can pick the stuff out, and I could have it sent over to Virginia's house. They wouldn't know it was from you, but at least they'd get it. Someday you'll be able to tell them."

"I wish I had your optimism." He sighed as he opened the door for her to go into the store. "I wonder about my kids. Are they happy?"

straight ahead. He didn't want to see any disappointment in Molly's eyes.

"God will answer, but it isn't always easy to know what God is trying to tell us. Sometimes, our prayers are answered in ways we least expect. We just have to have faith."

Kurt stole a glance at her. Her eyes were trained on the road ahead as the sun dipped below the horizon. The evening twilight closed around them. "Help me believe that."

She shook her head. "That's something you have to do for yourself. I can pray with you and for you, but I can't make you have faith that the prayers will be answered."

"I've been thinking about sharing my story with the people at church. Everyone's been so friendly. And last week when that man came forward and shared his problem with his wife so many people sought him out afterwards. I want to ask for their prayers."

Molly didn't respond immediately. The hum of the motor was the only sound as she drove in silence.

He puzzled over her lack of response. "Do you think I'm wrong?"

"Oh, no. You're right to do that."

"Then why the long silence?"

"I was just thinking how much the prayers of the church would help. There's so much power in prayer."

"Will you come with me when I go forward?" he asked.

"I'll stand up for you any time. I'll ask prayers for both of us because I'll be testifying on your behalf during the hearing."

Kurt released a long slow breath. "I'm feeling better already. Thanks."

"I hope you had fun today. That's what you wanted."

"I did. Thanks for coming."

"I'm glad you asked me. I've forgotten what a great city Boston is. We'll have to do it again."

Kurt smiled to himself. "We will."

***

The first chords of the final hymn rang through the auditorium as the congregation stood. Molly waited for Kurt to step out of the pew, but he didn't move. Was he still planning to tell the congregation his story? She wanted the church folks to pray about the petition to see his kids that would come before a judge soon, but they couldn't unless they knew about it. Was there some way to encourage him? She didn't want to push him into something he didn't want to do. He hadn't mentioned it this morning while they were driving to church, so maybe he had changed his mind since last night.

She glanced at him again, but he was looking straight forward, his mouth barely moving as he sang the hymn about being led to the cross of Jesus. Maybe he wasn't ready to share this Sunday. After all, he had mentioned it for the first time last night. He probably needed more time to think about it. She had to be patient and pray. She should certainly understand his reluctance to open up his life.

The congregation began to sing the last stanza, and without warning, Kurt grabbed her hand and stepped into the aisle. He gripped her hand as if he were hanging onto the edge of a cliff. He probably had no idea his large hand surrounded hers like a carpenter's vice. When they reached the front, he finally let go as he shook hands with Pastor Tom, who greeted Kurt with a smile.

The pastor indicated that they should take a seat on the front pew as he quietly talked with Kurt. While Molly waited, she prayed that the congregation would believe he was innocent and deserved to have his children with him.

The music ended. Kurt stood. The congregation sat. He motioned for her to join him as he faced the gathering with the pastor. She glanced at him, but his gaze was trained straight ahead. Her breath hitched and her heart stuttered as she watched him. When Pastor Tom indicated that Kurt wanted to be part of the congregation, the members smiled and applauded. Molly hoped they would still be smiling after Kurt told his story.

Pastor Tom stepped forward. "We're glad to welcome Kurt into our fellowship today, and he has a matter for prayer that he'd like to share with us."

After the pastor made his statement, curiosity hummed through the pews. Standing beside Kurt, Molly held her breath. Why was she worried when God was in control? She tried to keep the answer from penetrating her thoughts, but the guilt from not sharing her own story seeped in anyway. She let rationalization set in while Kurt explained his situation. She didn't have a family to think about. Kurt did.

Kurt finished speaking. Then Pastor Tom's prayer for Kurt ended the worship service. While many members filed forward to shake Kurt's hand and wish him well, Molly said her own prayer of thanksgiving for the way the congregation had accepted him. For a moment, she wished she had the courage to share her story, too, but her fears vanquished the thought as soon as it crossed her mind.

When the last of the well-wishers departed, Pastor Tom shook Kurt's hand. "If you let me know the date of the hearing, I'll say a special prayer for you on that day."

Kurt nodded. "I'm meeting with my lawyer sometime later this week. As soon as I know, I'll give you a call."

"Good. I'll be waiting to hear from you." Smiling, Pastor Tom glanced at Molly. "Don't work him too hard."

"I'll try not to." With a chuckle, Molly turned to Kurt. "Ready to go?" As he nodded, she drank in his happy demeanor. "I'm glad this all worked out. Now we have a lot of people praying for you."

"Thanks for standing by me. I almost didn't go forward."

"I figured you'd do it when you were ready— today or some other day."

"I'm glad I did it today." Kurt placed a hand on her elbow as they walked toward the back of the auditorium.

His touch set off a fluttery feeling in her stomach. Trying to ignore it, she took a deep breath and let it out slowly. She had to focus on the start of good things to come for the man she cared about more than was wise for either of them. He was dealing with enough without adding her baggage to his life.

***

The mahogany paneled walls and numerous bookshelves filled with law books, did little to calm Kurt's nerves as he waited for Nick to return to his office. The days had crawled since he'd asked for prayers at church. Did he dare hope for good news? Despite his prayers, he wasn't sure God was listening.

Kurt cast a sideways glance at Molly, who sat in the dark brown leather chair next to his. Even her presence didn't soothe his churning stomach, but her moral support and encouragement kept him focused on the good things in his life right now. She was one of them. He had come to rely on her more than he thought was wise sometimes, but she was a positive influence—one he couldn't ignore and wanted to relish.

The door opened, and Kurt held his breath as Nick settled behind his desk. "Good news. We have an expedited court date on Wednesday of next week."

"So what does that mean?"

"It means we have a judge who is willing to listen to our case because of the lies Virginia Spencer told your children."

"Do you think I have a chance to see my kids again?" With his insides still roiling, Kurt stared at Nick.

"There's no point in speculating." Shaking his head, Nick shrugged. "I can't give you an answer. I don't want to give you false hope or sugarcoat what we're up against. You've been convicted of killing your wife, so a judge most likely will be very reluctant to let you have contact with your children."

Kurt forced himself not to shout. This whole process was going to take a measure of self-control he wasn't sure he possessed. "But I'm not guilty. What about my innocence?"

Nick rubbed his chin. "Kurt, I know you want people to believe you're innocent, but that could complicate things right now."

"Nothing about this is fair."

"You're right, but we can't dwell on something you can't change. We aren't going to be there to retry your manslaughter case. We have to stick to what is happening currently. Not what happened in the past. Let's concentrate on making the best case for you to see your kids."

Kurt closed his eyes and imagined the possibility. If only he could wish the scenario into existence, but wishing wouldn't make it happen. Could prayer?

Molly scooted forward in her chair. "Will you need me as a character witness?"

Nick nodded. "Of course. We'll need you to tell the judge how Kurt is working for you."

"Do you think that's a good idea? Will I be the right kind of witness?" Molly knit her brow, concern evident in her eyes.

"You're just the kind of witness he needs. One who can tell the judge what a great job Kurt is doing on your house—how he's making a positive contribution to the community."

"You're right." Molly gave Nick a hesitant smile. "Courtrooms just make me nervous."

Kurt puzzled over Molly's question and the look that passed between her and Nick. Did they know something that he didn't? Kurt didn't want to ask for fear of confirming that the chances of seeing his children were nonexistent.

"We'll have Steve testify, and we'll ask some folks

from your church."

Negative thoughts continued to crowd Kurt's mind. Hadn't the members of his former church turned away after his indictment? People hadn't believed his story. He had to remember the positive response he had received the Sunday he'd given his testimony. The church had prayed for him. No one turned away. These folks were on his side. He had to remember that. He couldn't let the negativity win.

During the rest of their meeting, Nick planned the strategy for the hearing. They discussed each of the witnesses and how they could help Kurt's case. He listened to the plans with an equal amount of hope and apprehension. Coming face to face with Virginia Spencer worried him the most. She had always intimidated him. Did he have the fortitude to confront her?

***

While the judge shuffled through the papers in front of her, Kurt's heartbeat escalated, and he swallowed a huge lump in his throat. The quiet made him think that everyone could hear the pounding of his heart. He forced himself not to glance in Virginia Spencer's direction, but he wondered whether she was looking his way. Or was she focusing on the judge, too?

During the proceedings, Virginia had glared at him, hatred etching her face. Benton Turley, who had been the Spencers' attorney for years, sat next to the family law attorney Virginia had hired, as well. Benton's smug look made Kurt uneasy. It was the expression he'd seen whenever they were at the same gatherings during his marriage to Bonnie. Benton had looked down his nose at Kurt in the same way Virginia always did.

He remembered how Bonnie used to complain about Benton. She wasn't fond of him and said he reminded her of a snake oil salesman. She'd never understood why her mother had continued to retain his services. Benton's association with Bonnie's boss at the realty company, made her uncomfortable, too. She was suspicious that his dealings weren't always above board, but she'd never had any evidence to prove it—only her gut instinct.

Kurt pushed aside thoughts of Bonnie and Benton Turley. The present, not the past, had to fill his thoughts. Now that the judge had heard testimony from both sides, had she come to a decision, or would they have to wait to learn her ruling? He held his breath and tried to read the judge's expression as she surveyed the occupants of her courtroom. When she glanced his way, he wanted to shrink in his chair, but he forced himself to look her in the eye. He hoped to show her that he had nothing to hide—that he was innocent of any crime. He prayed that his demeanor would help to sway her opinion in his favor.

Adjusting her glasses, the judge cleared her throat and trained her gaze on the side of the courtroom where Virginia and her lawyers sat. "This is indeed a troubling case. I don't condone lying for any reason, Mrs. Spencer. The children should not have been told that their father was dead."

Kurt wanted to look at Virginia and see her reaction to the judge's statement, but again he restrained himself. As the judge turned her attention to Kurt, his mind raced along with his heart. Did this mean she would rule in his favor? Her laser-like gaze seemed to pin him to his chair. He was afraid to breathe.

"And you, Mr. Jansen, despite your troubled past, have served your time and appear to be making a positive contribution to society." The judge paused and glanced in Virginia's direction before turning back to him, then perused the entire room. "Although it pains me to do so because of Mr. Jansen's conviction in the death of his wife, I am granting the plaintiff limited supervised visitation with his children every Saturday for three hours, starting in two weeks."

A loud gasp echoed in the quiet. Murmurs swept through the room. Kurt's pulse pounded in his head. He was going to see his children. He looked at Nick, who was smiling.

Kurt jumped when the judge banged her gavel.

"Quiet until I am finished." The judge narrowed her gaze as she scanned the courtroom before continuing. "On the appointed day, the social worker assigned to this case will bring the children to a pre-determined place. The father shall meet them at said location at the time specified by the social worker. The children will also have a court-appointed counselor to help them deal with this situation."

The judge banged the gavel again. Before Kurt could gather his thoughts, the court adjourned and the judge hurried away. Finally feeling free to smile, he shook Nick's hand. Well-wishers immediately surrounded Kurt. He turned and hugged Molly without thinking. When she hugged him back, he knew it wasn't a mistake. While he held her in his arms, he wished he never had to let her go.

When the embrace ended, he stepped back. "Thank you."

She smiled, tears welling in her gray eyes. "Thank Nick."

"Yes, but if you hadn't discovered Virginia's lies, none of this would have happened."

Nodding and pressing her lips together, she wiped away a tear that trickled down her cheek. Tempted to reach out and wipe all her tears away, he remembered the day he'd come looking for a job. When she'd opened the door, her eyes had held that wary look. Now she was his biggest cheerleader. He wished he could show her how much he appreciated her help—how much he cared for her, but this wasn't the time or the place.

"I always cry over happy endings."

"I'm glad there was a happy ending for you to cry over." He chuckled, letting the reality of the judge's decision lift his spirit.

"Me, too." She fumbled in her purse until she brought out a tissue.

"I don't know how to tell everyone how much I appreciate their help." Kurt shook his head. "I've got so many people to thank—everyone who prayed—everyone who testified on my behalf."

"You'll have an opportunity to tell some of them at church on Sunday."

More hugging and backslapping ensued as joyful voices surrounded Kurt. He soaked in the happiness until he looked toward the other side of the courtroom. His stomach roiled as he caught a glimpse of Virginia huddled with her lawyers. He thought he'd feel triumph, but instead, an unexpected sorrow surrounded his heart like an impending storm. He beginning to feel at ease with her. While Nick had been talking about the other buildings, he had contemplated asking Molly's advice. For the first time, he felt like she was a friend he could confide in. He had even considered taking Nick's advice and asking Molly about her life. Now he didn't know. She would probably think he was overstepping his bounds. Was she his friend or just his employer?

Despite the sense that Molly might be his friend, he stood alone.

"Kurt." Molly's voice brought him out of his rumination.

He turned to gaze at her fearful that he would find a look of pity on her face. Instead, her gray eyes reflected an understanding he hadn't expected. "I'm sorry I questioned you, but I thought you and Nick—"

"You don't have to apologize again," she interrupted. "I can see how you could've misinterpreted our relationship. We have a bond that's hard to explain. It's like that scripture in Proverbs that talks about a friend who sticks closer than a brother. That's me and Nick."

"It must be nice to have a friend like that."

"Yes, it is. Nick can be your friend, too."

"Did you put him up to offering me this job?" Kurt shifted his weight from one foot to another.

Molly shook her head. "No, I didn't know a thing about it until today. Seems Steve suggested that Nick talk to you. They didn't consult me at all."

"How do you feel about it?"

"I think it's a great opportunity for you." Without looking him in the eyes, she busied herself by straightening some things on the counter.

"It could be, but I'm not sure I can handle all this

work. I know I can't do it by myself, and I don't want to short change the work I'm doing for you." He wondered about her lack of eye contact. Maybe she was concerned about how it would affect her house.

"You won't. It's all connected. One won't work without the other." Molly picked up a sponge and began wiping non-existent dirt from the counter tops.

"You're not happy that Nick asked me to do this project, are you?"

She stopped wiping and turned to look at him. "What makes you say that? I said it was a great opportunity for you."

Kurt released a muted chuckle. "But when you said it, your lack of enthusiasm told me a lot about how you feel."

"How can you know how I feel?"

"I don't." Kurt turned toward the mudroom. "Well, it seems I've done all I can to make myself unwelcome this afternoon. I'd better go search for that battery charger."

Molly touched his arm. "Please, don't go. I didn't mean for this conversation to take this turn. Let's try to understand one another."

He stopped in his tracks and turned around. Her touch was like a hot brand. He didn't want her to know how she affected him. He purposely avoided direct eye contact. "I'm not sure either one of us is ready to be open with the other."

She dropped her hand from his arm. "You're probably right, but that doesn't mean we can't make a little progress in that direction, especially if we share this project."

"If that's what you want." He finally allowed himself to look her in the eyes.

"From what I saw the other day, I'd say they are."

"This whole court deal could upset them."

"Don't think about that now. Let's think happy thoughts and pick out stuff for the baskets." Molly didn't wait to hear his protest.

Her refusal to allow him to speculate about the future gave him little choice other than to follow her lead. She moved through the store, showing him this and that as she asked him to make some choices for each child. When they had an armload full of toys and stuffed animals, she headed for the check out.

"Don't you think we've gone a little overboard?"

Molly glanced down at the things she had laid on the counter. "Yes, but that's okay. Some of this stuff I'm going to keep at the house for the future."

"Molly, I...I can't afford all this, and I can't expect you to pay for it."

"I insist, and I won't take no for an answer." She handed the clerk her credit card. "You can pay me later for your part."

"Are you always such a bully?"

She smiled. "Absolutely. I expect to get my way."

"I'll have to remember that." Kurt picked up the bags, knowing that he'd remember this day and the wonderful woman he shared it with forever. "We'd better get going, or we'll miss our reservation."

She glanced at her watch, then up at him with a sheepish grin. "You're right. I didn't mean to take so much time."

"No problem. If we hurry, we'll make it."

A few hours later, Molly drove away from the city. Everything about the day had been perfect—the game, the food, their walk, and the companionship. He hated for the evening to end. He wanted to box it up and save it because he didn't know what the future would hold. Shades of pink and orange surrounded the setting sun and reminded Kurt of the night he had taken her to the Lobster Shed. Would there be more days like these? He could only hope because his feelings for Molly were growing beyond what might be wise for a man in his situation, but there was no turning back now.

Somehow he had to clear his name. Having his children and gaining Molly's love depended on it. Desperation and despair settled over him. What could he do to change his circumstances?

Molly gave him a sideways glance. "You're awfully quiet."

"I've been doing a lot of thinking."

"About what?"

Kurt knew he didn't dare tell her how he felt about her, but he could share his thoughts about the upcoming court hearing. He had tied himself up in knots worrying about the outcome. "I can't help thinking about the hearing. Do you think I'm doing the right thing?"

"Absolutely. You deserve to know your children, and they should know you."

"But sometimes, I wonder whether it's in their best interest. If I am granted visitation, what will they think when they have to meet this stranger who says he's their dad? Especially when they thought I was dead. And worse yet, will they think I killed their mother? How can I explain that?"

"Kurt, you're borrowing trouble. Have you prayed about this?"

"I'm not sure how to pray, and maybe I'm not sure God will give me the answers." Kurt looked touched Molly's arm and nodded in that direction. "This isn't a happy ending for everyone."

Molly glanced over her shoulder, then returned her gaze to him. "It is sad for her, but she brought it on herself. I just hope it won't be a detriment to the children. She really has done a good job with them. You have to give her credit for that."

Kurt grimaced. "It won't be easy, but I'll try."

"None of this will be easy for anyone, but with God's help, we'll do all right." Molly stepped into the aisle. "I'm going to the ladies room. I'll meet you outside the courtroom."

"Okay." Kurt watched her go. She was the reason for so many good things in his life—seeing his kids, gaining new friends, and even finding a stronger faith. He was beginning to think of her as a permanent part of his life. He prayed that wasn't too much to hope for.

***

Molly emerged from the ladies' room and spied Kurt and Nick, who stood in the hallway on the other side of the courtroom door. She made her way toward them, but her insides knotted when Virginia Spencer came through the doors and turned in Molly's direction. The heels of Virginia's shoes clicked with an angry cadence as the older woman bore down on Molly. The sound matched the pounding of Molly's heart. She said a silent prayer that God would help her deal kindly with Kurt's former mother-in-law.

Virginia glared at Molly. "You have some nerve taking my money when you knew all along that man you have working for you killed my daughter."

Molly took a deep breath. "I'm sorry, Mrs. Spencer, that we have to be on the opposite side of this. I hope you can find it in your heart to accept the judge's decision without ill feelings for this project or me. It means so much to the women who will work there. Because of your donation, many women will be helped. We've decided to name the house where the women will live the Bonnie Spencer Jansen House."

"Do you think naming that house after my daughter is going to make up for your deception?"

"There was no deception. I never lied to you about anything."

"You may not have lied, but you failed to tell me the whole truth." Anger twisted the older woman's features.

Molly drew on all her willpower to remain calm. "I know you feel betrayed, but Kurt is not guilty. He deserves to get to know his children. You need to give him a chance—"

"He's had all the chances he needed, and he was found guilty," Virginia interrupted. "He's sucked you in just like he sucked in my daughter. Be warned, you'll be sorry you ever met him. You haven't heard the last of this."

Molly tried to keep her voice low and controlled. "I wish we could be on better terms for the children's sake."

"Those children have had a happy life with me. They don't need this disruption. But since you've seen fit to force it on them, you can be assured they will know the truth about their father." Virginia's voice raised until it echoed off the wall of the hallway. Several passersby stopped to watch.

"Please, Mrs. Spencer, don't do anything to poison the children's mind against their father. It will only hurt them."

"Don't lecture me." Virginia turned on her heel and marched out of the building without giving anyone a second glance.

After the door closed behind Virginia, Molly realized she was shaking. She sat down on the nearest bench. Immediately, Kurt and Nick were by her side. Kurt put his arm around her shoulders. "Are you okay?"

Nodding, Molly took another deep breath. Virginia had shaken her, but Kurt's nearness made her more weak-kneed than that woman ever could. "I'll be all right. She's just angry and upset. That's all."

Nick patted Molly's arm. "If I'd realized you were being accosted, I would have stepped in sooner. We didn't know she was talking to you until we heard her shouting."

Molly turned to Kurt. "Oh, Kurt, I'm afraid she's going to tell the children all kinds of bad things about you. They'll be scared to come near you."

Shaking his head, Kurt gazed at her. His expression remained calm. "I'm not worried. The Lord has opened this door to me, and I believe he'll help me deal with whatever Virginia throws my way. Sometimes I've had doubts about what God has in store for me, but I'm beginning to believe that He does have a plan."

"Yeah. I've got to remember that, too." Molly smiled.

Nick got up from the bench and gazed at her. "Remember the children have a court-appointed therapist who will be talking with them. They'll have some adjusting to do, but we're all here to help them. Let's go have our celebratory dinner. I called Allison, and she's going to meet us at the Wayside Inn in Sudbury. Steve and Lindy are coming, too."

"Great. I'm ready." Standing, Kurt took Molly's hand and pulled her to her feet. "How about you?"

Molly nodded. Kurt's touch made her speechless. She forced herself to put it into perspective. He was excited about the chance to see his children, and she shouldn't read anything into all the smiles and hugs. She could still feel his arms around her when the judge read her findings. Molly wished it had been more than happiness over the court's ruling.

Everything was falling into place for Kurt. That wasn't going to happen in her life until she had the courage to divulge her past to him. Now she feared that even more because he might not want her around his children if he knew.

She didn't want to find out. The status quo would hurt no one. The rationalization eased her conscience as they left the building.

***

Kurt watched Molly glance around the rustic dining room of the Wayside Inn. She was probably assessing every aspect of the historic bed-and-breakfast to get ideas for her own place. Then he looked around the table at Steve, Lindy, Nick, and Allison—the people sharing this joyous occasion with him. They had believed in him enough to offer their help. Without them the opportunity to get to know his children would never have come.

Especially Molly.

She had made it all happen—the job, the lawyer, the chance to see his kids again. He cared for her, but how could he tell her when he still carried the burden of his conviction. Clearing his name was the next hurdle in his life. But now wasn't the time to think about it. Now was the time to celebrate this victory.

Kurt tapped his fork on his water glass. Everyone at the table looked his way. "I just want to tell you how much I appreciate all you've done for me. This is one of the happiest days of my life. I'd like to say the blessing for the meal and all the events of this day."

"Shall we join hands?" Steve asked.

"Good idea," Nick replied.

Holding Molly's hand made it more difficult to keep his mind on the prayer, but he managed to thank the Lord for all the people sitting around the table and the food as well. Then he asked for the Lord's guidance in dealing with his children. After he said amen, Molly squeezed his hand. When he looked up, somehow he managed to swallow the lump in his throat.

While everyone helped themselves to the appetizers, Kurt thought about Molly's confrontation with his former mother-in-law. Molly had only told him that Virginia planned to say bad things about him, but what else had she said to Molly? She undoubtedly wanted to forget it, but he wanted to know Virginia's reaction to the judge's ruling. Did he dare bring it up? Maybe this was the best time to discuss it while they had other people to evaluate the situation.

Smiles and laughter swirled around him as he contemplated bringing up Molly's altercation with Virginia. He ate his food, but he wasn't enjoying it.

Despite all the good news today, he still felt a loss because Virginia thought he was guilty. Her distrust weighed heavily on his mind.

Molly touched his arm. "You're awfully quiet."

He glanced up from his meal. "Too busy eating."

"Is that all?"

"Well, since you've asked, no. I've been worried about how Virginia confronted you today. If she wanted to yell at someone, she should have yelled at me. She has no reason to be angry with you."

"Oh, yes, she does." Molly set her fork on her plate. "She's unhappy about the money we accepted from her for the foundation. She feels like we took it under false pretenses because you work for me."

"What else did she say?" A sinking feeling hit his gut as Molly recounted her entire conversation with Virginia. "I wonder what she plans to tell the children. The fact that she lied to them in the first place didn't set well with the judge."

"I think so, too, but how is she going to explain a dead father who's now alive? I hate to think what she might tell them." Molly twisted the napkin in her lap.

"I've been thinking the same thing. What should I tell the kids when I meet them?"

"The truth," Steve interjected.

"I agree with Steve," Nick said. "A lie lost this case for Virginia Spencer."

Nodding, Kurt grimaced. "But are the kids old enough to understand what happened? Can they handle it?"

Nick leaned forward in his chair so he could look Kurt in the eye. "I don't think you have to go into any gory details, but I think they can understand your unfair conviction."

"But I keep wondering why they would believe me when they've been living with Virginia all these years. She's all they know. I'm a stranger." Helplessness inundated Kurt.

Allison spoke for the first time. "You'll have to gain their trust. It took me a while after I got out of an abusive relationship to learn to trust, but over time I learned because everyone was patient with me. That's what it takes. Patience."

"You know what needs to happen here?" Everyone turned to look at Steve. "Prayer. It got us where we are today. There were a lot of people praying about this outcome. We can do it again for your first meeting with the kids."

"You're right," Kurt said. His earlier foreboding subsided.

Molly touched his arm again. "We'll request prayers again at church on Sunday."

Glancing in her direction, he swallowed hard and nodded. She had no idea how her touch affected him. The butterflies in his stomach over the thought of meeting his children for the first time doubled when she touched him. Somehow he had to make everything work out with his kids and Molly.

CHAPTER THIRTEEN

Kurt peered out the bay window in Molly's office. "I thought they'd be here by now."

"They'll be here any moment." Molly came to stand beside him. "Staring out the window isn't going to make them get here any faster."

Kurt walked back and forth across the Oriental rug in front of the fireplace. He glanced at his watch as his stomach churned. "What if they don't like me?"

"Kurt, they'll like you. Quit pacing. You're going to wear a hole in my rug." She gave him a perturbed look. "Are you the same man who told me that you could handle anything that Virginia Spencer dished out? And now you're worried about two little kids."

"I guess the reality has hit home." He stopped and looked at the woman he cared for more and more each day. If only he could tell her how he felt. "You'll answer the door, right?"

"Yes." She put her hand in front of her mouth as she tried to hide a smile. "We've gone over how we're going to handle the introductions. Say a prayer to calm your nerves."

"Good idea." Closing his eyes, Kurt took a deep breath and released it slowly. He prayed that God would give him wisdom in this first meeting with his children.

When he opened his eyes, Molly was watching him. "Feel better now?"

"Yeah, but I don't feel ready for this. What if I can't think of anything to say, and we just sit there and stare at each other?"

Molly chuckled. "Don't worry. I don't think Emily can be silent that long."

"I might scare her."

"You don't look scary to me."

"Yeah, but you're not three and half feet tall."

"Quit worrying." Molly glanced out the window. "I hope they get here soon, or you'll have me…look, here they come."

Kurt raced to the window and looked out. The gray day matched the gray sedan that stopped near the house. A middle-aged woman dressed in tan slacks and a navy blue jacket emerged from the driver's side and immediately opened the back door. Kurt figured she must be the court-appointed social worker who would observe each time the children came to visit. Eric got out first and waited for Emily. The children wore jeans and khaki jackets.

Emily clutched the fluffy white bunny with pink ears that he had given her in the Easter basket. His heart twisted at the sight even though she didn't know the bunny had come from him. She had probably brought it because they were coming to Molly's house. Eric carried a bag, and Kurt wondered whether the bag contained his Easter gift.

The social worker offered Emily her hand, and the little girl took it. The woman did the same for Eric, but he shook his head and walked stoically beside her. As they approached the front porch, Kurt continued to watch out the window while Molly made her way to the door. When the doorbell rang, she opened it immediately and greeted the social worker, who introduced herself as Diane Connolly. Hanging back, Kurt stood in the office doorway.

"Hi, Eric. Hi, Emily." Molly looked at the children. "Do you remember me?"

Emily nodded. "Yeah, you're Molly and you took us in the secret passage."

"Good," Molly replied.

"Are you going to be here when we meet our father?" Eric's lower lip quivered as he grabbed Emily's hand.

"Yes. Would you like to meet him now?"

"I suppose." Eric looked up at the social worker. "Is that okay?"

"It's okay." Diane glanced in Kurt's direction.

When the children turned to look, Kurt stepped into the front hall. He couldn't mistake the anxiety he read in their eyes. His worst fears had come to pass. What could he do to take away that look? With his heart in his throat, he walked slowly toward them. He prayed they wouldn't cower away from him.

When he stood just feet away, he hunkered down. "Hi, Eric. Hi, Emily. I guess you know that I'm your dad."

Eric stepped in front of Emily in a protective gesture. He held out his hand for Kurt to shake. "Hello, sir."

Kurt took the small hand of his son in his. Taking a deep breath, he fought back the emotions that threatened to bring tears to his eyes. He had never anticipated how much this would affect him. "I'm glad you're here to see me."

Emily stepped forward and looked Kurt right in the eyes. "My grandmother said we have to be polite to you, but that doesn't mean we have to like you."

Kurt went from near tears to holding back laughter at Emily's blunt assessment of the situation. He resisted the urge to pull her into his arms and laugh for joy at her gumption. She was her mother's child all over. How could he ever make up for the years without them? "That's fair enough. You have to get to know me before you'll know whether you like me or not. But I can tell that I like you already. Do you know why?"

With a serious look on her face, Emily shook her head as she clutched the bunny tighter. "Because you're my dad?"

"Well, yes, but also because you've been so honest with me. I like honest people. We have to be honest with each other, don't you think?" Kurt couldn't help thinking about the discussion that he would eventually have to have with them about their mother's death.

"Do you like me, too?" Eric asked as concern knit his little brow. "I can be honest, too. Grandma says our mom died because you were mean to her. Is that true?"

Kurt felt as if someone had ripped his heart out of his chest and stomped on it. At least Virginia hadn't told the kids that he had murdered their mother, but that was little consolation. Eric's question triggered doubts that he had had since Bonnie's death. If he hadn't rushed from the house in an angry huff, maybe Bonnie would be alive today. He would have been there to keep her safe. He had berated himself time and time again for leaving his wife and allowing someone to murder her. Now it seemed as though his child was raising that same point. How could he answer this honestly?

Kurt very carefully touched Eric's shoulder. When the little boy didn't flinch, Kurt breathed a sigh of relief. "I like you too, Eric. I'm glad to know you're just as honest as Emily. That makes me proud to be your father."

"But did you make our mother die?"

"No, Eric. I loved your mother."

"Then why did Grandma tell us that?"

Kurt gazed at his son and wondered how to explain this to him. As much as Kurt disliked Virginia Spencer, he couldn't denigrate his children's grandmother. They loved her just as much as he loved them and wanted that love in return. Standing to his full height, he turned to the social worker. "Is it okay if we go into Molly's office?"

"Sure. This is your time with the children. Make yourself comfortable." Diane smiled and helped the children off with their jackets. "Where can we put these?"

Molly stepped forward and took them. "I'll hang them in the mudroom. Make yourselves at home in my office."

Kurt welcomed the tension breaker as he followed the children and Diane through the double door into Molly's office.

Emily broke away from Diane and headed for the window seat. "This is where we sat when we came here with Grandma. I like this spot, especially with these new cushions." She settled onto one of the navy blue cushions Molly had arranged on the seat to go with the blues in the Oriental rug. Every day she added new touches to the interior of the house.

Molly returned just as Eric joined Emily. "You two look comfortable. May I sit here with you?"

Emily nodded and scooted closer to Eric. "There's room for three."

"Good. I like the window seat, too." Molly settled beside Emily then looked at Kurt. "You and Diane can bring the chairs over here so we can talk."

Diane gestured to Kurt as he moved the chairs. "I'll just sit over here in the corner. You go ahead and talk with the kids. Don't mind me."

"Okay." Kurt set a chair in front of the window seat.

As he settled on his own chair, he noticed that Emily had placed her bunny in the window between her and Molly. Eric had left his bag on the floor. Now that they were all sitting, Kurt didn't know what to say. He didn't want to answer their question, and he wondered whether he could wait for them to bring it up again. That seemed like the best option to him. He could always hope they would forget.

Before he could say anything, Emily turned to Molly and placed the bunny in her lap. The expression on Emily's face tore at his heart. "I forgot. Grandma said I should give the bunny back to you. She said I can't keep it. And Eric can't keep his toys either."

"Why?" Molly asked as Eric grabbed his bag and gave it to her.

Emily shrugged. "Just 'cause."

"Grandma says we have enough stuff, but thank you anyway." Eric nodded, his mouth forming a grim line.

"But I ate the chocolate bunny." Emily hid a little smile behind her hand. "Grandma got mad at that, but it was good."

Eric frowned. "She's always getting into trouble."

"You get into trouble, too." Emily stared daggers at Eric.

Kurt sat and watched his kids bicker. He loved it. It made him feel alive. He wanted to grab them in the circle of his arms and hug them and never let them go. How tough was it going to be to say goodbye when his three hours were up today? He didn't want to think about it.

Molly took the bunny and Eric's bag of toys. "Okay, since you can't keep these at your grandmother's, we'll keep them here. So each time you come, you can play with them."

"I like that idea." Emily bounced on the cushion and clapped her hands. "We get to come here every Saturday."

Eric shook Emily's arm and pointed to Kurt. "Emily, you're forgetting. He did bad things to our mother. We shouldn't want to visit him."

Looking contrite, Emily hung her head but snuck a peek at Kurt. "What did you do?"

Thanks, Eric. You're going to be one tough customer to win over. Kurt couldn't think of an answer to her question. His mind was blank. *God, help me.*

"He hurt our mother. Didn't you listen to Grandma?" Eric poked Emily.

Emily scooted away, and Molly pulled the little girl onto her lap. Then Molly gave Eric a stern look. "Eric, let's give your dad a chance to tell us what happened."

Kurt wasn't sure whether he was thankful for Molly giving him the opportunity to explain. He couldn't tell his children that someone had murdered their mother. They weren't old enough to understand murder. He didn't want to use those words. Virginia obviously hadn't wanted to use them either.

"Eric, Emily, someone did hurt your mother, but it wasn't me. But someone had to be blamed, and your grandmother blames me. I tried to tell her that I didn't do anything, but she wouldn't believe me. I hope you'll believe me."

"But Grandma said they sent you to prison because you hurt our mom."

There was no explaining away the time he had spent in prison. How could he make his children believe him when no one else had? The unfairness rankled, but he couldn't let it upset him. That would serve no purpose at all. He stared at his children as if an answer would come from their sweet faces. When Emily squirmed on Molly's lap an idea popped into his head. He focused his attention on the little troublemaker, as her brother had described her.

"Emily, Eric says you're always getting into trouble."

"He tattles on me all the time." Emily flashed her brother a perturbed look.

"Emily, did you ever get blamed for something you didn't do?" Kurt asked, trying to regain her attention.

She nodded. "Yeah, when I was hitting tennis balls on the garage door. Grandma told me not to do that anymore 'cause I could miss and break the window in the garage door. Then she found a broken window and blamed me. I kept telling her I didn't do it, but she wouldn't believe me."

"Did that make you angry?"

Emily nodded again. "And sad."

"Yeah, she cried," Eric said.

"So does your grandma still think you broke the window?" Kurt asked.

Emily shook her head. "No, 'cause she got it fixed, and it broke again."

"Did you get blamed for that, too?" Kurt gazed at his daughter with a sense that he was gaining some ground with her.

"No, Grandma took her tennis racket away after the first time, so I got blamed." Eric crossed his arms over his chest and stared at Kurt.

"So you both got blamed for something you didn't do?" Kurt found himself intrigued with the story. "Who did break the window?"

"No one." Emily sounded as though she was telling a ghost story.

"Then how did it break? Twice?" Molly joined in the questioning.

Emily scooted off Molly's lap and walked over to stand in front of Kurt. "The man who came to fix the window the second time told Grandma that it kept breaking 'cause there was something wrong with the garage door. It had the wrong pressure or something like that. And then Grandma told me she was sorry she blamed me."

"That's what happened to me, too. I got blamed for something someone else did. Do you understand that?"

Emily peered at him as if she was weighing what he said against what her grandmother had said. Then she slowly nodded. "It isn't fair, is it?"

Kurt's heart tripped over itself as he gazed at his daughter. She understood. Then he glanced at Eric. He didn't appear convinced, but with Emily's help, time would win him over. "No, it's not."

Eric joined Emily. "Then we got our tennis rackets back."

"So you lost your racket, too?" Looking at Eric, Kurt surmised that Eric might understand better than Kurt first suspected.

Eric nodded. "I'm glad Grandma gave our rackets back because we got to finish our lessons and get a certificate. We got our picture in the paper."

"I know."

Eric squinted at Kurt. "How do you know?"

"Let me show you." Kurt reached into his back pocket and brought out his wallet. He carefully took out the newspaper clipping and unfolded it and handed it to them. While they looked at it, he pulled the old tattered picture from its place in his wallet. "I've had it right here with this other picture."

Emily reached out and took the tattered photo. "Is this us?"

Kurt smiled at his daughter. "Yes, you were three years old when that was taken. Your Grandma Jansen took that picture and gave it to me. Do you remember her?"

Emily's expression turned thoughtful. Then she shook her head. "I don't remember any grandma except Grandma Spencer."

"Your Grandma Jansen was my mother."

"How come we never see her?" Eric handed the photo back to Kurt.

Taking a deep breath, Kurt tamped down the anger and sorrow that threatened to overwhelm him. "Your Grandma died last year. She was very sick with cancer."

"Is that why we couldn't see her?" Emily asked.

Kurt nodded. He wanted to tell his children how

their Grandma Spencer had made it impossible for his mother to see her grandchildren. But he couldn't say anything negative about Virginia no matter how much anger he felt toward her. "Yes, I'm very sorry you didn't get to see her."

"Me, too," Emily replied. "I bet she wasn't allergic to cats, was she?"

Kurt puzzled over Emily's out-of-the-blue statement. "No, she wasn't. Why do you ask?"

"'Cause Grandma Spencer is allergic to cats so we can't have one. But Molly has one." Emily turned to look at Molly. "Can we see your cat this time?"

Molly hopped up from the window seat. "Sure, if we can find him. He likes to hide."

"You said that last time." Emily put her hands on her hips. "Does that mean we won't get to see him?"

Molly smiled. "Today we have plenty of time to look for him. I'll show you all of his favorite hiding places."

"I bet I find him." Eric pulled on Kurt's arm, seemingly forgetting that he wasn't supposed to like his father. "Will you help us?"

Kurt stood. "You bet. Lead the way, Molly."

Kurt followed the little troop as they left the office in search of a gray cat. Love and pride filled every corner of his heart. He felt as though it could burst from happiness. This day was turning out better than he had ever hoped. He looked heavenward and said a silent prayer of thanks.

As they entered the kitchen, Kurt turned to Diane who was bringing up the rear of the procession. "I hope this is okay."

"The children seem to be fine," she said.

As Kurt watched Molly show the children Smoky's

favorite hiding place in the closet among the boots, he hoped that the social worker would give a good report on this meeting. He felt like it was going well, but he didn't know what this woman thought. And he certainly wasn't going to ask. While he worried about what might be in her report, a squeal of delight shook him from his thoughts.

Molly appeared in the doorway to the mudroom with Smoky. "Okay, Emily, you'll have to calm down or you'll scare him, and he'll run off again. Just pet him gently."

Emily ran her hand down the cat's back. "Can I hold him?"

Molly shook her head. "Not right now. Let's let him get used to all these new people. He might run off if you try to pick him up." Molly went over to the cupboard and brought out a can of cat treats. She handed it to Emily. "Open this, give a couple to Eric, and take a couple for yourself. I'll put Smoky down, and you can give him the treats."

Emily did as Molly instructed and soon made a friend. Smoky seemed to take to the children even when he had finished the treats. While they played with the cat, Molly and Kurt made sandwiches for lunch. They ate lunch while the cat circled under the table. After lunch, Emily and Eric helped Molly put the dishes in the dishwasher. They seemed eager to please. Kurt only hoped they would be eager to return next week.

When they finished the dishes, Emily turned and glanced around the kitchen until she spied Smoky. The cat lay across one of the kitchen chairs with his paws hanging over the end as he lazily observed the goings on in the room. Emily turned back to Molly.

"Can we play with Smoky some more?"

"Sure." Molly wiped her hands on a towel and hung it on the nearby rack. "I've got some toys for him to play with. Let me get them."

Emily and Eric followed Molly into the mudroom. His tail swishing in the air, Smoky jumped off the chair and moseyed after them. When the trio reappeared, Emily clutched a slender stick with a long purple feather attached to one end. Eric sported another toy that resembled a fishing pole with a little stuffed fish on the end. Molly held a stick with a ball on the end of it.

Kurt laughed. "Do you think Smoky has enough toys?"

"There's more in there, if you want one. You can play with us, too." Emily swung the feather in the air as Smoky tried to grab it with his paw.

Kurt's heart filled with joy. This was more than he had ever hoped for. "Thanks for asking me, but I think three people with toys are enough for now. I'll watch."

"Hey, kids, let's go in here." Molly pushed open the swinging door that led to the dining room. "If you take off your shoes, you can play in the dining room and living room."

"Wow, this is fun!" Eric shouted as he ran around the room with the fish trailing behind him and Smoky in hot pursuit.

Emily ran into the room and tried to capture Smoky's attention with her feather again. The cat danced in circles trying to grab one of the toys.

While Kurt leaned against the doorjamb and observed his children, Molly came up beside him. Her nearness made his heart beat in triple time. He didn't know if his heart could handle all this happiness.

Molly leaned close and whispered in his ear, "You can use my toy if you want to join them."

Kurt's breath caught in his throat along with his heart. Unable to speak, he shook his head. Then, finally catching his breath, he looked over at her. "I'd rather watch them having fun."

"They are so exuberant." Molly squeezed Kurt's arm.

He nodded again. The laughter and shrieks of delight echoed off the walls in the empty rooms. He wished he could hear that sound every day. Love for his children made his heart swell with pride, but his feelings for Molly made it race. He wondered if someone could die from too much happiness. He resisted the urge to slip his arm around Molly's waist while they stood together watching the children play.

After several minutes of chasing the toys, Smoky lay down. His tail slapped the floor and his eyes closed. Both children tried to rouse the cat by wiggling their toys in front of his paws. The cat only gave them a cursory glance and closed his eyes again.

Emily looked at Molly. "What's wrong with Smoky?"

"I think you wore him out." Molly chuckled. "You'll have to let him rest for a while."

"Okay." Emily proceeded to run around the room with the feather waving in the air. Eric followed right after her as they raced from the dining room into the living room and back again, making a big circle.

Diane stepped from the corner where she had been observing the happenings. Smiling, she approached Kurt and Molly. "They're a couple of live-wires, aren't they?"

Kurt nodded. "They have lots of energy. It does my heart good to see them enjoying themselves."

"Me, too." Diane looked at her watch. "Time's up for today. We'll see you next week."

"Okay," Kurt said, an ache in his heart.

"I'll get their jackets." Molly turned toward the kitchen.

***

When Molly returned she found Diane informing the children that it was time to go. Molly brought their jackets into the dining room. Emily pouted as she put on her jacket. Eric did just as he was told without protest.

Molly's heart went out to Kurt as they proceeded to the front door. She couldn't imagine how hard it was for him to let his children go. When they were all standing in the front hall, Eric stepped forward and held out his hand to Kurt. "Thank you, sir, for a very nice day."

"You're very welcome, Eric." Kurt shook his son's hand. "I'll look forward to your visit next Saturday."

As Kurt turned to Emily, she suddenly sprinted into the living room where Smoky lay curled up on the hearth in front of the fireplace. She put her little hands on either side of the cat's head and gave him a kiss full on the mouth.

"Bye, Smoky. I'll see you next week." She sprinted back to the front door and tugged on Kurt's arm. "I have a secret I want to tell you."

Kurt hunkered down so he was eye level with Emily. She leaned over and cupped her hands around his ear and whispered something that no one else could hear. When she finished she looked at Kurt with a sly little smile.

Kurt nodded and then whispered something back in her ear. Nodding, she giggled and flung her arms around Kurt's neck. The scene touched Molly, and she had to fight back the tears that welled up at the back of her eyes.

Diane opened the front door, and ushered Eric onto the front porch. Molly didn't know if she could contain the tears when Emily grabbed Kurt's hand and pulled him out the front door with her. They walked to the car together. Emily reluctantly got into the booster seat in the car. Eric got into the other booster seat without a word. As the car went down the lane, Emily bounced in her seat and waved until they were out of sight. Even Eric gave a little wave before the car disappeared.

Releasing a heavy sigh, Kurt turned toward the house. "What a day!"

Placing her hand over her heart, Molly walked beside him. "I don't know if my heart can take any more of this stuff."

"I know what you mean."

"Can I ask what Emily whispered to you? Or would you betray a confidence?" Molly asked.

"No, it's something you already know about." Kurt opened the door for Molly. "But it worries me."

"Why?"

"She recognized me as the one who rescued Smoky."

"Oh, I thought of that the first time they were here because I wondered whether they would recognize the cat. I never thought of it today. I should have." Molly closed the door behind her and leaned against it.

"Me, too." Kurt went into Molly's study and picked up the bunny that lay on the window seat. He stared out the window as he held the bunny to his chest. "I asked her to keep it our secret." He turned to Molly. "Do you think she'll do it?"

Molly nodded. "She seemed pretty satisfied with herself that she had a secret."

Shaking his head, Kurt blew out his breath. "Yeah, but if she doesn't, Virginia will jump on that information like a cat on a mouse."

"Appropriate analogy."

"Yeah," Kurt said with a half-hearted laugh. "I should never have stopped that day."

"Don't beat yourself up over it. Think positive. Besides, if you hadn't stopped, I wouldn't have Smoky."

"Yeah, think positive." Kurt tried to give himself a pep talk. He set the bunny back on the window seat. "That Emily is a corker. Bonnie could light up a room like that. Emily reminds me so much of her mother."

Kurt's talk about his dead wife created a myriad of jealous thoughts in Molly's mind. She hated feeling this way. Why did she let herself care for a man who couldn't get over his wife's death? She reminded herself that it didn't make any difference. She still wouldn't be able to declare her feelings for Kurt because she couldn't tell him about her past. So the whole thing was a wash. "Well, Eric is you in miniature. I bet you looked just like that when you were a kid."

Shrugging, Kurt smiled. "I don't know. But I do know that I've got to find out who killed Bonnie, or there will always be a chance that Virginia will come up with something to keep my kids from me."

"What do you want to do?"

Kurt knit his brow, thinking. He pounded a fist into his palm. "I want to pursue your idea about there being an embezzler. But I've also been thinking about those articles on that real estate development. There were a lot of court fights over the land before the deal finally went forward. Bonnie worked hard on that for a long time, but she was killed before she ever saw the first house go up. I keep wondering whether her death has some connection to her involvement."

"That's another possibility. What made you think that?"

"All the legal wrangling that went on. Someone had a lot invested in the deal, and if something went awry, then they had a lot to lose."

"Do you want me to do more research on that, too?"

Kurt shrugged as he shook his head. "I don't know. How can we prove anything? It was so long ago."

"Maybe we should just gather information for now and see where it leads. I'll do the research, and you can see if you can fit everything together." Molly hoped he would agree to her suggestion. She still didn't want him going back through the newspapers.

Kurt nodded. "That sounds like a plan. I'm not going to give up until I find the real killer."

Despite Kurt's determination, Molly wondered where all of this would take them. Would this search reveal her past? Would it lead them to a killer? Would it lead them into a dangerous situation they were ill-equipped to handle?

CHAPTER FOURTEEN

....

Kurt took his usual Saturday morning station in Molly's study to wait for Eric and Emily's arrival. Eight weeks had gone by since that first Saturday meeting, but the thrill of seeing his children hadn't worn off. Their Saturday routine was one he lived for all week. Molly did paperwork at her desk while Kurt kept his eyes trained out the window toward the lane.

Molly got up from her desk and joined Kurt at the window. "You can't wait for them to get here, can you?"

"I know. I like to see them as soon as they get out of the car. I don't want to miss one minute." Kurt gave Molly a sideways glance as she stood beside him.

He liked having her close. Keeping his distance grew more difficult with each passing day. He longed to let her know how he felt, but he still lived in the prison of his unjust conviction. Until that was overturned, he didn't feel free to pursue her. But the idea of a family sprouted in his mind as he spent time with Molly and the kids. He was asking for trouble if he pursued those feelings. Even after all of Molly's research over the past couple of months, they were no closer to finding clues that would lead them to the person who had killed Bonnie.

"They've grown to like and trust you, don't you think?" Molly asked as she touched his arm.

Although her touch took his focus away from the

troubling thoughts, he almost wished she wouldn't do that. He had learned that she made the gesture naturally with people as she talked with them. He saw her do it with the kids, even with the social worker. It didn't mean a thing beyond a friendly gesture, but he couldn't convince his heart not to race when she touched him.

Nodding, he breathed deeply, trying to calm his pounding heart. "Emily for sure, but Eric still holds back."

"I think he's just less expressive about how he feels. Emily wears her heart on her sleeve." Molly rubbed her shoulder.

"Like her mother."

Molly's lips tightened as she returned to her desk. "Maybe Eric's like his father. Could that be?"

"Are you saying I don't wear my heart on my sleeve?" Kurt wondered about Molly's quick change of mood.

"Take it however you'd like." Molly bent her head over her paperwork.

"I forgot to tell you my uncle who lives in Springfield called me the other day."

"How did he find you?"

"He got the number from Steve. He said Steve's number was in some of my mother's things. He was going through the stuff and wanted to see how I was doing. I didn't think any of my relatives cared what happened to me."

"Sometimes people surprise you," Molly said, without looking up.

"I guess. Anyway, he mailed me a couple of photo albums that belonged to my mother. There are lots of pictures of Bonnie and me and the kids. I'm going to show them to the kids today."

Molly glanced at him. "They'll enjoy that. Also they'll probably enjoy doing something outside. It's supposed to be in the seventies with lots of sunshine. It's time we've had some warmer weather. We've had a cool spring."

"Summer officially starts in two days. Warmer days are ahead. That means plenty of time to get some outside work done. I thought maybe Eric would like to help me tear out some of that old balustrade on the porch."

"I don't know. The social worker might consider that child labor."

"Do you think?"

Molly laughed. "I was only kidding. I think he'd like that, too."

"The last thing I want to do is get on the wrong side of Diane. So far Emily has kept her little secret, because if Virginia knew she would be in front of the court immediately to bring it up."

"So far so good."

"Why do you say that?"

"I know I said she probably wouldn't tell because she seemed satisfied that she had a secret, but I've gotten to know your daughter better. She is a very loquacious child, and she just might run off at the mouth someday without thinking."

"Don't you think that hasn't crossed my mind? When they show up every Saturday, I breathe a sigh of relief."

Kurt waved a hand in the air. "I could do away with all of this supervised visit stuff if we could just come up with some leads on the real killer."

"I'm still checking on some of the fundraisers

Bonnie was involved with. I'm beginning to think she had a charity of the week."

"Yeah, she was big on volunteering."

"I've followed up with more than half of them. So far no missing funds."

Kurt sighed. "Well, hopefully something will turn up. There's nothing to my theory about that land development. All the information you brought me on that leads nowhere. Once all the dust from the legal wrangling settled, the development sailed through without a hitch."

"Yeah, that's what I thought after reading through all the articles again." Molly wrinkled her brow. "I never did find anything more about the Jerry Malone you mentioned even after you helped me narrow down my search."

"That's another dead end." Kurt shook his head. "Sorry I forgot to mention it, but one of the suppliers mentioned that Jerry died in a construction accident a couple years ago."

"So if he's the guilty one, we'll never know. That can't be good."

"Yeah. That's what I thought. How can I prove I'm innocent if the real killer is dead?"

Molly pointed toward the window. "They're here."

Pushing aside his problems, Kurt stepped toward the front hall as Emily bounded into the house and dumped a shopping bag by the front door.

She gazed up at Kurt. "Where's Smoky?"

"I haven't seen him all morning."

"Come on, Eric. Let's find Smoky."

"Hi." Eric waved at Kurt, then immediately joined Emily in her search.

Kurt greeted Diane and turned to Molly when she joined them in the front hall. He chuckled. "Looks like they've come to see the cat and not me."

"At least you got a 'hi.' They didn't even stop to talk to me." Molly closed the front door and picked up Emily's bag. "What's this?"

"Emily brought some of her playthings with her today." Diane picked up the bag and set it near the office door. "I'm not sure she'll find time to play with them."

"If anyone will find time, it'll be Emily." Kurt went in search of his children. "Hey, kids, did you find the cat?"

Carrying Smoky, Emily came through the hallway leading from the kitchen to the front hall. "I found him. He was in the mudroom closet again."

Eric followed, carrying the cat toys. "Where are we going to play with Smoky? There's furniture all over now."

"Wow, when did all this stuff get here?" Emily peered into the living room.

Molly joined Emily in the entrance to the living room and leaned against one of the columns. "The Antique Trader delivered it all this week. We have furniture in every room now."

"I liked it better without furniture." Eric tugged on Emily's arm. "Let me see Smoky."

Kurt was surprised when Emily handed the cat to Eric and walked into the living room. Kurt watched while Molly followed. Emily sat on every sofa and chair. She pulled out every drawer and opened every cabinet. "This is cool stuff."

"Let me show you something else cool. Come look at this." Molly motioned for the little girl to join her in the dining room. "Your dad finished the French doors that go out to the porch this week."

"I want to see, too." Eric set Smoky on the floor and ran through the living room into the dining room. Smoky immediately went and made himself at home in the window seat.

Kurt joined the group as Molly opened the doors and walked onto the side porch.

Emily ran to greet her father as he came through the doors. "Dad, you did good." She turned her attention back to Molly. "What are you putting out here?"

"Nothing for a while. Your dad has to fix the railing all the way around the porch. We have to replace the trim and then paint." Molly pointed to all the rotted wood in the railing and pulled a piece of peeling paint from the side of the house.

"Then it will look just as good as the inside." Emily picked off another piece of peeling paint.

"After we finish that, we'll put tables and chairs out here so we can serve meals."

Emily raced up to Molly and pulled on her arm. "Can we eat our lunch out here today?"

Molly smiled indulgently. "I think we can arrange that."

"Oh, good. I'll help you make the sandwiches. Can we cut them in shapes like we did last time?"

"Sure." Molly ushered Emily back inside. "You can let Smoky play with his toys in the upstairs hallway, but don't open any of the doors up there. I don't want him in any of the rooms."

"Okay," Emily and Eric chorused as they raced for the office to retrieve the cat.

For the next half hour, Kurt joined the kids while

they ran the length of the hall with the cat's play toys. Smoky chased, the kids giggled, and Kurt savored every minute. When Smoky finally slunk down the stairs in an effort to find a little peace and quiet, Kurt waylaid the kids on their way to the first floor.

Kurt sat on the bottom step. "Smoky's tired. Let him rest, okay?"

"What can we do, then?" Emily whined.

"I've got something I want you to see."

"What?" Eric asked.

"Come into Molly's office, and I'll show you."

When Kurt was settled in the window seat with Eric and Emily on either side of him, he showed them the old photo albums. The children sat fascinated as Kurt pointed out the pictures of them as babies. They were especially intrigued by the picture that showed them with their Grandma Spencer and a woman they didn't recognize.

"Who's that lady?" Emily asked.

"That's my mother, your Grandma Jansen."

"But she's standing with Grandma Spencer." Eric looked at Kurt with a frown wrinkling his little brow.

"That's right. Both your grandmas were visiting that day."

Eric narrowed his gaze as he looked at Kurt. "Then how come we never saw them together any other time?"

Kurt wondered where Eric's question was leading. "You remember how I told you about Grandma Jansen getting cancer?"

Eric nodded. "But we never saw her."

"You did, but you don't remember. You were too little."

"I guess." Eric seemed satisfied with the

explanation. "Grandma Spencer says Grandpa Spencer died from cancer, too. He died before we were born. That's a bad disease."

Kurt nodded. "Yes, it is. And your Grandpa Jansen died before you were born, too."

"Do you have pictures of him?" Eric asked.

"Not in these albums, but maybe I can find some for you." Kurt wondered whether his uncle might have more of their family albums.

Kurt showed the children the rest of the album and hoped they didn't ask more questions about his mother. He hated thinking about how Virginia had kept his mother from seeing Eric and Emily. While Kurt showed them the second album, he tamped down the anger that threatened to surface when he thought of his mother's unfair treatment. She should have had the comfort of seeing her grandchildren in her last days, but she had been denied that pleasure. He wanted Virginia to feel that pain, but he couldn't let that wrong-headed desire take root in his heart. He remembered how often Molly had told him to get over the past. With her help, he could do it. He had to do it if he intended to win her heart.

When they were finished, Emily hopped down off the window seat and retrieved her bag from the floor. Coming back over to Kurt, she held the bag open. "See what I have?"

"Show me." Kurt looked into the bag.

Emily brought what looked like an old jewelry box out of the bag. She sat on the floor and opened it up. "This is my treasure."

Eric looked disgusted. "It's just dumb old jewelry. It's stuff Grandma didn't want anymore."

Emily lifted her chin. "I like it."

As she brought out the necklaces, bracelets, and pins from the box, Kurt suddenly realized that the jewelry box had once belonged to Bonnie. He watched with more interest while Emily continued to empty it. He looked to see whether any of the things she brought out had been Bonnie's. He had never had the heart to go through her things after she died. Then after he was arrested, he'd never had the chance. He couldn't imagine Virginia would let Emily have anything that he had given Bonnie, but he continued to watch closely. When Emily pulled out a gold locket, Kurt's heart jumped into his throat. He was almost sure it was one that he had given Bonnie while they were dating. Once they were married she had rarely worn it.

Kurt joined Emily on the floor. "May I see that, Emily?"

"Okay, but let me show you this first." She opened the locket and pulled out a tiny key. "This is for my secret drawer."

Kurt examined the locket and knew for certain it was the one he had given Bonnie. He puzzled over the little key. "Where's the drawer?"

"In my desk. I keep my secret stuff in there. Would you like to see it?" She looked at him as though seeing this stuff would be a great honor.

"Well, if you feel like showing me your secret stuff, I'd like to see it."

"Okay, I'll bring it next week."

"That's a bunch of dumb stuff, too." Eric wrinkled his nose. "Girls like all kinds of dumb things."

Kurt wanted to laugh at his son's assessment of the situation. In a few years, he would change his tune, and Kurt wanted to be there to help him when he wanted advice on girls. Although the way he was feeling right now, he wasn't sure he was much good at giving that advice. He hadn't done a very good job with Bonnie, and he didn't know where to start with Molly. He glanced at her, and she smiled. Her smile told him he'd better figure that out.

Kurt turned his attention to Eric. "How would you like to do some spindle testing with me?"

"What's that?" Eric's eyebrows knit together.

"The railing out on the porch has spindles. Some of them are okay and some are rotten. I have to replace the rotten ones, but I have to test them first. Would you like me to show you?"

"Yeah." Eric jumped up from the window seat.

Emily pulled on Kurt's arm. "I want to go, too."

"Who's going to help me with the sandwiches?" Molly asked.

"Yeah, you said you'd help Molly." Eric stuck his face right in front of Emily's.

Kurt separated the children before a full-blown confrontation occurred. "We'll all help Molly with the sandwiches. Then after lunch, we'll all do the spindle testing."

"Okay," the children chorused as Kurt ushered them into the kitchen.

After they made the sandwiches, Kurt set up a card table and chairs out on the porch. They ate their lunch, and afterwards, they all tested the spindles on the porch. All too soon, the time came for Eric and Emily to leave. With each passing week saying goodbye became more difficult. Somehow, someway, he had to find Bonnie's killer.

While he'd been focused on seeing his kids, he had let that task slide. Long work hours and little knowledge of how to go about finding a murderer did nothing to help him pursue the truly guilty party. In so many things, he had been trying to rely on himself rather than asking God for help. When he'd finally started praying, things had changed. He'd found a better job, gotten visitation with his children, and gained their love. He'd prayed about all those things. Why had he forgotten to pray about discovering the identity of the person who had ruined his life? If he prayed, would he find the answer?

Despite all the affirmatively answered prayer he had experienced over the past few months, he still let doubts slip into his thoughts. Doubts would get him nowhere. He had to replace them with faith—faith in a God who answered prayer even when things seemed impossible.

***

The following Saturday, Molly looked out her office window. Kurt stood in the yard and waved goodbye to Emily and Eric. After the car disappeared onto the main road, Kurt turned toward the house. His shoulders slumped as he walked across the yard. Molly's heart ached for him. She knew his frustration at only seeing his children for a few hours each week. His children should be living with him, not with their grandmother. Each week, the children grew closer to Kurt, but Molly knew that made parting more difficult.

As she stood looking out the window, Kurt came into her office. He plopped his large frame onto the chair closest to her desk. "I love those kids. I've been thinking about getting a puppy for them. What do you think?"

"I think Smoky will be jealous, and Virginia won't be pleased."

"I don't care what Virginia thinks." Kurt drummed his fingers on the arm of the chair. "I could never please her no matter what I did. Do you disapprove of the dog?"

"It's not my call, but I wouldn't want to make Virginia angry." Molly shrugged as she sat behind her desk. "I've got lots of invoices and orders to file and reconcile with the computer files."

"Doesn't sound like fun." He shook his head. "I'm going to do some more work outside."

Molly picked up some papers from her desk. "You know you don't have to work on Saturdays."

Kurt pushed himself up from the chair. "I know, but I've got to do something to keep my mind off the kids." He walked to the door. "I'm not sure working is even the answer."

"Well, don't work too hard, and remember I'm having one of my deluxe dinners tonight. You're expected promptly at six-thirty."

"And if I'm late?" he asked with a smile.

Molly didn't answer immediately. When he smiled, her stomach did little flip-flops. She just wanted to look at him.

"Are you trying to think up my punishment?"

She shrugged. "Maybe. Were you planning to be late?"

"No, but if I don't get a move on, it'll be six-thirty before I know it."

"Okay, I'll see you later." As he left the room, she glanced down at the papers she had picked up from the desk. They were Emily's. She had left them. Molly ran to catch him. "Kurt."

When she reached the front hall, he had just stepped out the door. He turned. "Did I forget something?"

"These." She held up the papers. "They're Emily's. She left them. What do you want me to do with them?"

"What are they?"

Molly looked through them. "You remember the papers she brought from her secret drawer? She was going to show them to you, but she laid them on the desk when she first got here. Then Smoky showed up, and she forgot all about them. And so did we."

"We'd better keep them for her until next week." Kurt stepped back into the house.

Molly flipped through the eight-by-eleven sheets of paper. "Oh, look, she drew a picture of you."

Kurt took the paper. "That's me?"

"Sure. See, here's your hammer. Besides, she labeled it DAD. And Smoky's right here." Molly pointed to the gray blob that resembled a cat.

"Did she draw a picture of you?"

"I don't know. Let me look." While Molly searched the papers, she spied a picture that resembled her house with Kurt working on the porch and two kids helping. "This is a good one."

"Let me see."

Molly held it up. As she did, she saw writing on the back. "Emily must have used some old office paper."

Kurt turned the page over and perused the text, then glanced up with a puzzled expression. "Are there more papers with writing on the back?"

"I don't know. Let me look." Molly turned the

papers over. "Yeah, it looks like all of them have something on the back."

"Do you see what it says here?" Kurt pointed to some boldface print.

After she read it, she looked at him. "Do you suppose this is connected to Bonnie's death?"

"I don't know, but this report mentions the presence of toxic materials on the land where they put that development."

"Where do you suppose Emily got these papers?"

Kurt slowly shook his head. "She said they were her secret drawer papers, but it doesn't matter. Don't you see? This is a clue. Something to go on."

"Do you think?"

"Yes!" He threw his arms up in a triumphant pose. When he brought them down, he grabbed Molly in a big bear hug and lifted her off her feet.

As Kurt set her back on the floor, her heart pounded. Her head felt light. She clung to him until he released her. Their gazes locked, and she knew he was going to kiss her. When their lips met, she savored every sensation. She didn't want to think about why he was kissing her, just that he was. How many times had she imagined this moment?

He ended the kiss but continued to hold her close. He whispered in her ear, "I probably shouldn't have done that."

"I didn't mind," she said, loving the feel of his arms around her.

"Good." He held her at arms' length. "Because I'm going to kiss you again."

Closing her eyes, Molly let the world and its cares fade into the background. Nothing existed except Kurt and her. She melted into his embrace. His kiss completely captured her mind.

When it ended, she gazed into his sky-blue eyes. She tried not to think of anything but him, but reality burst the bubble. Kurt's joy at the moment didn't abide in her, but in newly found information that could mean getting his kids back. Where did they go from here? She didn't want to think too far ahead. Her past stood like a wall between her and future happiness.

"Was that for celebration?" she asked, trying to lighten the moment. She didn't want to read too much into his kisses.

He gazed into her eyes. "No, I kissed you because I don't know what I'd do without you. You've made everything possible. You've become very important to me."

"Not everything."

"Well, maybe not everything." He chuckled. "You didn't bring me these papers. This is what I've been hoping for—praying for. I finally started praying that God would help us find the real killer. I care about you, but I don't believe I can move forward with a relationship unless I clear my name."

Molly smiled, but she didn't want to hope too much that there was a future for Kurt and her. Too many things stood in the way—her own secret, his desire to prove his innocence, and his love for his deceased wife. Bonnie's memory would always be there, and Molly would have to deal with it. Eric and Emily would want to learn about their mother, and Kurt wasn't going to forget the woman he had loved. Molly knew if she wanted a relationship with Kurt that Bonnie's memory would be part of the equation. She had to accept it.

"What are you going to do with the papers?" she asked.

"First of all, we should both read through them. Then we can compare notes."

"Right now?"

"Absolutely."

While Molly sat at her desk, Kurt sat in a nearby chair as they read through the papers. Just as he handed her the last page, the phone rang. She picked it up.

"Hello, Emily." Molly looked at Kurt. "You want to talk with your dad? He's right here."

Kurt took the phone. "Hi, Em. What's up?"

Molly listened while Kurt talked with Emily about the papers. From what she gathered, he was reassuring her that he would keep them safe until her next visit. After another minute of small talk, Molly could tell Kurt was talking with Eric. When the conversation ended, Kurt smiled wryly as he hung up. "I can't believe Virginia let Emily call."

Molly laughed. "Think about it. You know Emily. She would badger her grandmother until she got to call you."

"You're right." Kurt nodded. "My daughter doesn't give up easily when she wants something."

"I'd say it runs in the family." Molly glanced over the last paper before laying them on her desk. "You mentioned before that Emily said the papers came from her secret drawer? What secret drawer?"

"She told me she has Bonnie's old desk. It was a little writing desk with a single drawer that Bonnie had in the spare room she used as an office at home. I saw that Emily had the key last week, but I didn't remember the desk until Emily told me. It seems she'd been using the desk to play office. She told me she likes to be the boss."

"Now why doesn't that surprise me?" Molly couldn't help grinning. "Were the papers in the drawer?"

"Yes, but she discovered the false bottom by accident. She said it was cool and a good place to hide her stuff from Eric."

Molly chuckled then raised her eyebrows as she tapped the papers. "Oh, wow. This must mean we really are on to something with these."

"You got it. Bonnie must've hidden them there for safe keeping." Kurt looked thoughtful. "When I came home the night of the murder, the house was a mess. Drawers were open and stuff slung everywhere. Even Bonnie's desk. She never used that lock. I think the key was taped inside the drawer. I thought it looked like a robbery, but I bet whoever killed Bonnie was looking for those papers."

Molly picked up the stack of papers. "We have to find out who knew about this."

"And how do we do that?"

"Find a list of the investors." She got up from the desk and handed the papers to him. "It should be part of the public record. I can do that on Monday."

"Then what do we do with those names?"

"I'm not sure, but we'll figure that out when we get the information."

CHAPTER FIFTEEN

Three days after the discovery concerning the real estate development, Molly approached the real estate office owned by Bonnie Spencer's former boss, Connor Drake. Molly had spent the morning searching through records of real estate transactions, and his name was on the list of investors for the deal. Kurt's list of suspects included Connor, but the two other suspects on Kurt's list weren't mentioned. Because Connor had a close association with Bonnie, he was at the top of Molly's list. She hoped her appointment with Mr. Drake might give her a clue as to his guilt or innocence.

Birds chirped as a breeze ruffled the leaves on the branches, forming a canopy over the walk that led to the building. Flower boxes filled with pink and purple petunias hung under the windows on either side of the door. The idyllic setting did little to calm her nerves. The thought that she might come face to face with a killer made her stomach churn. Taking a deep breath, she opened the door and stepped into the reception area. A secretary sitting at a large walnut desk looked her way.

Molly walked to the desk, her heels clicking on the tile floor in an ominous tempo. "I'm here to see Connor Drake."

"He can see you in a few minutes. Have a seat."

"Thanks."

Molly sat on one of the chairs that lined the wall opposite the reception desk and grabbed a magazine from a nearby table. As she thumbed through it, her mind buzzed with suspicions. Although Connor Drake was only one of several investors on the list, he would have known more about Bonnie's daily activities. She would have invited him into her home without a second thought.

While she tried to concentrate on the magazine, someone entered the front door. She looked up. Benton Turley, Virginia Spencer's lawyer, stood only a few feet away. Even on a warm summer day he was dressed impeccably in a gray suit. His silver hair was cut in the latest style. Despite his good looks, Molly cringed inwardly. She didn't want a confrontation.

He stopped in front of her chair and gazed down at her. "Well, well. If it isn't our little do-gooder. What brings you here?"

Molly put on her best smile. "I could ask you the same."

"I'm here to look at some land."

"I hope you find what you're looking for." She focused her attention back on the magazine.

Before Benton could make another comment, an agent came out and greeted him, and the two of them went into a nearby room. Moments later, Connor Drake appeared in the reception area.

He walked across the room and extended his hand. "It's good to see you, Ms. Finnerty. Come into my office."

"Thanks." Generating a smile, Molly forced herself not to shrink from shaking his hand. It could have Bonnie's blood on it.

Molly had to get a grip. This man could be just as

innocent as Kurt. Just because he was one of the major investors in the real estate development didn't mean he had done anything to Bonnie.

"Please sit down." He pointed to the chair at the side of his desk. "What can I do for you?"

Molly held her breath then slowly released it as she sat down. "A little over a year ago, I bought some property over in Hawthorne. I'm restoring an old Victorian and making another house and old barn on the property livable. I intend to use these facilities for a women's shelter." Molly twisted the strap of her purse as it lay in her lap. "We're naming the shelter after a woman who was murdered some years ago. I think she used to work for you. Bonnie Jansen?" Molly tried to gauge whether Connor flinched at the mention of Bonnie's name, but Molly saw no visible evidence that the mention of the name bothered him. "Is that right?"

Connor rubbed his chin. "Yes, it was a terrible tragedy. She was a real go-getter—one of my best agents. Naming the shelter after her will be a nice memorial. In fact, I think I remember reading about a big donation that her mother made. Was that your foundation?"

"Yes, my partner handles all the fundraising."

"If you're here seeking funds, I'd be happy to make a contribution to your cause. Please leave your card, and I'll have my accountant take care of it."

Molly wondered if he was making a contribution to salve his guilty conscience. "That's very generous of you, Mr. Drake, but I'm also interested in finding other pieces of property where I might do the same thing."

"That's what I'm here for." He smiled. "Call me

Connor."

"And you may call me Molly."

"Certainly." He nodded. "You are championing a wonderful project. Were you thinking of a particular town?"

"I was hoping to find something near here or a neighboring town."

"Fair enough, Molly. Let's see what I can find." He turned to his computer and typed in some information. "It'll take me just a minute to bring up some properties that might work."

The tapping of the computer keyboard filled the otherwise silent room. Molly wished she could mention the toxic waste and get Connor's reaction, but bringing up that topic might seem too obvious. Was there a good way to get the subject into the conversation? If she mentioned environmental issues in general, would he show any signs of guilt?

"Connor, I want to stay away from any properties that might have historical restrictions or environmental issues. I don't want to buy property that might have problems down the road. Do you have many problems with those kinds of things?"

His gaze narrowed as he turned from the computer to look at her. "If we know about anything that might impact the buyer's use of the property, we always let the client know. Then they can make an informed decision about whether they want to go ahead with the purchase. Can you be more specific?"

Thoughts tumbling through Molly's mind matched the beating of her heart. Did she dare mention the toxic waste specifically? "I was thinking of things like wetlands, toxic waste, or access easements. I've talked to people who have had problems with all of those."

Connor nodded in a matter-of-fact way. "You're right to be concerned about those issues. I always advise clients concerning details like that. Wetlands are okay as long as you still have plenty of room to build or if they are on a part of the property that you don't plan to change in any way."

"What about the other two problems?" Molly held her breath as she waited for his response.

Connor turned back to the computer and began typing as he answered the question. "I wouldn't touch property that involves toxic waste, but easements come in all shapes and sizes. Those have to be looked at on a case-by-case basis. Some easements should give the buyer no problem. A buyer may have to look carefully at other easements. It depends on what the easements are for."

Even though he had turned away, he didn't give any other signs that her question had bothered him. Still, she wondered whether he turned away because he didn't want to look her in the eye when he answered.

Molly wasn't sure this visit had accomplished anything. But possibly, if he was somehow involved in the cover-up and Bonnie's murder, maybe her questions might make him wonder whether someone had discovered problems with the golf course development. "Did you find anything?"

"I have one property that might interest you. If you'd like to look at it today, we could go now."

Would it be safe to go anywhere with this man? "Um, where is this property?"

"It's about fifteen miles from here. If you don't have time today, we can schedule you for another time. The property isn't occupied and it's our listing, so we don't have to call another agent. That makes scheduling very easy." He raised his brows as he waited for her response.

"Can you give me some information on the property? I'd like to share it with my partner. If he thinks it seems like a viable property, he'll want to look at it, too."

"Sure. It's about twenty acres. It was a small working farm until a few years ago. There's a farmhouse with four bedrooms and a barn." He read from the computer screen. "We actually sold this property to some folks from Boston, but they decided they didn't like the country life so they're selling."

"It sounds like a possibility. I'll share this with my partner." Molly reached into her purse and looked for one of her cards. When she found one, she wrote Nick's number on the back and handed it to Connor. "My partner's name and number are on the back."

"Thanks. Here's my card. Give me a call when you're ready to look."

"I'll do that." Molly stood, eager to get away.

"Good." Connor walked her to the door and opened it. He accompanied her out into the reception area and extended his hand to her. "I hope we can do business."

"I'm sure we can." She shook his hand with less fear this time. He seemed like a nice man. What would Kurt think of her assessment?

Just as she turned to go, Benton strode out of the next office. "Well, I see you're still here." He turned to Connor. "Did you help this young lady?"

"We're trying to," Connor replied.

"Good. Connor, if you have a few minutes, I'd like

to talk with you about that legal advice you were seeking."

"Okay. We can talk now." Connor looked back at Molly. "Give me a call when you want to look at that property."

"I sure will." As she turned to go, the two men went back into Connor's office. She wondered what kind of legal advice Connor needed.

When Molly arrived home, she found Kurt scraping paint from the siding. She jogged up the front steps and around to the side of the house where he was working. Stopping, she watched for a minute. His muscles rippled beneath his t-shirt as he worked, and she couldn't help admiring them.

Her thoughts wandered back to the day in her office when they had discovered the information on the toxic waste. She remembered the gentle touch of his lips on hers, and she longed for more. She knew a relationship wouldn't progress between them until the issue of Bonnie's killer was resolved. When that happened, Molly would have to deal with her past. She wanted to tell him, but whenever she tried to summon the courage, she failed. Some days, she felt like this secret was separating her from God as well as Kurt. Still, she couldn't bring up the subject because she didn't want to see the disappointment in his eyes. He turned, wiping the sweat from his brow. "Are you watching me work?"

Stepping closer she looked up at him. "A good boss always checks on the workers."

He set the scraper on the window ledge. "So, boss, am I doing a good job?"

"A very good job." Despite her sobering thoughts, he always made her smile.

"What happened when you went to see Connor Drake?" He sat in the porch swing and patted the seat beside him.

She gladly joined him. "You'll never guess who I ran into there."

"Virginia?"

"No, but almost as bad. Her attorney, Benton Turley. He made some snide remarks about me being a do-gooder." Molly grabbed the chain that held up the swing. The links bit into her hand. The missing link. That's what they were looking for. Would they ever find it?

Kurt shook his head. "We just have to ignore him and Virginia. They aren't going to get over you taking that charitable donation or my visitation with the kids."

"I know, but I don't like his attitude. He thinks he's better than everyone else."

Kurt smiled. "Funny. Bonnie used to say the same thing about him. She didn't have much use for him."

Molly tried not to let Kurt's talking about Bonnie make her jealous. If she wanted a relationship with Kurt, she would have to realize he wasn't going to forget Bonnie. She had been a very big part of his life—the mother of his children. "Anyway, to get to your question." Molly told Kurt about her meeting.

"Did he have any reaction?" Kurt interrupted.

"I don't think so." She wrinkled her brow in frustration. "To be honest, I couldn't tell. I'm not a very good detective. He actually seemed like a very nice man."

"If he's been carrying around this secret for over six years, you know he's got to have no conscience and nerves of steel. So he probably wouldn't have a reaction." Kurt sighed as he made the swing move back and forth. "If he's guilty, he might start to worry that someone could discover the toxic waste in that development. Maybe he'll tip his hand somehow. All we can do is pray."

Molly nodded, but Kurt's words, 'carrying around this secret,' echoed in her brain like a gunshot. At least she knew her conscience was working because it was beginning to hurt, even though her past wasn't really a secret. Nick, Allison, Steve, and Lindy all knew about it. Lots of people knew. Just not Kurt.

Standing, Kurt grabbed Molly's hand and brought her up with him. For a minute she thought maybe he would kiss her again, but he turned away.

"Time to get back to work." He picked up the scraper.

"Oh, one more thing. Benton asked to speak with Connor as I was leaving. Do you suppose he's going to inform Connor about my relationship to you?"

Kurt shrugged. "I'd say so, but that's to our advantage. If Connor learned that we know each other, he might think I have information about Bonnie's murder and shared it with you."

"I don't know. The whole thing seems hopeless."

"Don't give up. I'm going to keep praying until the day I find out who killed Bonnie." Kurt scraped the house as if he was trying to scrape away the pain of losing his wife. Then he stopped for a moment. "Molly, don't go look at property with that guy. If he's guilty, you might not be safe."

Molly basked in the unspoken words his message conveyed. He didn't want anything to happen to her. "I won't. If I go, I was planning to take Nick with me."

"That sounds like a plan. Whatever you do, be

careful. A nervous killer can be dangerous."

Molly released a shaky breath. "I know, but now it's a waiting game. And if he's not the killer, then who is? I want you to be vindicated so badly."

"You and me both."

***

Eager to get the rest of her order, Molly entered the Antique Trader. The house was nearly done, and everything was falling into place except identifying the person who had killed Bonnie. A week had passed since Molly had talked with Connor Drake, but she still had no clue whether he had anything to do with Bonnie's murder.

The bell over the door jingled as Molly entered, and Bev came out of her office. She smiled, but she appeared nervous and ill at ease, shifting her weight from one foot to the other. When Virginia Spencer stepped from behind Bev, Molly understood why.

"I do need to talk with you about your order, but Virginia insisted on coming over." Bev retreated to her office as if something scary was chasing her.

"Hello, Virginia." Molly tried to prepare herself for whatever the older woman had to say. "I hope you're doing well."

Virginia smiled, but unlike Bev's smile, Virginia's had a Cheshire-cat quality to it. "Hello, Molly. Or should I say Mary?"

Molly's heart sank. She wanted to run out of the house, but she had to face her past. She had been running too long. "My real name is Molly."

"But you don't deny that you're also known as Mary Finn."

"No. I once went by that name. How did you discover this?" Molly prayed that she could remain calm.

"Emily needed pictures for a poster she's doing for a day camp project. I had some old magazines in the attic, and your face was on the cover of one."

"I'm surprised you recognized me. I don't look the same."

"The resemblance was strong enough." Virginia smirked. "Then I remembered the news stories about your arrest. I think the court might find this information interesting, don't you?"

"It has nothing to do with Kurt and his children."

"Yes, it does when you see them every week. I don't want my grandchildren hanging around a drug abuser."

Feeling sick inside, Molly shook her head. "That was a long time ago. I'm not the same person."

"We'll see what the court has to say."

Molly took a deep breath. "You don't want to do that."

"I do and I will." Virginia's gaze narrowed. "It's interesting that two felons found each other. You and Kurt are a perfect match."

"Don't take my past out on him. He's innocent."

Virginia wagged her finger at Molly. "That's not what a jury decided six years ago."

"Juries have been wrong."

"Not that one. I knew Kurt Jansen was no good, but I couldn't convince my daughter of that. You two deserve each other." Virginia's mouth twisted in a malicious smile. "I'll see you in court."

As Virginia walked out the front door, Molly's legs nearly gave out from under her. She sought the nearest chair and plopped down on it. Putting her elbow on the arm of the chair, she laid her head on her hand. This wasn't happening. She would surely wake up and find it was all a bad dream.

"Are you all right?"

Molly looked up. Concern on her face, Bev stood beside her. "I've been better. Why didn't you warn me about her?"

"I couldn't. She was standing right there when I called you. She's my friend, and I couldn't go against her. I'm sorry."

"I know she's your friend, but she is twisted with hate. It isn't going to do anyone any good to keep those children from their father. They love him," Molly said. She loved him, too. "Virginia doesn't realize what she's doing."

"I agree. I live next door to them, and I've heard the children talk about their father. They adore him." Bev sighed. "What can we do?"

"The only thing I can think of. Pray." Molly stood. "I'd better get going."

"Don't you want to talk about your order? I do have it."

Molly shook her head. "No, I can't deal with that right now. I'll call you later in the week."

"Okay. My prayers are with you," Bev called after Molly as she left.

Molly got into her car and leaned her head against the steering wheel. She could hear Nick's voice. *I hope you don't live to see the day you'll regret not telling this man about your past.* That day had come. Now she'd have to deal with the past she had been running from for far too long. She wondered why she had kidded herself all these months thinking somehow she would never have to tell Kurt. Now her actions could jeopardize his contact with his children. She would have to separate herself from Kurt in order for him to keep seeing his kids. Once again, she had lost the family she hoped to have.

She finally started her car and drove away from the Antique Trader. When she passed the children's school, the tears came unbidden to her eyes. Unable to drive further, she pulled over. Misery welled up inside her. Putting her face in her hands, she sobbed uncontrollably. How could she ever say goodbye to Kurt and his kids?

God, please help me through this. I can't do it without you.

When the tears finally subsided, Molly drove out of Oakton, but she couldn't bring herself to go home. Going home meant telling Kurt about her past. She had no option except to tell him, but she didn't know how she was going to do it. As she drove the long way home, she tried to formulate a plan. There was no easy way to inform the man she loved that in a drug-induced stupor she had let her husband die. She'd had a miscarriage and nearly died herself. After Kurt heard these things, Virginia wouldn't be the only one who didn't want her around the children.

At the Hawthorne town line, she took the turn-off that went toward the center of town and away from her house. She couldn't go home yet. Her stomach churned. She needed more time to think. Besides, as she looked at herself in the rearview mirror, she knew she couldn't let Kurt see her with red, swollen eyes. When she faced him, she wanted to look her best.

She stopped at the local pizza parlor to kill more time. When she was fairly certain that Kurt would be finished working, she headed for home. He usually quit around dusk and would be gone from the house when she got back. She needed the night to summon the courage to face him first thing in the morning.

The sun was setting as she drove the few miles to her house. The colorful sky promised a good day ahead for the weather, but Molly could only see storm clouds ahead for herself.

When she drove down the lane, she saw lights illuminating her office. A dark blue sedan that she didn't recognize sat near the house. Kurt must be talking with one of the contractors about the work they were doing. At least she wouldn't be alone with him. After parking her car in the carriage house, she walked with deliberate slowness to the house. She considered just going up to her apartment without stopping by her office, but Kurt would definitely guess that something was wrong if she did that.

Instead of going in the back door as she usually did, she took the long way around to the front. She noticed that Kurt had finished replacing all the rotten spindles today. As she climbed the steps, she tried to peer in the window to see if she could tell who was in the office before she went in. Kurt sat at her desk and another man stood in front of it. She tried to make out who the other man was, but his back was to her. Something flashed in the light. When she looked harder, she realized the other man had a gun pointed at Kurt.

Molly shrank away from the window. Leaning against the house, she put her hands over her mouth. Her heart raced. The unidentified man had to be Bonnie's killer. They had flushed him out. Now he was going to kill Kurt, too. She should call 911, or she could charge in and take the man by surprise. But maybe he had seen her car come down the drive. She had to call 911.

She fumbled in her purse for her cell phone. After she punched in the numbers, she suddenly realized that the man might hear her talking. But if she left the porch, she wouldn't be able to see what was happening inside. She had to make the call from here.

The phone rang. The dispatcher answered while Molly's heart pounded. She was sure he could hear it. Cupping her hands around her mouth and the phone, she spoke barely above a whisper. "There's a gunman in my house."

As Molly gave the dispatcher the information he requested, she prayed and tried to remain calm. The dispatcher assured her that the police were on their way. His unflappable voice helped to soothe Molly's nerves, but her tranquility was short-lived when she saw the man wave the gun in the air as he motioned for Kurt to stand. The man kept the gun trained on Kurt while he walked across the room.

Then the man turned. She saw his face and gasped.

Molly blinked, not believing what she saw. The gunman was Benton Turley. Maybe she should've guessed. From the first time she had seen him in court, he had made her uneasy.

Then she realized they were leaving the study. Where were they going? She couldn't let them get away. Panic scrambled her thoughts as she squeezed the phone tighter. What should she do now?

"They're moving. I can't talk." Her pulse pounding in her head, she looked around for a weapon. She spied a leftover spindle lying nearby. As she picked it up, she left her purse and phone next to the railing. She gripped the spindle like a batter eager to hit a home run and tiptoed toward the front door. Just before she reached it, the screen door swung open. Her heart in her throat, she jumped back into the shadows.

Kurt walked out first. Hoping no one could see her, Molly pressed her body against the side of the house. She held her breath as the gunman stepped out of the door.

"All right. Don't make any sudden moves." Benton's voice dripped with malice. "Let's find your friend. I saw her car come down the lane."

"I won't let you touch her."

"We'll see about that. You're both dead. It'll look like a murder-suicide when I get done. Since they think you killed your wife, they'll have no problem believing you killed another woman."

Ready to strike, Molly waited until they reached the front steps. While they descended the stairs, she made her move. She held the spindle high, planning to bring it down on Benton's head.

She charged. The floorboards on the porch creaked, and Benton turned. Before she could bring the spindle down, his gun fired. She lunged forward and swung the spindle as hard as she could.

Everything went black.

***

With the gunshot still ringing in his ears, Kurt watched in disbelieving horror while a bright red blotch of blood fanned out on Molly's blue shirt. Somehow, even after the bullet struck her, she'd continued forward and smashed Benton over the head with the spindle. Molly and Benton crumpled to the floor as the spindle and the gun hit the porch with a thud.

Kurt rushed to her and knelt by her side. Holding his breath, he lifted her upper body into his arms. His stomach in knots, he held her close as he listened for signs of life. Relief washed over him when he heard her shallow breathing. Despite his relief, worry scrambled his thoughts. He couldn't think.

He had to do something, but what? Could he stop the bleeding, or would he just make things worse? He didn't know anything about first aid.

"Molly, Molly, do you hear me? Please don't die. I love you." Kurt blinked away the tears, but he couldn't blink away his forebodings.

Benton groaned. Kurt grabbed the gun and pointed it toward him. The temptation to squeeze the trigger crawled through Kurt's mind, but he willed the thought away. Acting on the impulse would make him no better than Bonnie's killer. "Don't you move an inch."

Benton moaned but remained still.

Kurt wanted to call 911, but he couldn't leave Benton in order to get to a phone. Then he spied Molly's cell phone lying on the porch. He carefully laid her down and inched toward the phone while keeping the gun pointed at Benton. When Kurt picked up the phone, he noticed that it was already connected to a call. Had Molly called 911?

The answer to his question came in the form of flashing lights atop a police car that came down the lane. Kurt looked at Benton, who groaned again. Kurt didn't dare leave Molly. He knelt beside her as he waited for the police to come to him.

When they emerged from their vehicle, Kurt yelled, "Call an ambulance. My friend's been shot."

One officer continued to approach while the other one went back to the car. As the officer came up to the porch, he surveyed the area. "How did this happen?"

Kurt motioned toward Benton. "That man shot her, and she managed to hit him over the head with the spindle lying there."

"That's a lie." Benton shot up from the porch and pointed at Kurt. "Don't believe him. He's the one who did the shooting. He's an ex-con who killed his own wife."

His stomach sinking, Kurt couldn't believe what he was hearing. Benton couldn't possibly think he would get away with that story. Kurt shook his head and pointed at Benton. "He's a liar. Molly will tell you what happened."

The officer stared at Kurt. "Who's Molly?"

"This is Molly." Kurt held her in his arms and tried to explain the events of the evening while Benton disputed every statement.

"Looks like we'll have to take you both into custody until we can sort this out." The first officer pointed to Benton as the second officer joined them. "You cuff that one, and I'll take care of this one."

The snap of the handcuffs brought back the unwanted memories of prison. If only he could wake up and find this was all a horrible nightmare. Surely Molly would survive and be able to confirm his story. Otherwise, who would believe him over a respected attorney? To make matters worse, Kurt had picked up the murder weapon. But he wouldn't have gunshot residue on his hands because he had never fired the gun. He clung to that fact.

A backup patrol car arrived just as the flashing lights of an ambulance appeared on the main road. It turned into the lane. In minutes, the paramedics had Molly in the back of the ambulance while Kurt stood by, helplessly wishing he could join her. As the ambulance sped away, Kurt prayed that God wouldn't let him spend even one more night in jail, but most importantly wouldn't let another woman he loved die.

CHAPTER SIXTEEN

Molly sat on the hospital bed and looked out the window as the sun rose. The two weeks since the shooting had gone by in a blur, but she was alive and recovering well. Today she would be discharged from the hospital.

She should be happy, but dread filled her heart. Now that she wasn't groggy from the pain medicine, the time had come to tell Kurt the story of her past. She tried to decide the best way to bring it up when he arrived today. Not one satisfactory idea came to mind, but she had to tell him.

Now that Kurt would be exonerated in Bonnie's murder, Virginia wouldn't have a chance in court against him unless she could convince the court that Molly's presence would be a bad influence on the children. She had to tell Kurt before that happened.

When Kurt walked into the room, the scripture she had read the day before popped into her mind. *Then you will know the truth, and the truth will set you free.* She wasn't going to hide behind her fears. She was ready to face the truth.

"Hi." He smiled. "I think I saw them getting your chariot ready."

"My chariot?"

"Yeah, your wheelchair. You know you can't motor out of this hospital on your own." Kurt greeted her with a kiss. "Is your mother coming to get you?"

"Yes. She thinks I need pampering during the rest of my recovery. Thanks to you." Molly hopped off the bed. "See? I'm fine. That's why the doctor said I could go home. You hear those last two words, 'go home'?"

"Yes, but we both know what you would do if you went home. You'd want to make sure everything's just right for the opening in two weeks. You need that time to rest." He put his arm around her shoulders. "Kayla's back and Allison's coming out to help, too. And folks from church are making sure everything will be ready. We've got it all under control."

"But I do need to be there. I promise I won't overdo it." Molly walked away from his embrace. His nearness always muddled her mind. She needed clear thoughts if she wanted to bring up her past. If she didn't do it soon, her mother would show up, and the moment would be lost again.

"Sorry, it's settled. You're going home with your mother." He gave her a satisfied smile. "You're looking good today."

"Thanks." She wished this could be easy. She was afraid that what she had to say would take the smile off his face. "I feel much better. The painkillers were almost as bad as the pain. I hated feeling so groggy."

"Yeah, that stuff made you kind of goofy."

"Goofy?"

"You couldn't put two coherent sentences together."

"Did I say anything strange?" Molly wondered what she had talked about while under the influence of the painkillers. Maybe it would have been easier to tell him then. At least, she wouldn't have been aware of his reaction.

Kurt shrugged. "Not strange. You didn't make much sense. I like you much better this way."

"That's good." Molly forced herself to smile and wondered if he'd still feel the same way after he learned the truth.

He reached into his back pocket and brought out a couple of envelopes. "I almost forgot. I brought you cards the kids made for you when they came on Saturday. They wanted to visit you, but Virginia wouldn't let them. I don't understand her."

Taking the cards and sitting back on the bed, Molly realized this was the perfect opening for her story. She put it off for only a moment as she read the cards. She smiled even though worry curdled her stomach. "They're wonderful. Tell the kids thank you."

"They're eager to see you."

Molly closed her eyes for a moment as she summoned the courage to speak.

Kurt touched her arm. "Are you feeling okay?"

Nodding, she opened her eyes. "I'm fine, but there's something I need to tell you."

"What?" Concern wrinkled his brow.

"I know why Virginia doesn't want the children to see me."

"What could that possibly be?"

Molly took a deep breath as she tried to tamp down the apprehension that ate away at her courage. "It's not a pretty story."

"What story?"

"The story of my life before I met you."

"What about it?" Kurt's gaze narrowed as he leaned forward in the chair.

"Do you remember a fashion model named Mary Finn?"

Raising his eyebrows, he slowly nodded. "Vaguely. She was arrested for something about the time of Bonnie's murder. What does that have to do with you?"

Molly lowered her head, afraid to look Kurt in the eye. "I'm Mary Finn. My real name is Molly Finnerty, but I took the name Mary Finn when I started modeling."

"I thought there was something familiar about you when we first met. What were you arrested for?"

"Possession of drugs. I was guilty."

Kurt didn't say anything, so Molly continued.

"I took diet pills to keep my weight down, then graduated to other things to get me through the day. I didn't want to feel anything. My marriage was a disaster, and I didn't want to face reality. Drugs were an easy way out until they nearly killed me. They did kill my unborn baby, and my husband died because I was too strung out on drugs to care." She covered her face with her hands and sobbed, "And God forgive me, I didn't care if he died."

Misery welling up inside her, Molly raised her head. Kurt still sat there without speaking. She prayed that he would somehow understand. "I didn't want to tell you any of this because I thought you would resent me for not serving any time when you served six years for something you didn't do."

Kurt got up and walked to the window. He jammed his hands in the pockets of his khaki pants. After what seemed like years, he spoke. "Maybe in the beginning that was wise."

A flicker of hope ignited in her heart until he

turned and looked at her. Disappointment radiated from his eyes. She wanted to cover her face again, but she forced herself to meet his gaze. Pain more powerful than the pain she had suffered from the gunshot wound squeezed her heart. "I was hoping you'd understand why I didn't tell you."

He turned toward her. "And you're telling me now because—?"

"Because Virginia threatened to use my conviction and our association to keep you from seeing Eric and Emily." Molly hung her head. She couldn't keep looking at the disillusionment in Kurt's expression. "Virginia confronted me the night that we had our run-in with Benton. I intended to tell you that night."

"After all these months and all the things we've shared together, I can't believe you didn't trust me enough to tell me your story. You kept telling me to trust people, and you couldn't do it yourself."

"I didn't want you to hate me for what I've done."

Kurt shook his head, a sad disbelief written on his face. "Why would you think I would hate you?"

"My family died because I was negligent, but your family was taken from you through no fault of your own. I thought you'd resent me for that."

"I can understand why you wouldn't share that kind of thing with me when we first met, but after months of working together and getting to know each other, you should've known me well enough to realize I wouldn't. I feel more betrayed by your lack of trust than anything else you've ever done."

"Please understand."

"I'm trying." Kurt frowned. "Did you honestly think that your long-ago conviction would hurt my cause now that you've turned your life around?"

"I wasn't sure what to think. Once Virginia found out, I was afraid of her threats. I didn't want to take the chance that it could ruin everything for you." Molly shrugged.

"I trusted you. I trusted you enough to share everything, but you didn't do the same. Just like Bonnie, you couldn't share with me. She didn't tell me what was going on in her life, and she wound up dead." Kurt let out a heavy sigh, his face grim, as he turned toward the window for a second time.

Molly closed her eyes. Bonnie again. Would the mention of his dead wife always make her cringe? Some day she was going to have to talk about it with Kurt, but now definitely wasn't the time. She opened her eyes. "I wish I'd been more open. I could've jeopardized your visitation with Emily and Eric. Can you forgive me?"

He turned but remained silent as he started to pace in front of the window. Just when she thought he wasn't going to say anything to her at all, he stopped and stared at her. "I don't know what I'm feeling right now. You had the right to your privacy, but it still hurts that you didn't think I'd understand. I know I'd be wrong to hold it against you."

"I'm sorry I hurt you—that I was only thinking about myself instead of how this would affect you and your children." Molly tried to smile. He hadn't exactly said the words, "I forgive you," but he had indicated that it would be wrong not to do so. Was that enough? It would have to be for now.

Kurt grew quiet again as he stared out the window again. He obviously didn't want to look at her. Molly's heart ached. Her confession had complicated their developing relationship. She didn't want to make things worse, but she still didn't want to do anything that would cause difficulties for him and his children.

"Even though you don't think my past would be a problem as you try to get Emily and Eric back, I think you're right. I need to fully recuperate at my mother's place. This time apart will give each of us space to figure out where our relationship is going."

Kurt nodded, sadness settling on his features. "That's probably for the best."

Molly wished that he hadn't been so agreeable, but what else could she expect?

***

Kurt worked in Molly's office, making sure things were in order for the next day's final inspection on the properties. The opening was just days away. The Hawthorne Valley Inn was fully booked.

Kayla and Allison would be here for the opening, but not Molly. She should be here, but she stayed away to make sure nothing would stand between him and his children. The place wasn't the same without her, but he would do his best to make the inn something she could be proud of. He wanted her to be happy, and he wanted to be a part of that happiness. Even though she had suggested their separation, he had done nothing to discourage it. He hadn't been willing to say he'd forgiven her when she asked.

Would his association with Molly keep him from seeing his children? Nothing would be right until Eric and Emily were with him again. He only wished that Virginia would stop fighting him. He didn't understand the woman at all. Did she really want a court battle that would only make things worse for her grandchildren?

While he pondered the question, he heard a car come down the lane. Could Molly have changed her mind? His heart skipped a beat at the thought. He glanced out the window, hoping to see a blue SUV. Instead, a black Town Car parked near the house. The only person he knew who owned a car like that was Virginia Spencer. What would she be doing here?

He watched as Virginia emerged from the car and came up the front walk. Dressed in her fashionable summer pantsuit, she paused and looked around before she climbed the steps. He went to the front door and braced himself for a confrontation. He didn't need this.

When the doorbell rang, he took a deep breath and opened the door. No one was there. He stepped outside and found Virginia walking to the end of the porch as she looked over the place.

For a moment he thought about going back inside and not speaking to her, but his better nature made him stay put. She turned around.

"Oh." She put her hand over her heart. "I didn't hear you come out."

"What do you want?" His question held no welcome.

"I'd like to talk with you."

"About what?"

"A lot of things," she said as she approached. "First of all, I'd like to tell you what a beautiful job you've done with this house. I'm sorry I never appreciated your work before."

Kurt blinked. Why was she being so nice? This

wasn't the Virginia Spencer he knew. He didn't trust her compliments or her apology. "I'm sorry, too."

She stopped a few feet from where he stood. "I know we've never been on very good terms, even when Bonnie was alive, but we need to change that."

"Why do you feel the need to do that now?"

"Because I was wrong. Very wrong."

"That's right. You treated me like scum the whole time Bonnie and I were married. I didn't deserve that." Kurt tried to tamp down the anger and resentment that surfaced when he thought about all the years he'd spent in prison and how he'd been cheated out of having his children. "Now you're here to say you're sorry. Well, isn't that just fantastic. Does that take away the years I was in prison? Does that restore the time I missed with my children? The time you stole?"

Virginia shook her head. "No, and there's nothing I can do to change the past, but I want to do what's right for the future."

"And what is that?"

"I talked with your attorney and told him I want you to have the children. He said he'd take care of the paperwork." Tears welled up in Virginia's eyes, but she maintained a stiff upper lip as she continued. "He wanted to tell you, but I asked him to let me do it. I know that you can keep me from ever seeing the children again, but I'm begging you not to. They're all I have. I love them. I thought I was doing the best thing for them when I wanted to keep them away from you. I thought you had killed my daughter."

For a moment, Kurt couldn't believe what he was hearing. He was actually going to get his kids back without a fight. And she was begging him to let the children see her. His heart filled with happiness, but the bitterness lingered in the dark corners. He wanted to treat her the same way she had treated him, but the image of his children's smiling faces crossed his mind. Could he keep them from their grandmother, the woman who had been the center of their lives for six years? He didn't want to deal with that question.

"I don't know what I want to do. I'll have to think about it." He couldn't bring himself to look her in the eye. He didn't want to see the tears.

"Kurt, please." Her voice cracked as she spoke. "Please forgive me. I know that's a lot to ask, but I'm throwing myself on your Christian mercy. I don't deserve it, but I think that's why it's called mercy."

Virginia had a lot of nerve talking to him about Christian mercy. She never had any for him, and he didn't have any for her at the moment either. His thoughts weren't filled with much Christian thinking. He had drifted back into his old negative thoughts. This must be what Jesus meant by turning the other cheek. Kurt didn't want to turn the other cheek, but God had just made it possible for him to have his children. The good and bad warred within him. Doing what the Lord expected wasn't easy.

Trying to summon the forgiveness Virginia asked for, Kurt walked to the balustrade and looked out at the property in its full summer glory. The breeze ruffled the leaves in the tree branches overhead. The sun shining in the bright blue sky reminded him of God's glorious creation. All this made Kurt remember God's forgiveness and how He expected Kurt to forgive as he had been forgiven. But forgiving this woman who had treated him so badly went against every natural instinct.

"Kurt." Virginia came to stand beside him, her hands gripping the rail. "I can live without the forgiveness if you'll just let me see the children."

Taking a deep breath, Kurt finally turned to face her. "I've got to be honest with you. What you're asking of me is something I'm finding very difficult to do. But because of Emily and Eric, I'm going to work on forgiving you. It's going to take some time for me to work through all this. I will let you see the children as often as they want to see you. After all, you are their grandmother, and they love you."

Virginia didn't say a word. She just threw her arms around Kurt and sobbed on his shoulder. He didn't know how to react. Her totally unexpected reaction took him completely off guard. Slowly he put his arms around her and patted her on the back until she pulled away.

Wiping her eyes, she stared up at him as though she couldn't believe what she had just done. She ran her hand over her hair and shook her head. "I'm so sorry. I don't know what came over me. I can never repay your kindness."

"I did it for the kids. They're my main concern."

"Mine, too." She held out her hand. "Truce?"

Kurt couldn't help smiling. For just an instant he saw a little bit of Emily in Virginia. Or maybe it was the other way around. He took her hand. "Truce."

Virginia went down the steps then turned back to Kurt. "Oh, by the way, the kids are begging me daily to see your friend Molly. How is she doing?"

Kurt's heart twisted at the mention of Molly's name. "She's doing fine. She's staying with her mother and getting some well-deserved pampering until she's completely recovered."

"When she gets back, will you let me know? I have some fences to mend there, too."

"I will."

"Good. The children can see her when she gets back." Virginia came back up the steps. "As long as I'm here, I think you should give me a tour of the house. While we do that, we can talk about how we'll make this transition of the children coming to live with you."

Again, Virginia's out of character request took him off guard. "Okay."

He showed her through the Victorian, and she raved about the house and its furnishings. Then he took her out to the women's shelter and toured the Bonnie Spencer Jansen House. When Virginia saw the sign at the entrance, tears welled up in her eyes again. "Thank you so much for this memorial to Bonnie."

"Don't thank me. Your donation made it possible. I only supervised the work."

"You really loved her, didn't you?" she asked as they walked back down the lane to the main house.

The question caught him by surprise. "Yes, but I know it's time to move on."

"With Molly?"

He wished he could answer that. He had made the same mistake with Molly that he had with Bonnie. He had let his anger get the best of him. Who would have guessed that Virginia would be the one to teach him about forgiveness? He needed to tell Molly that he had forgiven her and ask for her forgiveness in return. He lifted his head toward heaven in a silent prayer thanking God for showing him the way through a most unexpected source.

"I hope so."

"I hope so, too. The children adore her." Virginia glanced at him. "I completely misjudged her. She wants to help these women because she knows about abuse firsthand. I don't know how she survived."

Kurt knit his brow in a puzzled frown. "Abuse?"

"She didn't tell you?"

"She told me that her husband had died, but she didn't go into detail."

Virginia slowed her step and released a loud sigh. "I feel even worse because I trusted the man who actually killed my daughter instead of trusting you. Benton Turley fooled me completely. He finally confessed that he killed Bonnie to keep her from telling Connor about the toxic waste. Now there is a big mess to clean up. Benton hurt so many people." Virginia shook her head. "And I've misjudged so many people."

"I've done the same."

Virginia touched Kurt's arm. "I mentioned my misjudgment of Molly to your attorney when I went to see him. He helped me understand why she has been such an advocate for abused women."

Then Virginia told Kurt what she had learned from Nick about Byron's verbal and physical abuse of Molly and how she was afraid to admit to anyone her supposedly fairytale marriage was a sham. Without pausing, Virginia continued her account of the day Byron died and Molly was arrested. "He took a gun and played Russian roulette. He alternated putting the gun to her head, then his. He shot himself, but Nick told me Molly still blames herself. She deserves some happiness. I hope you can make her happy."

"Me, too," Kurt replied, unable to imagine what she had gone through while her husband held a gun to her head. Somehow he had to make amends. He loved Molly, and so did his kids. They should be a family. He had to make that happen.

***

Kurt made his way through Boston's Public Garden as Eric and Emily skipped down the sidewalk ahead of him. The sun shone brightly on the warm, late August afternoon. Kurt tried to calm his nerves while he watched his happy children. They had been living with him for a whole week now, and he thanked God every day for the folks who had helped make that happen. He was especially grateful for Molly's help. She had aided him even when he had tried to push her away. The thought of meeting Molly had his stomach tied in knots. The last time he'd seen her in the hospital, he had planned to ask her to marry him. He'd been so sure of the answer then. Today he planned to ask that same question, but he had no idea how she would respond. Of course, before he asked that question, he had to convince her that they belonged together. He just prayed she would listen.

"Eric and Emily, you two need to stay with me," Kurt called after them.

Eric stopped and turned. "But we want to see Molly."

"You won't see her at all if you run ahead. You don't know where to go."

"You said by the big church. I see it right there." Emily pointed to the steeple of the Park Street Church that rose above one corner of Boston Common.

"Yes, that's it, but we have to walk all the way through the Common to get there," Kurt explained.

"Do you have the present?" Eric asked.

"Yes, I've got the present." Kurt held up the colorful bag stuffed full of tissue paper along with the gifts the children had made for Molly at day camp.

"Do you think she'll like them?" Emily asked.

"Yes." Kurt prayed for patience for him and his children.

As they left the Public Garden, they crossed Charles Street to the Boston Common. The sound of laughter, shouts and car horns filled the air. The sounds of the city made Kurt feel alive. Street vendors, whose carts lined the sidewalk, sold T-shirts, popcorn, and various other items. Fearing he would lose Eric and Emily in the crowd, Kurt grabbed their hands.

Eric pointed to a cart selling Frisbees. "Can we buy one, Dad?"

"Maybe later." Kurt continued through the Common with his gaze trained toward the corner where he had instructed Nick to bring Molly.

When they were two-thirds through the Common, Kurt spied Molly sitting on a blanket with her back to them. He couldn't mistake that strawberry-blond hair, pulled back in one of those fancy braids. She wore a blue and white striped shirt and blue capri pants. Nick, Allison, and a woman Kurt didn't know sat on the other side.

Who was the stranger? Was she a friend of Molly's? Was this unknown woman going to ruin all of Kurt's plans to be alone with Molly? Kurt had to quit thinking of himself. The kids were just as excited to see Molly as he was.

He looked down at the kids to see if they had seen Molly. He feared they would run ahead when they saw her. Maybe that wouldn't be all bad. They could break the ice.

Emily yanked on his arm. "Dad, Dad, I see her. Let's hurry."

Both kids pulled on his arms as they tried to make him move faster. Before they got there, Nick saw them and waved. When he waved, Molly turned around. At that point, the kids left Kurt behind as they ran to greet her. He deliberately slowed his pace while he watched the children hug her. He wanted to do the same. He just hoped he'd get his turn.

When the embrace ended, Molly appeared to be introducing the children to the dark-haired woman. Eric shook the lady's hand, and Emily grinned, then turned as she waved and pointed at him.

Molly looked his way. Their gazes met. She didn't smile, and his heart broke. She wasn't happy to see him. He waved and pasted a smile on his face as he drew closer. When he was standing next to Eric and Emily, Kurt held out the gift. "In your hurry, you forgot something."

Emily grabbed the bag and handed it to Molly. "Happy birthday, Molly. We know it's not your birthday for five more days, but we couldn't wait." Emily jumped up and down. "Open it now."

Smiling, Molly hugged the children again. "You didn't have to do this."

"But we wanted to." Eric was his serious self. "If you don't like it, you don't have to use it. I made it for your desk."

Molly removed the tissue paper and fished around in the bag until she pulled out a crooked ceramic bowl about the size of a tennis ball. She held it up. "It's lovely. I especially like the blue color. I'll definitely put it on my desk."

"It's for paperclips," Eric stated.

"It's just what I needed. Thank you, Eric." Molly looked in the bag again and brought out a cylindrical ceramic piece also in the color blue. She turned to Emily, who for once was quiet. "Is this for my desk, too?"

Emily nodded. "It's for your pens and pencils."

"It's perfect." Molly once again folded the children in her embrace. "Thanks so much. I love you."

Kurt watched the exchange, hoping he would hear the same words, but he wasn't sure that would happen, especially with the unknown woman standing there. Molly had yet to introduce him to this stranger. He stepped forward. "Okay, kids. Here." He handed each of them a ten-dollar bill. "Go with Nick and Allison, and they'll help you buy your Frisbee now."

"We'll find some bargains." Nick and Allison held out their hands for the kids. "We'll be back in a few minutes."

As Nick, Allison, and the children walked away, Molly glanced at him, then turned to the other woman. "Heather, this is Kurt Jansen. He's Eric and Emily's dad, and he's the one who restored my house. Kurt, this is Heather Watson. She moved here from Montana a few months ago. She's an oncology nurse, and she's been working on a cancer fundraiser that I've decided to join."

Kurt nodded and shook Heather's hand. "It's nice to meet you. And you won't find a better fundraiser to help you with your cause than Molly."

"I'm finding that out." Heather smiled, her brown eyes holding a curious look as she glanced from Molly to him. "It's nice to meet you, Kurt." Heather turned to Molly. "I'm glad you're doing better, and I'm glad we could get together for lunch."

"Me, too. We'll have to do this again soon."

"You can count on it." Heather held up an envelope. "And thanks so much for the donation. Now I'd better get going."

As soon as Heather was out of earshot, Molly turned to Kurt, her gaze narrowed. "Why are you here?"

"The kids wanted to see you. They've been asking ever since you went to the hospital. They miss you."

"I missed them, too." She picked up the blanket, quickly folded it and held it in front of her like a protective barrier. "I'm glad you brought them by."

"That's not the only reason." Kurt's heart pounded so fiercely he figured she must be able to hear it. "Molly, we need to talk. Everything has changed since we last saw each other."

"I know. Nick told me that the kids are living with you now and that Virginia isn't going to fight you. It's what you wanted, and I'm happy for you." Molly lowered her gaze.

"Thanks. That's not the whole story. Virginia asked that I forgive her for the way she has treated me over the years. She begged me to let her continue to see the children. When I said yes, can you believe she threw her arms around me and cried?"

"I'd like to have seen that." Shaking her head, Molly chuckled as she looked up at him. "I have news about Virginia myself."

"Really?"

"Yeah. She came to see me and asked for my forgiveness, too."

"Wow!" Kurt hoped all this forgiveness boded well for him and Molly. "She told me she intended to mend fences with you."

"She not only did that, but that's how I met Heather. Virginia introduced us. She wants to help with the women's shelter, too."

"God works in ways we would never guess."

"He does." Molly smiled.

"It's good to see you smile and hear you laugh." Kurt took the chance and placed his arm around her shoulders. "I've missed you."

She didn't say anything, but she didn't pull away.

His heart lightened with hope. "I told you the story about Virginia because when she asked me to forgive her that was the last thing I wanted to do. But she wouldn't give up. She said she was appealing to my Christian mercy." Kurt stopped and brought Molly around to face him. As he gazed into her wary gray eyes, he said a silent prayer that she would find it in her heart to forgive him. "When I realized I was forgiving Virginia Spencer, I knew I had to tell you how sorry I am that I didn't tell you right there in the hospital that you were forgiven when you asked. I was hurt that you didn't share with me, and I took it out on you. I realize now I didn't handle things well. I was wrong. Can you forgive me?"

Molly still didn't say anything, but Kurt saw a tear start to trickle down her cheek. She pressed her lips together and nodded. She let the blanket fall away as she wiped the tear away. "I've missed you, too."

With relief washing over him, he pulled her into

his embrace and held her close. She clung to him, and his heart soared. "I was such a fool. I let one little thing make me forget all the good things. You were my lifeline when I got out of prison. You taught me how to love again."

Her arms tightened around him. "And you did the same for me."

Kurt held her at arms' length. "I didn't know for sure if I'd have the nerve to do this in front of God and everyone in the Common, but here it goes."

Pulling a ring case from his pocket, he dropped to one knee. He opened the case and a diamond ring sparkled in the summer sun. "Molly Finnerty, I love you. I want you to marry me. Forgive me. Love me. I could beg you to consider it for the children, but I don't want you to do it for that reason. I want you to do it because I love you. I need you. I promise I won't turn away again if you give me a second chance to do it right."

"Yes, yes, I'll marry you," Molly replied. He stood and she flung her arms around him and held him close. She whispered in his ear, "We all need a second chance. You're my second chance."

A smattering of applause made them end their embrace. "Congratulations!" some interested bystanders yelled as they waved and went on their way.

"Here, let's get this ring on your finger." Kurt took the ring out of the box and put it on her left ring finger.

She held her hand out in front of her as she admired the ring. "I love it. I can hardly believe this is happening. It's amazing how God can take our mistakes and make them into something good. My mother and I are closer than ever. She helped me see how all these years I've never forgiven myself for Byron's death. There's a lot of forgiving I have to do."

"There's a lot of forgiving we all have to do. But with God's help we'll make it." He kissed her.

"Why are you guys kissing?" Eric's voice made them spring apart.

Kurt hunkered down in front of his children who were holding their new Frisbees while Nick and Allison remained in the background. "We were kissing because Molly said she'd marry me. Do you know what that means?"

"I do! I do!" Emily jumped up and down and waved her hand in the air. "She gets to be our mom. You know what, Molly?"

"What Emily?"

"God answered my prayers. I prayed you could be my mom."

"And you know what, Emily and Eric? I prayed God would let me be your mom." Molly folded them in her embrace.

When she released them, Eric looked up at Kurt with his little-man seriousness. "God's good at answering prayers, isn't he?"

Kurt ruffled his son's hair. "Yes, He is, Eric. Yes, He is."

Dear Readers,

Thank you for reading *A Place to Call Home*. I hope you enjoyed Molly and Kurt's journey to love and cheered for Kurt to get his children back and find the person who killed Bonnie. Forgiveness can be hard, especially when people have wronged you and the hurt runs deep. Relying on God when things don't seem to be going your way is sometimes difficult. Kurt and Molly both learn to forgive others and themselves in their goal to let God rule in their lives.

I would love for you to let other readers know what you think about *A Place to Call Home*. You can do so by posting an honest review wherever you purchased this book and also on Goodreads or Book Bub. Please consider mentioning *A Place to Call Home* on your social media sites, especially where you talk about reading! Word of mouth is the number one reason people pick up unfamiliar books. Every review and mention helps.

If you haven't read the other books in the Front Porch Promises series, I hope you'll look for them. Although each book can be read without having read the others, I enjoy connecting the books through characters and settings. You can find a list of the Front Porch Promises books below, as well as a list of my other books.

You can sign up for my newsletter on my website. https://www.merrilleewhren.com/

Blessings,
Merrillee Whren

ABOUT THE AUTHOR

Merrillee Whren is an award-winning and a *USA Today* bestselling author who writes inspirational romance. She is the winner of the 2003 Golden Heart Award for best inspirational romance manuscript presented by Romance Writers of America. She has also been the recipient of the RT Reviewers' Choice Award and the Inspirational Reader's Choice Award. She is married to her own personal hero, her husband of forty plus years, and has two grown daughters. She has lived in Atlanta, Boston, Dallas, Chicago and Florida but now makes her home in the Arizona desert. She spends her free time playing tennis or walking while she does the plotting for her novels. Please visit her website, www.merrilleewhren.com or connect with her on social media sites.

https://twitter.com/MerrilleeWhren

https://www.facebook.com/MerrilleeWhren.Author/

OTHER BOOKS by MERRILLEE WHREN

Dalton Brothers Series
Four Little Blessings
Country Blessings
Homecoming Blessings

Kellersburg Series
Hometown Promise
Hometown Proposal
Hometown Dad
Hometown Cowboy

Front Porch Promises Series
A Match to Call Ours
A Place to Call Home
A Love to Call Mine
A Family to Call Ours
A Song to Call Ours
A Baby to Call Ours
A Place to Find Love

Novellas Happiness in Hallburg
Puppy Love and Mistletoe
Puppy Love and Jingle Bells
Puppy Love and Christmas Cookies

The Village of Hope
Annie's Hope
Kirsten's Mission
Melody's Resolve

Non-series books
Miracle Baby
Second Chance Christmas